playing it
SAFE

playing it
SAFE

AMY
ANDREWS

Entangled Publishing, LLC
10940 S Parker Rd
Suite 327
Parker, CO 80134
rights@entangledpublishing.com

Brazen is an imprint of Entangled Publishing, LLC.

Edited by Liz Pelletier and Lydia Sharp
Cover design by LJ Anderson/Mayhem Cover Creations
Cover photography by MikeOrlov/Deposit Photos

Manufactured in the United States of America

First Edition September 2021

ENTANGLED
BRAZEN

To Daniel de Lorne and Courtney Clark Michaels for reading, loving and believing in this book and guiding me where it was needed. I couldn't have done it without your help. Big love to you both.

At Entangled, we want our readers to be well-informed. If you would like to know if this book contains any elements that might be of concern for you, please check the book's webpage for details.

https://entangledpublishing.com/books/playing-it-safe

Chapter One

Donovan Bane loved women. He loved his fourteen-year-old daughter and the sassy young woman she was becoming so much more than he would ever be capable of articulating. He loved his high school best friend-cum-ex-wife. He loved his mother and his three sisters and his multiple aunties and female cousins. He loved the women his Sydney Smoke teammates had chosen as life partners and considered them friends.

He loved the way women laughed and moved and put themselves together. He loved how they smelled and the great way they took care of themselves and that innate feminine confidence they exuded. Like they were born with their shit together instead of cluelessly stumbling through life like so many guys—including himself—he knew. He loved the way they talked and their circuitous way of telling a story that was both evocative and entertaining.

He loved all their shapes and sizes. Tall and short. Slender and curvy. Soft and toned. All things in between. Redhead, blonde, brunette. He loved them all.

He just didn't love them like *that*.

"What about him?" Valerie King asked fellow WAG Harper Nugent.

"Hubba hubba," Harper murmured in a reverent tone. "I don't know who he is, but I want to."

Donovan was sitting at an outside table with them at the café tucked in on the ground floor beneath the overhang of the stadium at Henley, the home ground of the Sydney Smoke rugby union team. It was a pleasant spot with a spectacular view over the pitch and, currently, a cool winter breeze blowing through the open, shaded area ruffled his sweat-dampened hair.

He'd been passing by on his way out of the stadium after the Smoke's training session when he'd spotted them and stopped to say hi. Val was waiting for her father—Griffin King, coach of the Sydney Smoke—to be finished with a press conference, and Harper had just finished a meeting with the big bosses about the murals she'd been commissioned to paint on the tunnel that led from the locker rooms to the pitch.

They'd invited Donovan to sit and chat for a while, and he'd obliged. He wasn't much of a chatter, but Val and Harper were great company, there was nothing pressing to be done on this glorious Monday, and hell, if they wanted to sit and converse with his sweaty ass, then who was he to deny them? But he'd been barely registering their chit-chat about finding a suitable date for a mutual friend in deference to cooing at Val's nine-month-old.

He was bouncing Griffin—or Little Griff as he was affectionately known by the players, so as not to confuse the kid with his grandfather—on his knee, his big hands almost completely enclosing the baby's torso. The kid was grinning his gummy smile, all flaming red hair sticking up like a troll doll and twin trails of drool running down his chin.

"Do you know who that guy is, Dono?" Harper asked.

Reluctantly, he glanced up from the cherubic face, following Val's and Harper's line of sight to find a tall blond guy in a suit and tie, tray in hand, scanning the tables.

And then the buzzing started and nothing else registered.

The air sucked from Donovan's lungs, his throat tightened, his heart bonged like a gong—a *warning* gong—inside his chest. Goddamn it. *He wasn't prepared for this.* Why hadn't there been some kind of sign from the universe that today would be the day he'd see a man that made the whole world tilt on its axis?

He'd always figured—*hoped*—that it would happen. One day. That it would be possible to experience that instantaneous *something* people who were together talked about in hushed tones. But he hadn't been looking for it. Not with his career at an all-time high. He'd resigned himself to being alone until after he'd hung up his boots. He'd made peace with it.

Blond Suit Guy was inconvenient.

Donovan pulled his gaze back to Harper, ignoring how jammed up everything felt in his chest. "Never seen him before," he said over the buzzing in his ears, injecting as much boredom and disinterest into his tone as he could muster. Then he returned his attention to Little Griff, who was dribbling like it was his superpower. "Dude, you gotta get control of that."

Given how close Donovan had come to drooling just now, he wasn't sure if the warning was for the kid or for himself.

"I think we need to find out more about him," Val said, and involuntarily, Donovan's eyes flicked back to Blond Suit.

This time there was a jolt to his chest as he watched the other man's gaze sweep closer to their table. It wasn't unusual to see a guy in a suit at the café, but it *was* unusual for Donovan to feel sucker-punched by one. The suit was a conservative charcoal and fit like a glove, the jacket hugging broad shoulders, the trousers hugging lean thighs. His shirt was a crisp white, leaving the job of flair solely to a tie, which reminded Donovan of peacock feathers.

Blond Suit's eyes skimmed over their table as it had all the others, moving quickly over Val and Harper then Donovan before moving on. It had been a nanosecond, yet it blasted like a white-hot spotlight into his soul, searing and searching. Illuminating all the lonely places. Making him want things he couldn't have.

Just as quickly, and before Donovan could catch his breath or recover enough to look away, the gaze cut back. To Donovan. It cut back and *held*. Not on Val—a stunning redhead—or Harper—a curvy goddess—it held on *him*. Settled on *him*. One second. Two seconds. Three. But in those blips of time an entire understanding was being communicated. An array of possibilities was being offered. A doorway was being cracked opened.

He smiled then. A casual smile that could have been interpreted as friendly by everyone else in the café, but those eyes said differently, and fucking hell, Donovan's head swam. He was so lightheaded every muscle in his body tensed to counteract the sensation, including his hands around the baby, who squeaked in protest.

Although it hadn't been Donovan's intention to python squeeze *the coach's grandson in the presence of his mother*, he was grateful for the distraction. Ignoring his galloping heart, he dropped his gaze like a stone, smiling blindly at Little Griff.

"He's looking this way," Harper murmured. "No time like the present."

In his peripheral vision, Donovan could see her smiling. God, *no,* please. *Don't.* Just *don't.* But then she was half standing and gesturing, and he shut his eyes.

Fuck.

Donovan didn't need to look up to know the other man was approaching. He could *feel* it in the way the air suddenly hummed with electricity and how every breath he took sizzled in his lungs.

"Hey," Harper said, addressing the guy Donovan was studiously avoiding as he came to their table. "Looking for some company?"

"Thanks." He placed his tray down. "Don't mind if I do." He undid the two buttons holding his jacket together, revealing a plastic ID tag sporting the Sydney Smoke logo attached to his belt. Which meant...Blond Suit worked here.

The place Donovan was at almost every day of his life during footy season.

"I'm Val," she said, carrying on like the whole damn world wasn't suddenly shifting and every cell in Donovan's body wasn't humming with awareness. "That's Harper." She nodded at Harper.

"Hi," he said, shaking both their hands. "I'm Beck. Nice to meet you."

"Is that short for something?" Harper asked.

"Beckett. But only my mother and grandmother call me that."

"Okay." Harper nodded. "Beck it is. And this mountain of sweat"—she poked Donovan's meaty right bicep sporting a half sleeve of black warrior-esque tattoos—"is Donovan Bane."

Donovan took a beat to stem the riot of feelings inside before glancing up from Little Griff and meeting Beck's eyes. The *zap* that arced between them would have put Donovan on his ass if he hadn't already been sitting. Unthinkingly, he squeezed the baby again as Beck offered his hand and said, "Hey, man."

Easing his grip as Little Griff let out another squawk, Donovan swallowed. "Hey," he said, his voice practically fucking *cracking* as he reached across to take the proffered hand. The hot current that sizzled up his arm was shocking in its intensity.

Much to Donovan's relief, Beck didn't hold for longer than was normal, releasing straight away, turning his gaze to the baby. "Your kid?" There was a twinkle in his eye and a half smile that was friendly, not flirty, but there was still this *thing* buzzing between them, and Donovan didn't have to ask to know that Beck was feeling it, too.

"Ha!" Val laughed. "As if with that hair." She ruffled her son's soft ginger mop. "Although Dono does have an adorable fourteen-year-old daughter, which is why he's so good with babies."

"I concur," Harper said. She and Dex had an eighteen-month-old, Gemma, who adored Donovan.

Little Griff, however, wasn't so sure, as Donovan gave a third involuntary squeeze to the baby's rib cage. A flash of something that looked like uncertainty in Beck's gaze put an itch up Donovan's spine. Was the other man puzzled as to how Donovan could have a *teenager*, or was he wondering if he'd been mistaken about Donovan being into dudes?

Val cooed at her son, leaning over to grab him off Donovan's lap. "Come on, grizzle bum, you hungry?"

Nobody at the table—including Beck—batted an eyelid as Val quickly reached in under her long-sleeve T-shirt and undid the snap of her maternity bra. Little Griff, cradled in her arm, was already searching for his snack as she lifted the shirt enough on that side for him to find what he was looking for but not enough for anyone to know she was feeding unless they looked really, *really* closely.

The baby, who was absently fondling a cluster of sequins on his mother's shirt, just looked like he was snuggling. Donovan had loved watching his daughter, Amiria—Miri for short—breastfeed. It had been endlessly fascinating and further confirmation of the might and majesty of women.

"So, you work here?" Harper asked as she passed over a bottle of water to Val.

"That's right." Beck pried the lid of his coffee cup off and reached for the sugar. "It's my first day. I'm in the finance department."

Finance? Donovan had *no* idea why a finance guy would be ticking all his boxes. Finance guys weren't his type. Not that he'd ever been with *any* guy to know what exactly his type was or, for that matter, allowed himself to wonder such things. He'd never let himself go there. Had a gun been put to his head, Donovan would have thought his type would be some buff, outdoorsy guy. A fellow athlete probably. Or someone who worked with their hands.

Not a desk jockey.

Someone more like him in build and physicality. Beck, who looked about six-foot-two, wasn't a small guy by any stretch, but at six-four and built like a tank, Donovan tended to dwarf most men.

His dick, however, was saying this guy was definitely his type.

"So, you pay these guys?" Harper said with a smile, inclining her head toward Donovan.

"Ah," he laughed. "I guess, yeah."

"This is who you have to suck up to, Dono," she said.

Oh Christ… *Do not think about sucking anything on this man!*

Beck's gaze flitted briefly to Donovan and back, and he felt the *awareness* in that glance down to his bones. Thankfully, Val jumped in, negating the need for Donovan, usually sparse in his communication, to say anything.

"Are you from Sydney?" Val said.

"Yep." Beck stirred his coffee. "The southern beaches originally. I've been working at a firm in the city for the past decade. But I was starting to feel the barnacles growing on my ass, so I knew I needed to change things up and"—he shrugged—"here I am."

Yep. Here he was. With his sandy blond hair and his body-hugging suit and the power to fucking *sizzle* air. Oh, and a really, really nice mouth. Full lips, the bow of the top lip beautifully delineated and flashy as fuck. The bottom lip extra lush. It made Donovan wonder what it would be like to grab that sexy tie and yank Beck closer. Kiss those lips. Bite that bottom, fuller one. To lick it and suck it into his mouth and savour it's taste.

To hear Beck groan as he did it.

Donovan blinked. *Jesus. Do* not *look at his mouth, dickhead.* But that was easier said than done. He'd never kissed a guy. Never been kissed by one, either. He fantasised about it—a lot. More than fucking or wanking or blowjobs. Just the sheer pleasure of being able to kiss someone freely and wantonly and without thought or hesitation...

"Nothing boring about a rugby club," Val said with a smile.

Beck laughed as his gaze once again cut to Donovan's for the briefest second. *Christ.* He had dimples. They were more elongated than pointed, bracketing his mouth rather than punctuating it, but they were on full flash now. "So I'm learning."

His gaze moved away quickly. But it lingered in Donovan's gut, sitting warm and solid and full of potential.

"Are you a rugby fan?" Harper enquired.

The other man shot her a sheepish grin and leaned in conspiratorially. "Don't tell anyone, but I'm more of an AFL guy." He flicked his gaze to Donovan. "Sorry," he apologised, that damn smile hovering on his bottom lip.

Donovan sought for a witty reply, but witty replies had never been his forte—hell, *conversation* wasn't his forte—and this guy had him all at sea. Thankfully, both women were exceptionally capable of defending the game.

Val shot him a faux-scandalised look. "Hush your mouth. You want this stadium to collapse on top of us?"

"Don't worry," Harper assured, patting Beck's hand. "You'll be converted before you know it, right, Dono?"

Donovan nodded awkwardly, words stuck in his throat. But now that there was no baby to hide behind, he didn't know what to do with his hands, so he went to his default tic when he was nervous, cracking his knuckles, absently making his way through each finger.

On both hands.

Neither woman seemed to notice his discombobulation, but Beck's gaze flicked from Donovan's face to his hands and back again, his eyes—they were blue—soft with understanding and assurance, which was even more dangerous to Donovan's equilibrium.

God, he should go. Just excuse himself and go.

"You'll have to come to the home game on Saturday night. Join us in the corporate box," Harper invited, drawing Beck's attention. *Thank Christ.* "The view up there is amazing, and if Dono marauding through a pack of opposition players like they're Skittles doesn't make you a fan," she teased, "then there is no hope for you."

Beck's attention returned to Donovan. "You're that good, huh?"

Donavan avoided Beck's gaze. Still cracking his knuckles, he said a little more gruffly than intended, "I do all right."

Which was a lie. Donovan Bane was fucking magic to watch, and he knew it. He just didn't brag about his prowess like fellow teammate Lincoln Quinn, who practically rented a billboard every time he scored a goddamn try. But Donovan did know his worth and wasn't afraid to own it. He just couldn't do it in front of this guy. Not when he felt ridiculously awkward and tongue-tied and…and…discom-*fucking*-bobulated.

He felt fifteen years old again, beset with confusing feelings about his PE teacher and the dawning realisation that it might be connected to the nagging sense of *other*ness he'd felt too often in his life.

Jesus, Donovan. Just leave already. Shift your ass!

Firing up his legs to do just that, he was pulled up short by Val saying, "So…Beck, you're what? Early thirties?"

"Thirty-one."

"Are you"—her eyes moved to the bare ring finger on his left hand—"married? Or have a girlfriend?"

Donovan cracked his knuckles some more, his pulse washing loudly through his ears as he waited—*sweated*—on the answer. Maybe he'd gotten it all wrong and this vibe he was feeling was all one-sided? All in his head? Because his libido had gone rogue.

Beck grinned and oh-good-fucking-Christ, those dimples! "No," he said. "To both."

"Because"—Harper continued leaning in on her elbows—"you prefer to stay foot loose and fancy free, or you just haven't found the right woman yet?"

Beck mimicked Harper's pose leaning in conspiratorially. "Because," he said in a loud, theatrical stage whisper, "I'm gay."

And there it was. *Not* Donovan's rogue libido. Not his wishful thinking, either. Beck was into guys. Donovan ran through his knuckle-cracking ritual again as relief loosened the tension in his shoulders, followed closely by a flood of envy. How would it be to just casually and freely admit your sexual orientation? Not have to hide it or worry that someone would yank open the closet door and expose you?

Harper blinked, sitting back in her chair. "Really?"

"Yes."

Val also blinked. "*Really*?" She glanced at Harper. "I did *not* get that vibe."

"Yes, really." Beck grinned. "You want to see my gay card?"

Recovering quickly, Val laughed. "Does it have little rainbows all over it?"

"It does not." More grinning that made those dimples deep, irresistible grooves. "But it does play 'It's Raining Men' every time I pull it out of my wallet."

All three of them laughed this time. Little Griff stirred at the sound, and Donovan cracked his knuckles faster.

"Well…damn," Harper said, "I don't guess you'd be interested in our friend, Elizabeth, then?"

He smiled. "No." Grabbing his boxed sandwiches, he pulled the plastic cover off and picked the first half up. "Is the invitation to join you in the box withdrawn?"

"Hell no," Val hastened to assure him. "Do you have a husband? Or boyfriend? You can bring him along if you want."

"No to that as well." Beck bit into the sandwich, flicking his gaze to Donovan for a beat or two as he chewed. "I split with my last boyfriend six months ago." He returned his attention to Val. "I'm free as a bird."

Donovan swallowed as his heart skipped a beat. *Dumb fucking heart.* It didn't matter if Beck was free or not. This thing, him and Beck, *couldn't* happen. He had zero intention of coming out while he was playing. He'd waited this long. He could wait a few more years. So there was no point in beat-skipping.

But how he envied the ease with which the other man said *boyfriend* without tripping over the word. It just slid out, smooth and effortless.

"And was it one of those sworn-off-men-for-the-rest-of-your-life splits or are you wanting to get back on the horse?"

Val asked.

"*Val.*" Harper bugged her eyes at her friend. "Maybe Beck doesn't want to talk about it."

"Oh god, sorry," Val said, instantly contrite as she eased her now-sleeping son away, pulled down her shirt, and cradled him close again, all without disturbing his slumber. "Harper's right. I'm one of those terrible I'm-in-love-so-I-want-everyone-else-to-be-too, people. Ignore me."

Beck laughed. "It's fine. The split was mutual and amicable, and I'm up for dating again."

Dating. Donovan couldn't even allow himself the luxury of *thinking* about going on a date with this guy. *Any* guy.

Val glanced at Harper. "Is that muralist friend of yours…what's his name…Alan or something? Is he seeing anyone at the moment?"

Harper narrowed her eyes as if she was thinking. "I'm not sure. I'll ask. What about John Trimble's brother?"

Donovan's heart rate spiked. John Trimble was a teammate and a good bloke, but his brother Devon was an unbearably entitled dick.

Their conversation continued for the next two minutes as names were tossed around. Beck ate his sandwich, letting them prattle on, glancing between the two women with a bemused look on his face that softened his bottom lip. Donovan, *who wished he could get off his ass and just leave already*, seemed to be temporarily frozen while his thoughts churned thick as soup and he did a year's worth of damage to his knuckles.

"Are they always like this?" Beck asked, interrupting the chaos going on inside Donovan's brain.

The knuckle cracking ceased as Donovan stilled, feeling ridiculously tongue-tied beneath the warmth of Beck's gaze. Despite the quagmire, Donovan admired the way the other man was unfazed by—indulging, even—Harper and Val's matchmaking. It seemed Beck was also comfortable around chatty women.

"Pretty much," Donovan said.

"Oh, I know." Harper held up a finger to punctuate her announcement. "One of the wait staff that usually works the corporate boxes. The cute one…Harry, I think? He's gay."

"Oh yes." Val's eyes lit up as she addressed Beck. "He's a great guy. Now you have to come to the game."

"Hey, you had me at corporate box."

She grinned. "Perfect."

Yeah. *Perfect.*

Not.

Now he was going to have to perform on field on Saturday night knowing that Beck was up there watching.

"I'll get Eve—that's my dad's PA—to put you on the door list."

"Thanks," Beck said as he drank from his coffee cup, his gaze lifting to Donovan's, his eyes flashing hot and intense. It was only for a moment before he returned his attention to Val, but he felt that look all the way down to his testicles.

His dick got hard. A state, he suspected, he was going to have to get used to.

Great. Just *great.* Donovan had played under all kinds of pressure. He'd played injured and unwell, he'd played while his contract was being renegotiated and once when his father had been admitted to hospital for a heart attack.

But he'd never played knowing a guy he had the hots for was watching him from the corporate box. And he'd *never ever* played with a hard-on.

Was that even possible?

Chapter Two

On Wednesday night, Donovan's trip across the city took him past Henley Stadium, which made him think about Beck. *Again.* He'd thought about little else other than Beck the past couple of days. Considering he didn't even know the guy's last name, it was getting a little embarrassing.

And it'd been noticed.

He'd been so distracted during training earlier today, Griff had thrown a football at his head when he'd been staring out to space, thinking about wrapping a hand around a certain tie and kissing a certain mouth.

You got something else you'd rather be doing, Dono? he'd barked as the football had bounced off Donovan's head and Linc had doubled over with laughter.

Linc was such an asshole.

Donovan had loved rugby union from the day he'd first laced up his boots in the under sevens—he'd been a star player from then, too. But the truth was, since Monday, his focus on rugby had played second fiddle to his focus on Suit Guy.

And the thought of *doing* him? Donovan's guts twisted

and his hands went clammy around the steering wheel as he drove cautiously through pelting rain. He couldn't see a world where that could ever happen for him, and even in an alternate universe, Donovan wouldn't know where to start.

He had zero game.

Beck, on the other hand, oozed confidence and openness. He was clearly comfortable in his own skin, freely admitting he was gay and talking easily about an ex-boyfriend. Hell, the guy was on Grindr. Donovan knew because, sitting in his dual cab in the stadium car park after training yesterday, he'd briefly reactivated his long-deactivated account.

BeckInRealLife had popped up immediately on screen as being under a kilometre away. The profile pic, which was so current it could have been snapped during Monday's lunch, was of a smiling Beck, his dimples on full flash. It had caused an unwanted flutter in Donovan's chest, although his bio had quickly put a stop to the flutter.

I like real. *Happy to kiss as many frogs as needed on my journey to the one.*

And his likes were listed as clubbing, Mardi Gras, going out to dinner with friends, and dirty weekends away.

In other words, the exact opposite of Donovan, who was a big fat fake, hiding behind everyone's assumptions about his sexuality because he'd been married and had a kid. He'd never been kissed by one man, let alone multiple. And his weekends were usually spent either playing rugby or obsessively watching replays of the last game whilst nursing some bump or bruise or strain.

Unless Miri was visiting, then it was laser tag or hanging at the beach or watching age-appropriate movie marathons on his big-screen TV.

Whilst nursing some bump or bruise or strain.

But it still didn't stop Donovan wanting to *do* Suit Guy. Well…kissing that mouth, anyway. The mere thought of that had kept him awake—and hard—at night.

Christ, he was worse than Miri mooning over her latest Hollywood crush. It was fucking pathetic for a thirty-two-year-old man. But also a...revelation. For the first time ever, he actually had feelings for a guy that couldn't be ignored. That refused to bow to his steely determination to keep a lid on his true self.

Okay, maybe the feelings were just sexual. Maybe it was his libido talking, but still, it had never happened before. He'd just...never let himself go there and had kept any stray lust or desires locked down tight, only doing something about them when they could no longer be channelled into his footy. Or when it felt like he was in imminent danger of busting a nut.

And only then by his own hand in the privacy of his house.

If Donovan was being honest with himself, there really hadn't been anyone who had made him feel like this... excited and terrified all at once. He'd assumed that years of self-denial had somehow blocked that path for him. But this vortex of feelings, where possibility mixed with hopelessness to leave a hot ache in the pit of his stomach and a stranglehold on his throat, gave him hope that maybe all wasn't lost.

That maybe he wasn't totally emotionally stunted, and when his career was over and he'd faded from the limelight, he *did* have the capacity to find the one and settle down.

But for now, it was a problem. Mainly because it didn't matter how he felt—it couldn't happen. There was not, nor had there ever been, any elite, *current*, rugby players in Australia who had come out as gay.

And he had no intention of being the first.

He was here to play rugby. Until he couldn't play it any longer due to age and form. He was not here for being judged over who he chose to love. Maintaining an elite career was hard enough with normal pressures without the extra bullshit he knew would be inevitable if he came out while he was still playing.

Not to mention how it could affect his major sponsor relationships. Lucrative relationships that were setting him up to be able to continue to provide for his daughter in the years after his retirement.

So he needed to forget Suit Guy and that mouth and those dimples and get his shit together.

Fate, though, had other ideas, as he made his way closer to home, crawling along in a line of traffic, rain lashing the windscreen. The traffic lights turned red up ahead, and a row of brake lights glinting blurrily illuminated the gloom as Donovan slowed to a halt, leaving a safe distance between him and the car in front.

Motion from the corner of his eye caught his attention, and Donovan flicked a glance at the cyclist to his left walking his bike along the bright green path on the edge of the road. He was in cycling pants and shirt, which were both completely soaked—along with his hair—as he put one foot in front of the other. Frowning, Donovan glanced at the bike as the cyclist got ahead of his stationery vehicle.

Flat tyre. Bummer.

But, suddenly, something about the way the guy held himself—even in the dark and the rain—pinged his antennae. And then a horn sounded from somewhere, and the guy, who was passing under a streetlight at the time, looked over his shoulder as if trying to identify where it was coming from, and Donovan's heart practically stopped in his chest.

Fuck. *Beck*.

"Oh god," he muttered under his breath, shutting his eyes, trying to rid himself of the image, hoping that when he opened them again the figure was just some trick of the rainy night spurred on by his excessive fucking longing.

But no. As Donovan opened his eyes, the man was real,

and it was, without a doubt, the guy Donovan had been salivating over for the last two days.

Fuck. Fuck. *Fuck!*

Donovan gripped and ungripped the steering wheel. *Just drive on, man. Just pretend you haven't seen him.* He sucked in a breath and let it blow out steadily, impatient now for the light to change. Impatient to drive past and get home where it was safe and familiar and he could give himself permission to feel something.

But even as he thought it, a hundred different scenarios of Beckett dying heroically and quietly of pneumonia or... consumption, like some tragic nineteenth-century gentleman accountant on an English estate, beat against the inside of his skull.

Oh for the love of...*consumption*? This was the hazard of growing up in a houseful of sisters who were Bronte fangirls. *Pull your shit together!*

Donovan turned up the air-con. It was suddenly stuffy inside the cab, his breathing hot and husky, the windscreen starting to fog. He tapped his fingers against the wheel as the figure ahead trudged along in the rain.

C'mon, turn green, already, damn it!

As if the universe had heard his entreaties, the lights changed, and Donovan took his foot off the brake, inching slowly forward. "Just drive straight past," he muttered under his breath. "It's only rain."

A bit of rain never killed anybody.

Besides, there was nowhere really to pull over safely, particularly not in this weather and certainly not without pissing off the line of traffic behind him. But as Donovan neared Beck, a bus stop loomed ahead, the road widening to create a pull-in lane, and Donovan knew it was a sign to do the right thing. To stop, pull over, offer the guy a lift. He had a dual cab ute—the bike would easily fit in the back.

Hell, he'd have probably stopped and offered a stranger a lift. Why wouldn't he do the same for a guy he vaguely knew? Why should his inconvenient physical attraction change that? One thing had nothing to do with the other.

It was just…being a good person. Doing his civic duty to a fellow human being in need of assistance.

Sighing, Donovan indicated and pulled into the bus stop. Switching off his engine, he took a moment to still himself. *Jesus…not a good idea.* But he opened the door anyway.

The rain was cool and plentiful, and Donovan was soaked to his skin within seconds as he called, "Beck," to the soaking wet man just ahead.

He didn't turn, and Donovan's chest tightened, which he immediately dismissed. It wasn't some kind of rejection, for fuck's sake. It was raining—hard. The dude probably hadn't heard him.

"*Beckett!*" Donovan repeated, louder this time, walking around to the other side of the car closest to the bus stop.

The other man stopped and glanced over his shoulder, his brow furrowing for a moment as he peered into the gloom between them. Then the lines relaxed, and a slow smile broke out across his features, and yes, it was dark and it was raining, but damn if Donovan didn't feel an instant triple whammy.

A punch to his throat. A squeeze to his chest. A stroke to his groin.

Turning his bike around, he reached Donovan in a dozen long, loose strides, and he wished he could look away. Alas, he was not that strong. Beck emerged from the poorer visibility up ahead into the glow from the street lighting positioned at either end of the bus stop like a goddamn fucking angel. He smiled as he halted about a foot from the car bumper.

"Donovan," he said, using his full name, which felt *right*. Just as calling him Beckett had felt right.

His eyes ran over Donovan in a way they *had not* at

the stadium on Monday. Two days ago, he'd been very circumspect, but here he obviously felt no such need for propriety. And hell, if that wasn't exciting in the pissing-down rain on the side of a major road in the middle of Sydney.

Hell if Donovan wasn't returning the favour, taking in narrow hips and flat abs framing a very nice bulge between legs that were long and lean. Those Lycra bike pants, extra skintight from the rain, left nothing to the imagination. Same went for the shirt. Every muscle in Beckett's lean body had been moulded to within an inch of its life.

Beckett dragged his gaze back to Donovan's. "Aren't you a sight for sore eyes."

Donovan's gut clenched, and he felt stupidly tongue-tied again as he took in the beads of rain splashing Beckett's cheeks and running from his hair into his eyes, clinging to his lashes. Nervously, he cracked his knuckles, the clash of feelings in his chest forming a tight band of anxiety. "You have a flat."

Oh, good Christ. Way to state the fucking obvious, dude. He might as well have said, *I carried a watermelon.*

Beckett's lips twitched, but he just said, "Yes," all calm and easy like roadside conversations in the rain were nothing unusual.

But nothing about this was usual for Donovan—at least not with *this* guy. And it was like an irritant pricking beneath his skin. "Why are you riding your bike in this shitty weather?" he asked, goaded by Beck's composure.

More calmness, more lip twitching. "It wasn't shitty when I started out fifteen minutes ago."

"It's been threatening to storm for hours," Donovan said.

Why he was choosing to debate this now was a mystery to Donovan, but seriously…did the guy not have some kind of weather app? Or a fucking window in his office?

Had he not heard of consumption?

Beck shrugged. "I thought I could beat it home. Probably would have, too, if it wasn't for the flat."

The explanation sounded reasonable in Beckett's calm baritone backed up by his measured, watchful gaze. A gaze that drew Donovan in, the blue of his eyes illuminated by the streetlighting and tempting in ways he didn't fully understand.

How could *eyes* be tempting? Unless it was the possibility he saw there.

Realising he was staring—*they* were staring—in the pouring rain, getting wetter and wetter, not that it was possible to get any wetter, Donovan dragged his mind off Beckett's lips. "I'll give you a lift to your place. You can put your bike in the back."

The twitch of those lips turned to a slow, lazy smile lighting the other man's features, as the grooves on either side of his mouth deepened. "My mother told me I should never accept rides from strangers."

Donovan suddenly wanted to laugh at the quick, easy comeback, but he was too nervous because, was Beckett flirting? And what the hell did he do about that? He searched his brain for something equally cool and flirty to say. Given his already klutzy attempts at conversation, he didn't hold out much hope.

"Are we?" He swallowed. "Strangers?" Which wasn't cool or flirty, but it felt like he'd known this man all his life or had, at least, been waiting for him all his life.

"I guess not," he said, with a slight smile playing on his mouth before he glanced at Donovan's Ranger dual cab. "I don't know if you noticed, but I'm kinda wet, and I don't exactly live close. I'd hate to ruin your seats."

Donovan's gaze flicked up and down again of its own volition. "I noticed." Unfortunately, he'd noticed *every* detail of Beckett's physique. He pulled his sodden T-shirt shirt out and let it slap back against his chest. "Me too."

His lips quirked. "I noticed."

Donovan wouldn't have thought it possible to get a hard-on in this very public, very un-romantic situation, but he was wrong. And given his shorts were now clinging to everything he owned, they weren't going to be any help in disguising his condition.

"The seats are leather," he said, injecting a no-nonsense gruffness into his voice. "Put your bike in the back."

He turned then, striding around to the tailgate and opening it with brisk efficiency. No need to pop the lid—the bike would slide straight in. When he turned, Beckett was behind, bike in tow, removing the helmet from the handlebar. Without preamble, or really even looking at the other man, Donovan lifted it up and pushed it into the empty tray, tossing the helmet in, too, then snapping the tailgate back into place.

"Get in," he said, voice still gruff, before heading down the driver's side to the door and yanking it open.

By the time he was in and buckled up, Beckett's door was opening and he was stashing the small backpack he'd been wearing on the floor as he slid into the cab. Instantly, it felt like there wasn't enough air, and Donovan's left hand gripped the steering wheel hard as he turned the key with his right. The cool relief of fresh air from the vents helped as the radio station he'd been listening to blared to life, and he automatically reached to turn the volume down.

"Hand towels in the glove box."

Beckett quirked an eyebrow, clearly amused by the admission. "Really?" he murmured, his voice loaded with amusement and innuendo as he reached for the handle.

"For after practice," he clarified. "I sweat a lot." He'd learned a long time ago to always have some spare towels on hand.

"I guess it's sweaty work," Beck said.

"Yes."

"Want one?"

He leaned forward and pulled out two towels, offering one to Donovan, who took it with a grunt of thanks. The towels were only double the size of a face washer, but at least he'd be able to dry off his hair.

Once he'd towelled off enough to stop droplets from running into his eyes, Donovan threw the towel on the console between them. "Where do you live?"

"Parramatta. Sorry, it's probably well out of your way."

It was. "It's fine." It was more than fine, actually. It might be inconvenient right now, but it was best in the long run that Beckett lived out of easy reach.

The temptation had he lived closer might be overwhelming.

Donovan pretended to consult his side mirror even though he couldn't see a good goddamn anything through the driving rain and with the other man's scent being pushed around the cab by the air con. It was something rich and warm and spicy and did funny things to Donovan's equilibrium, and in his mind's eye, he could see himself leaning over and nuzzling the other man's neck to acquaint himself with the fragrance.

His heartbeat quickened at the fantasy. Yeah, Parramatta was *definitely* a good thing.

A car slowed, opening up a break in the traffic for Donovan, and he pounced on it, gesturing a thank-you with his hand even though he doubted it could be seen.

They didn't speak for what felt like minutes, but Donovan could *feel* Beckett's eyes on him, studying him. Like twin lasers, they roamed his face and hair and neck then down his body to his chest and abs and thighs where his wet shorts clung like a second skin. It skipped to his hands next, which were gripping the steering wheel like they were riding the corkscrew section of a roller coaster instead of being stuck in a long line of stop/start traffic.

His scrutiny was equal turns terrifying and exhilarating. A mix that was both scary and arousing all at once.

And utterly nerve-wrecking.

Jesus…what was Beckett thinking? Did he have questions? Or was it purely just ogling? Just one man checking out another in the most frankly sexual way possible? And was he as horny as Donovan was at the moment? More importantly, how did Donovan stack up? Did Beckett think he was *he-man hot* like that *Dick-a-licious Donovan* Facebook fan page that was out there on the internet that Linc always gave him shit about?

Did he like what he saw?

Donovan cringed internally. How fucking pathetic. The guy was *obviously* checking him out. There was a *vibe* between them. What did he want? A fucking handwritten confirmation? When he had eyes. And his gut. And a dick that was currently like a divining rod of sexual interest and as stiff as one.

Thank god it was dark enough in the cab and the overhang of his T-shirt covered the evidence. But good Christ, the stretching silence was like nails down a chalkboard. Was Beckett ever going to say something? *Anything.* Instead of watching and…waiting. For who knew what? Maybe for Donovan to say something?

Yes. Good idea. He could say something. *Anything.* Just break this unending silence that was fraught with things he couldn't speak about.

He opened his mouth to say something as he slowly drew the car to a halt again, but Beckett got in before him. "So…" He let the word stretch for a while as if he was thinking about how to complete the sentence. "You're not out, then?"

Donovan almost sagged despite the tightening of his fingers around the wheel. Okay. Maybe he *could* speak about them. Here. In the confines of his pickup. On this dark, rainy night. Just the two of them. It was a strange notion when he'd always played his hand close to his chest and his instinct to deny was strong. But not as strong, suddenly, as his desire to finally speak the words out loud.

To another man.

He'd only ever told one other person—*not* a man—and he hadn't planned on changing that. Not until after his career was done, anyway. But it was overwhelming how much he wanted to tell Beckett.

Blowing out a thick, unsteady breath, he addressed the windscreen. "No."

There. *He'd done it.* Donovan's fingers loosened around the steering wheel, and the knot in his traps at either side of his neck melted away. In fact, what felt like two decades of tension dissolved away in an instant.

Okay, he hadn't come out and said it directly. *I am gay.* But it was tacit acknowledgment.

Donovan glanced across the cab, risking a look at the man who in two days had turned his life upside down. Looking at Beckett seemed much easier now there was truth between them. He was nodding slowly, a small smile playing on his mouth. "This is the first time you've had this conversation with anybody, isn't it?"

"No." Donovan shook his head. "My ex-wife knows." That conversation had only been marginally less difficult than this one. "You're the first...guy."

Donovan wished immediately he could take the admission back. Why would he confess how much of a freak/fraud he was to a guy who was clearly very comfortable in his sexuality? A guy on whom he had a king-size crush.

Luckily, Beckett didn't seem fazed. There was just more nodding and that small smile telegraphing understanding and admiration all in one, which was *all the things*. Donovan wanted to kiss it right off his mouth. But admitting his sexuality to this man and exploring it with him were two different things.

"Congratulations," Beckett said, his smile bigger, a light tease to his voice. "How does it feel?"

Donovan huffed out a laugh. "I don't know. Ask me in the morning." Immediately after the words were out of his mouth, he wished he could take them back. Oh Christ...what had he just implied? "I mean," he blurted quickly, "I didn't mean—"

Beckett's laugh interrupted him. "It's okay, I know what you meant."

And then a horn blared from behind, giving Donovan the perfect circuit breaker to his faux pas as he whipped his attention back to the road and the forward momentum of the traffic. The familiar tension returned to his muscles. The respite from years of not being able to express his identity was wonderful but...now what? He'd just told a guy, in a roundabout way, he was gay.

It still didn't change anything.

He was still Donovan Bane, star rugby player. He still wasn't able to do anything about it. Not now.

Not *yet*.

His brain grappled with that as the silence built between them again, and he felt Beckett's gentle scrutiny once more. Jesus...why did he have to be so fucking awkward about this? Why couldn't he just have a normal conversation? Not about why he was thirty-two and not out yet or how much he wanted to kiss the guy.

But about the weather. Or his bike. Or Beckett's new job.

It was a blessed relief when his phone rang via the car audio system. He glanced at the screen to find it was Mrs. Connor, his elderly next-door neighbour. She was a nice woman who'd been widowed for several years and baked muffins every Wednesday morning and always made extra for him. She didn't ring unnecessarily, and with the storm, he was instantly concerned.

Plus, he'd have answered the phone to the devil himself right now to break the awkward silence. Except he didn't need to—the devil was sitting only a few feet away...

"I need to get this," he said, addressing the windscreen with a gruffness he hadn't planned or understood.

He noticed Beckett nodding in his peripheral vision. "Of course."

Donovan punched the answer button. "Hi, Mrs Connor. Everything okay?"

"Oh Donovan, dear." Her crackly voice rang clear down the line. "I'm so sorry to bother you."

"It's fine." And it was fine. Miri would certainly never forgive him for ignoring her phone call. His daughter adored her, because the old woman spoiled her rotten whenever she came to stay.

"It's just that the storm has sent Wally haywire, and he's gone up that tree again and won't come down, and he's meowing like the world's about to end because he's utterly terrified, and I'm so scared he's going to die of fright up there. He's not a young cat, you know. But if you're nowhere near home, I can call the fire department or the rescue people."

Grimacing, Donovan shook his head. That bloody cat. This would be the third time Donovan would have to get his ass down from the tree in Mrs. Connor's front yard. But he imagined on a night like tonight the emergency services were probably busy enough without getting random *my-cat-is-stuck-up-a-tree* calls.

And they were only a few minutes away from where Donovan lived.

He glanced at Beckett, startled again by the lurch in his pulse at the mere sight of the other man. "Do you mind?" he mouthed.

"Of course not," he mouthed back.

Donovan nodded his thanks. "I'm five minutes away," he said. "Stay inside, in case there's any lightning." There hadn't been yet, but the forecast was for increasing severity of the storms.

And then of course, there was consumption...

• • •

Beck still didn't know what to make of the big guy in the driver's seat. Those interesting tats that added a layer of yum to his bronzed skin and that hard, square jaw. Not to mention his dark wavy hair, long enough to be pulled back into a man bun. Oh, and a small white scar that bisected his left eyebrow.

On one hand, he looked totally badass. The kind of guy a person wouldn't want to meet in a dark alley.

Unless it was for a clandestine root or quickie blowjob...

On the other, there was clearly a gentle, sensitive soul amongst all that brawn. For Christ's sake, they were currently heading to get a cat down from a tree. But he was a man of few words—he hadn't said a thing since he'd hung up the phone—and strong, silent types weren't usually Beck's deal. He liked guys who were easy in their skin and could carry an interesting conversation.

And guys *not* out of the closest were definitely not his deal.

Been there, done that. Wasn't heading down that route ever again.

But there was no denying ever since he'd laid eyes on Donovan Bane two days ago, he'd been captivated. Hell, he'd Googled him almost obsessively and had jacked off several times to footage on a Facebook page called Dick-a-licious Donovan featuring several minutes of spliced together footage of Donovan tackling—*hard*.

Christ, that was some he-man shit right there, and Beck had been surprised to discover it got him all revved up. Or *Donovan* did anyway as he brought down guys almost as big as himself like a lion lunging at a wildebeest.

He had no idea why it worked for him suddenly—it just did.

As did the man's…shyness. Or maybe awkwardness was a better descriptor. The way he'd avoided eye contact with Beck at the café on Monday, the obvious reluctance in his gaze tonight as if pulling over to help had been a line-ball call, the absent way he cracked his knuckles. Clearly, there was a vibe between them of which Donovan was excruciatingly aware and, not being out yet, didn't know how to handle.

Maybe Donovan was anxious that Beck might out him. Or that Beck's *interest* might, anyway. Which was why he'd kept himself strictly in check that day at the café. Normally, if there was a vibe with a guy and Beck was single, he'd have flirted like crazy. Beck was an excellent flirt. But it had been obvious from the way Donovan had looked away after that first electric meeting of their eyes that flirting was off the table.

Beck understood that. He'd been lucky in life to have known early—to have always known, really—and had supportive friends and family, but he knew many guys who had not been so lucky and that coming out could be fraught. That the reasons gay people didn't come out were many and varied and that it wasn't any of his goddamn business.

But tonight, in the car, the way those big shoulders had sagged when Donovan had said *no* had hit Beck hard in the chest. He'd been sure the tough guy pro athlete was going to deny the very premise of the question. Deny being gay. The fact that he didn't had been *big*. But not as big as his admission that he'd never confided in another man.

Because that meant he'd chosen *Beck* as his confidant. *Him*. Beckett.

The relief in this cab had been palpable, and Beck's heart had gone out to the guy he'd developed a serious crush on. It couldn't have been easy for him, and he felt both honoured and privileged.

And also, if he was being honest, just a tiny bit hopeful. Which was ridiculous, because Donovan's admission didn't mean he was going to suddenly come out of the closet or do anything about the attraction flaring between them. In fact, Beck would put money on him doing the opposite.

So, pinning his hopes on something serious developing between them wouldn't be smart. He was done with guys who were publicly denying their true selves. But he could settle for some dirty making out if Donovan was particularly horny for it and, if he'd never indulged before—which was Beck's gut feeling—then he must be *gagging* for some guy-on-guy action.

Even the thought of it made Beck hard, and he thanked god for that discarded hand towel sitting in his lap.

The car slowing and turning off the main road yanked Beck's head out of his—and Donovan's—laps as leafy streets all named after birds came into focus through the rain-spattered windows. A few more turns and they were driving onto Finch Street, where Donovan pulled into the driveway of a suburban house.

Beck hadn't known what to expect, but modest, low-set, unremarkable brick with neat shrubs and gardens affording some privacy at the front and a well-kept lawn had not been it. Maybe something huge and modern and...flashy, with lots of glass and expensive architectural flourishes?

Okay, sure, nothing about Donovan was flashy, but he knew how much the guy earned. He could certainly afford something much swankier.

He didn't give a shit. It was just…curious. Donovan Bane was an enigma.

The engine cut out, and Donovan handed his keys across the space between them. "Go inside and get dry," he instructed.

It wasn't a suggestion; it was a command. Just as his *I'll give you a lift to your place* had been. Clearly Donovan was used to being listened to, to being in charge. But his gruff voice had a husky edge, causing it to rumble around the warm cab, stirring the heavy silence between them, roughening it into something far more intimate.

"Towels in the bathroom cupboard," he continued. "And there's a bunch of clean clothes folded in the laundry if you can find something that fits."

He looked Beck up and down, obviously assessing the unlikelihood of that happening, but his gaze snagged and lingered over every inch of Beck's body. It wasn't frank, but it was thorough, the *yearning* swirling in Donovan's gaze more potent than anything overtly sexual.

It was the most innocent eye fucking Beck had ever endured, but he felt it *everywhere*. Filling his chest, tightening his lungs, squeezing his gut. And yeah, wrapping like a fist around his cock. Donovan's hunger was lying dormant, like a banked fire. What would it take, Beck wondered, to get that flame flickering to life and burning out of control?

Exploding into a fireball?

"I'll see to Wally," Donovan said, oblivious to the thoughts sliding seductively through Beck's hyperactive imagination. "Then I'll drive you home."

Beck shook his head. "And miss out on seeing you climb up a tree to save a little old lady's cat?" He grinned as he opened the door. "Not in a million years."

Chapter Three

Beck didn't think there was a gay man alive capable of *not* checking out Donovan Bane's ass as he climbed the massive Japanese maple tree that seemed to take up the entire front yard of his neighbour's property. He sure as shit did. It might have been raining and dark, but Mrs. Connor had handed him a torch and told him to light Donovan's way, and who was he to disappoint a sweet, little old lady?

Was it his fault that the powerful beam managed to spotlight the climbing man to perfection, allowing him to ogle all that magnificence? It was hard not to, what with the cling of those very wet shorts showcasing glutes that were so round and taut Beck actually salivated at the thought of sinking his teeth into them. And then there was the back view of his thick legs, hamstrings and calves working in beautiful tandem.

Yes, indeed—Donovan was one very big boy.

God knew, Beck was no sapling. At six-foot-two and a hundred kilos, he was broad-chested with well-defined abs. And quads and calves (thanks to cycling) that most would consider big. But compared to Donovan, who probably had him by thirty kilos or so and was just plain *thick* through the chest and abs and legs, Beck was positively lean.

For a guy built like a tank, he was surprisingly agile, though, his step light as he powered upward toward the cat. If it had been any other tree, Beck might have worried that the branches would break under the strain of supporting such a huge frame, but the big limbs were solid and gnarled with age, barely giving at all beneath Donovan's weight.

"He's such a good boy to me," Mrs. Connor said affectionately, projecting her crackly voice over the noise of the rain.

They were standing under the overhang of the roof that extended out from the front door to form a porch. There was no light, other than the outward beam of the torch, but it kept them relatively dry in the inclement weather. "I'm very lucky to have him as a neighbour."

Lucky to have that kind of eye candy on call night and day? Hell yes, she was. "Good neighbours are a godsend," Beck replied, smiling down at the woman, who beamed back, clearly thrilled they were on the same wavelength.

Beck was great with grandmothers. Flirting and grandmothers.

And blowjobs.

Because it was difficult to be getting such a glorious view of Donovan's back and not think about *the front*. About how much he'd like to take what he was sure would be a very impressive erection in his mouth and blow both Donovan's cock *and* his mind. Had he ever had a blowjob by a man before? Just because he'd never admitted out loud he was gay to a guy before didn't mean he didn't have an arrangement with some discrete dude or service, perhaps, for the purpose of sexual release.

Although Beck hoped not. Because he couldn't deny,

the idea of *him* being Donovan's first was fast becoming an obsession. Sure, closeted guys were off Beck's relationship radar, but potentially introducing *this* guy to the delights of another man's body was firmly on his sexy-times radar.

Not that such thoughts were exactly respectable, standing next to a woman who'd proudly told him she was eighty-six and a great-grandmother six times over. Beck filed those thoughts under *spank bank* and ordered the horny little devil that had been riding his shoulder since Monday to shut up.

"He's nearly there," Mrs. Connor said.

Her hand fluttered absently near her throat as she watched Donovan inch closer to her very bedraggled cat. Wally's fur was soaked and clinging to his body like Donovan's shorts were clinging to his ass. Except beneath the fur the cat was impressively skinny, and beneath those shorts, Donovan was impressively *not*.

Even through the shroud of pissing rain, the cat was visibly trembling as Donovan reached out his hand. It didn't move from its spot, however, and Beck watched as Donovan inched a little closer, sliding his arm around the cat's middle and lifting. Wally, though, was not having any of it as he clung to the branch for grim death, protesting the intervention with hissing and a meow loud enough to be heard over the rain. But Donovan persisted, and eventually, the cat unfurled his claws.

"Oh...he did it!" Mrs. Connor exclaimed, clapping her hands.

Beck smiled. "He did." And he thanked the universe that he'd been here to witness *the* Donovan Bane, pro rugby god, in the role of cat rescuer.

Tucking the animal beneath his arm, Donovan shimmied much more cautiously down the tree, which meant Beck got to watch the show all over again—in reverse. *And* slow motion. He wasn't sure which one he appreciated more, but for *damn* sure he'd be turning that conundrum over and over in his head.

Often. At night. In bed.

Bloody hell. *Get a grip.* He was wearing Lycra for fuck's sake. When it was dry, that stuff showed every line and bump of his body. When it was wet? The damn thing showed which side he dressed.

About a foot from the ground, Wally obviously decided he was close enough to make a break for it. He squirmed before leaping out of Donovan's arms and splashing down in the sodden grass that surrounded the base of the tree.

"Wally!" Mrs. Connor bent over and clicked a few times in the cat's direction. "Here, my darling. You poor thing. Come to Mummy."

The cat *strutted* over, tail flicking, like he'd just returned fit and fabulous from a day at the spa, *not* looking like he'd just cashed in one of his nine lives.

"There, there," she soothed as she swept Wally into her arms, kissing the wet fur between his eyes several times. "That was so naughty, Wally. Naughty. Naughty. Naughty." She emphasised each *naughty* with another kiss.

Beck vaguely heard the cat purring appreciatively, but he only had eyes for Donovan coming toward him through the heavy cloak of rain centred in the beam of the torch. His sodden clothes revealed the full extent of his mass, his T-shirt streaked with grime from the bark like some kind of arboreal skid mark.

A potent rush of desire whammied Beck, kicking up his heartbeat and flooding heat to his groin. He'd been attracted to Donovan from the get-go, but striding toward him like a superhero from the dark, complete with shiny fucking halo over his head?

Christ…he wanted this man.

A fact that was patently obvious now to anyone who

bothered to look in the general vicinity of his crotch. Beck thanked his lucky stars for the lack of light as he switched off the torch and used it as a prop to hide his erection.

"Oh, thank you," Mrs. Connor said, her voice thick with emotion as Donovan joined them under the porch. "I'm terribly sorry about this. You are so good to me." She looked down at Wally. "Say thank you, Wally."

Wally eyed his rescuer with disdain but did manage to mutter a tiny meow, which earned him a beaming smile from *Mummy*. "Why don't you both come in and get dry? I can make some hot chocolate, and I have some jam drops I made this afternoon looking to make themselves at home in some stomachs."

"No thanks, Mrs. Connor," Donovan said with a smile. "We'll get dry at my place then I need to get Beckett home."

His announcement rang with finality and maybe desperation. And even though Donovan wasn't looking at him, Beck was getting the message, loud and clear. He was drawing a line under their night. Signalling this deviation from their journey was over.

Beck suppressed a smile. Donovan needn't have bothered. As much as Beck would love to stage a seduction, Donovan had probably come far enough for one night. He was going to need to process a bunch of *stuff.*

They bade goodbye to Mrs. Connor, who picked up Wally's paw and waved it at them before heading inside. It took a matter of seconds to cross to Donovan's house, and Beck waited patiently for the door to open. A light snapped on and was temporarily blocked as Donovan stepped through the doorway, taking up nearly all the space. Beck followed him in, shutting the door then leaning his ass against it while he took in the surroundings.

He was standing in a large, open floorplan with four distinct zones. A living area dominated by a huge wall-mounted television to his left. Behind that, a dining area, with a solid wooden table. Along the back wall to the right ran a modern kitchen with white marble benchtops, gleaming fixtures, and a long breakfast bar that housed the sink and sectioned off the last zone to Beck's immediate right, which had several bookshelves, a low couch with plump, comfy cushions, two colourful bean bags, and a desk with a computer.

A hallway ran off an open doorway between the kitchen and dining areas, where Beck presumed the bedrooms and bathroom could be found. The high raked ceilings were dominated by large wooden beams, the furnishings and fixtures were excellent quality, the tiles underfoot were glossy, and the colour scheme had the subtle classiness that came with an expensive interior decorator.

Clearly what the house lacked in panache on the outside, it made up for in quality on the inside, yet it was also unexpected. Beck figured there'd be more overt signs of masculinity. Framed football jerseys on the walls. Impossibly heavy weights strewn on the floor. Sporting trophies cluttering shelves.

There *were* a couple of trophies in the bookshelves, but both seemed to be for swimming with a female figure on top of each one. There were also several medals hanging over the edge of one shelf, their neck ribbons anchored around the base of a pink-and-blue unicorn statue.

Donovan's daughter's, Beck presumed.

The house was impressively clean and neat. No dishes cluttered the sink, no discarded pizza boxes or beer cans littered the living areas, and there was no pile up of mail or other paraphernalia on either the dining table or the breakfast bar. Was he a slob who employed a cleaning service? Or was he a neat freak?

Beck's gaze drifted over to Donovan, who was dumping

his keys on the breakfast bar and toeing off his wet shoes at the same time. He contemplated asking him to not stop at the shoes but didn't. "My hero," he said instead, smiling a little as Donovan's frame stiffened.

Slowly, the man turned to face him. "Beckett."

Beckett. Man, even with the warning in his voice, Beck liked the way Donovan called him by his full name. When only two other people in the entire world called him that, it imbued the name with an intimacy that he really, *really* liked.

It sure a shit wasn't helping the state of his dick.

"Yes, Donovan?" Beck grinned with an expression of faux innocence. He liked the way that name rolled off his tongue.

Donovan liked it, too, if the flare of his nostrils was any indication. He opened his mouth then shut it again, their gazes locking for long moments before Donovan broke the contact. But he didn't look away. Oh no. He looked *down.* His gaze *dropped* to travel over Beck's body with breath-snatching intensity.

Beck forgot about how soaked he was and the water running off him into a puddle on Donovan's floor as his flesh lit up, long licks of flame evaporating every water droplet in its path. His neck, his chest, his abs, his thighs all touched by the heat. The taut sling of muscle stretching from one hip bone to the other and, between, the hard line of his cock.

It was impossible to hide the erection, so Beck didn't even try. In fact, he shoved his hands on his hips, framing his arousal, and lifted his chin as the other man looked his fill. He refused to be ashamed of a perfectly normal bodily function. And maybe, if Donovan could see how comfortable Beck was about the situation, he'd start to open himself up to possibilities.

After long, excruciating moments, Donovan dragged his gaze back to Beck's face, his throat bobbing as he swallowed hard. "*Beckett.*"

Beck shut his eyes briefly as he dropped his hands to his side. *God*…this guy. The husky ache in his voice was so damn raw it hurt *Beck's* throat. The clash of emotions in his eyes was just as painful to witness. The desire was plain, but so was the hesitancy. The anxiety. And maybe even a little fear.

Of the unknown? Of stepping into something new. Of what he wanted?

Of *how much* he wanted it?

Beck wouldn't have thought it possible to see such a big, vital guy so damn motionless. Torn between what he wanted and what he wouldn't allow himself to have, the limitations that held him in precarious check stretching thinner and thinner with each passing second making him cling even harder.

The competing forces played out in his tormented gaze, and hell if Beck didn't want to cross the damn room and launch himself at Donovan. Make the first move. Take that big hand and shove it down his Lycra bike pants, wrap those big fingers around his throbbing erection while he kissed Donovan within an inch of his life.

But…not tonight.

Donovan needed some time and space now. Nothing much might have happened on the surface, but underneath it all, it had been a big night for the big guy. The conflict in his gaze said it all, and Beck didn't want to be that guy. The one who took advantage of a situation to fulfill his own selfish needs.

He had no doubt he could show Donovan Bane a damn good time. Hell, the mere thought of initiating him into the delights of guy-on-guy was keeping his erection fully loaded. But their coming together would be so much better when Donovan came to him of his own volition.

If Donovan came to him of his own volition.

Clearing his throat, Beck said, "Is the bathroom"—he pointed at the door leading to the hallway—"through there?"

The enquiry snapped Donovan out of his inertia, and he straightened, leaning against the bench as he blew out a steady breath. "Second door on the right. Laundry is third on the right for the clean clothes."

Beck nodded as he toed off his sodden shoes. "Thanks." And he headed for the open doorway, conscious of Donovan's gaze like a laser burning right between his shoulder blades.

· · ·

Donovan had been pacing the floor near the front door for five minutes, the car keys in his pocket jingling with each footfall. He'd waited until he'd heard the bathroom door close and had bolted to his bedroom and the attached en suite to dry off and change his clothes. All while trying not to think about Beckett.

About how he'd asked the question tonight without asking the question—gently and without judgment. About his teasing and his flirting and how good he'd been with Mrs. Connor. And about that fucking erection. About the way he'd put his hands on his hips, emphasising its existence and daring Donovan to keep looking.

Jesus. How could he not when presented with the blatant evidence of the other man's arousal? Even torn between the urge to walk right over, sink to his knees, pull down those flimsy, wet shorts, and suck that cock deep into his mouth and blind panic, he couldn't drag his gaze away.

Knowing Beckett was in that state because of him had been terrifying and dizzying all at once. Especially given he'd not done or said anything remotely sexy. He hadn't gotten close enough to touch, and he'd barely said a word to him since Mrs. Connor's phone call.

Donovan had lived long enough to know that arousal didn't need any overt provocation, but really, he'd been... whatever the opposite of a turn-on was? A bucket of cold water? Not to mention supremely fucking awkward.

Which meant Beckett must just plain *desire* him.

Sure, he'd been aware of the vibe between them from the start, had sensed the other man's interest from the get-go. God knew he'd had quite a few Beckett-induced erections himself. But surely someone getting it as often as Beckett must be wasn't in the kind of hair-trigger state that was all too familiar to Donovan.

Surely he had better control?

Okay, yeah, scrap that bullshit. Donovan shook his head free of the preposterous thought. Since when, if ever, had Donovan's dick *obeyed* him? That fucker had a mind of its own. Penises weren't known for their controllability, and where Beckett was concerned, Donovan's had gone totally rogue.

Which was why he was driving the dude home then avoiding him like the plague.

"What washing powder do you use in your machine? Your clothes are soft as down, and they smell like strawberries and sweet, warm milk."

Donovan startled a little. He'd been so deep in thought he hadn't heard Beckett pad into the room with his bare feet. Glancing at him as he approached, whatever the other man had said stopped computing. Donovan was not prepared for the sight of Beckett in *his* clothes. He looked fucking *hot* in the plain navy T-shirt and a pair of drawstring basketball shorts that always sat just above his knee, but on Beckett, they came to just under.

Unlike his bike clothes, these were definitely on the baggy side—thankfully hiding any residual hard-on—but a swell of possession stormed Donovan's defences. The kind of sensation he usually only got when he'd plucked the ball from the air just before it got to an opponent's fingers and ran it down to the try line with the crowd screaming his name.

Mine. Mine. *Mine.*

It roared through his ears and filled his chest, rising like helium, lodging in his throat.

"Donovan?" The question was low and silky, Beckett's eyebrow quirked, a small, playful smile on his mouth. "Your laundry detergent?" he prompted.

"Oh." Donovan blinked. "I use..." Fuck? What did he use? He'd never been asked before, and the way Beckett's hair, no longer plastered to his head but still damp, tended to curl on top was exceedingly distracting. "Lux soap flakes."

Beckett's smiled grew. "Soap flakes? I didn't expect that."

Donovan wanted to ask what he *did* expect. Something he-man like bleach or Borax? Or an admission that he washed his clothes using rocks down by the river? People made assumptions about him because of his size and what he did.

It didn't usually bother him, but it *did* with this guy.

He'd never be some refined gentleman, didn't want to be. But he also didn't want Beckett to think he was some kind of Neanderthal. No matter how much *caveman* stirred in his blood every time he looked at the other man.

"My daughter had bad eczema for the first few years of her life, still does from time to time. It's the only detergent that doesn't exacerbate her condition, so I've just always used it."

"I'm sorry, I've forgotten how old your daughter is?"

The question seemed inquisitive, not wary. Beckett didn't seem weirded out by the fact he had a kid. "She's fourteen."

"She lives with her mother?"

Donovan nodded. "Yes. In New Zealand. She comes to

Australia for the school holidays."

Which was much easier now she was older, and at this age she still enjoyed the trip across the ditch to stay with her dad. Donovan always went home to Auckland for Christmas so Miri didn't have to feel split in two on what was an important family day. Annie, his ex, who had remarried and had two other children—Miri's brothers—and Dale, her husband, always welcomed him to their house for the day. He and Annie were still great mates, and Dale was a good bloke who was secure enough in his love for Annie and their marriage to not be a jealous asshole.

But none of that was Beckett's business. Pulling his keys out of his pocket, he asked, "You ready?"

"It's fine. I called an Uber." Beckett held up his phone, the screen showing a map with a little virtual car moving along a virtual street. "It'll be here in six minutes."

"Oh…right." He shoved his keys back in his pocket and started cracking his knuckles. Now what?

"Rain's been forecast for the next couple of days," Beckett said, clearly *not* disconcerted by the *six* whole minutes they had together.

Unlike Donovan.

A *lot* could happen in six minutes. A hundred push-ups could be achieved. A try could be scored. Two soft-boiled eggs could be cooked. One-minute rice could be cooked six times over.

A kiss could be given. Hell, a kiss could get out of control.

"So I won't be needing my bike," he continued, oblivious to the machine gun *rat-a-tat* of Donovan's thoughts. "Is it okay if I get it on the weekend?"

No. God, *no*. His pulse spiked. It was *not* okay. They couldn't be alone like this again. He wanted things that weren't possible whenever the other man was in sight. Best not to tempt fate. But Beckett didn't give him an option as he said, "Here," and handed over his phone. "Put your number in my contacts, and I'll call later to arrange a time."

Donovan took the phone on autopilot, staring at it like it was a live bomb or a hand grenade with the pin pulled. Why had he taken it? Why hadn't he refused? And *why*, in God's name, was he inputting his number? Probably because it gave him something to do with his hands other than crack his knuckles.

Or put them all over Beckett.

Maybe also something to do with the illicit hitch in his breathing and bump in his pulse at the thought of Beckett having his number.

Handing it back, Donovan returned to cracking his knuckles under Beckett's steady, unnerving gaze. The other man didn't bother to hide his attraction. It was there, frank and real, backed up by that wide, easy smile, causing an ache in Donovan's bones and a shiver through his blood.

Jesus—why did being with Beckett make him feel like he was coming down with a communicable disease?

How many minutes were left, damn it? Three? Four?

"So," Beckett said, his smile gentling, his gaze flicking to Donovan's fingers briefly before returning to his face, "I'm going to take a wild guess and say you've never been with a guy, have you?"

Donovan paused mid–knuckle crack, his heart thudding like gunfire in his chest now. He swallowed, panicking for a moment over how to answer. Should he be honest and tell him about his one and only foray into exploring his sexuality with a man that had made sure he *never* tried again? Should he lie and brag about how much dick he got? Or tell the guy to mind his own fucking business.

And go wait out in the rain for his Uber.

In the end, with his brain all a'jumble, he blurted out the truth. "No." He refused to count that one disaster as an example.

But, almost immediately, he wished he could take the *no* back. He felt gauche admitting his lack of experience to a man who clearly had a plethora of it. The same way he'd felt at seventeen admitting to his mates that he was still a virgin despite having been with Annie for two years. He'd been embarrassed back then. Left with the feeling of not being normal because he hadn't *done the deed* yet. And confused because he hadn't *wanted* to.

Desperate to not be *ab*normal, he'd been...vulnerable to their friendly jibes. Which was pretty much how Miri had happened. And here he was, fifteen years later, feeling awkward and abnormal all over again.

But this time for his lack of gay credentials.

"Have you never even been"—Beckett dropped his eyes to Donovan's mouth, lingering a little longer than necessary before locking gazes—"kissed by a man?"

Donovan swallowed against a lump in his throat big as a fist. The sounds of knuckles being cracked filled the silence that had ballooned between them. Kissing a man was the thing he fantasised about the most when he was lying in his bed at night.

It was his go-to fantasy during his sexy *alone* times.

The other sex stuff he was never sure about, but the yearning to feel a man's mouth on his? To taste him? To feel the softness of lips and the roughness of whiskers? To hear a low male groan filling his head? Smell the rich, heavy notes of aftershave? Feel the stroke of his tongue, swallow the husky timbre of his pants?

That well went *deep.*

The man in his fantasies had always been faceless. Anonymous. As of Monday, he'd worn a suit and had a pair of dimples that didn't quit.

"No."

"Well, now," Beckett said with a slow, rueful kind of smile, his gaze fleetingly touching Donovan's lips again. "*That* is a great shame."

The well got deeper even as the lump turned sharp and pointy. "I can't." The words were blunt, almost harsh in their finality as he set his jaw, ignoring the leap in his pulse and the clear invitation in Beckett's eyes.

He was thirty-two, damn it. He refused to be vulnerable again.

Beckett just nodded thoughtfully. No judgment. "Because of rugby?"

"Yes."

"There are"—he took a step closer—"gay footballers."

Donovan's belly clenched as Beckett came within touching distance, and he cracked faster, the dull creak loud as his knuckles succumbed to their regular torture. It was entirely possible he'd have none left at the end of this six minutes. "Not any of them that are out. Not at an elite level."

If there was precedence, his coming out wouldn't be such a curiosity. The interest would probably be less and abate faster. But there wasn't. He would be it. Standing out on his own like a fucking *maypole* in the middle of the rugby pitch.

"And you want to be known as the best rugby pro, not the best gay rugby pro."

"Yes." Jesus, *yes*. Beckett *got* it. "I also don't want who I sleep with—" Donovan stumbled over his choice of phrasing. Like he slept with dudes all the time instead of being a... big, gay, virgin *liar*. "*Off* the field, to be the story. To be what defines me *on* the field. Because it will be."

Donovan knew that as sure as God made little green apples. And he didn't want to be a spectacle. The pressures of the elite game were hard enough without media bullshit and homophobic crap as well. Rugby was still a *man's* game in a lot of ways—scratch the surface and old attitudes wouldn't be hard to find.

Again, Beckett just nodded, empathy and understanding in his gaze. Until he dropped it to Donovan's knuckles. Reaching out a hand, he slid it over Donovan's busy fingers, and every nerve ending in Donovan's body went into overload, sizzling from the tips of his fingers up and out, branching everywhere until he was humming and *burning* all over with the current. His breath hitched as the whole damn world stood still.

Gripping Donovan's hand a little firmer, Beckett took another step closer until there was only a handspan between them. Compared to Donovan, he was two inches shorter, a little less broad across the shoulders, and generally leaner, but right now, Beckett seemed to take up all the space. Inside Donovan's head as well as inside the room.

Tipping his chin up slightly, Beckett looked him straight in the eyes and said, "You know knuckle cracking is really bad for you, right?"

Donovan's breathing roughened, and his belly felt like it was made from tangled fishing nets pulling tauter and tauter into cold, wet knots. He swallowed even though it hurt, his throat suddenly as parched as three-day-old toast. "So I've heard."

He tugged then, loosening Donovan's top hand and bringing it slowly, *slowly* to his mouth. Donovan could do nothing but watch the progress, his breath thick as soup in his lungs. It was ridiculous—he had the other man by a good thirty kilos, yet he was powerless to resist.

Their gazes locked—blue on brown—a rough, pent-up breath escaping Donovan's mouth as Beckett's full lips touched down on the knuckle of his index finger. His heart thudded loud in his chest and ears, and his vision blurred as the world tilted on its axis. His dick turned hard as granite, and he had to lock his knees to stop from swaying.

"*Beckett*," he murmured, his voice low and so fucking needy he'd have cringed had he been in his right mind.

Clearly, he was not.

Why he'd spoken the other man's name, he wasn't sure. As a protest? An encouragement? Whatever it was, Beckett didn't respond, just kept his gaze locked with Donovan's and continued the onslaught, moving to the next knuckle, whispering his lips over it. The third knuckle felt the scrape of Beckett's teeth then the quick soothing wet of his tongue. The last one got similar treatment.

Donovan's breathing was so husky now he was sure Mrs. Connor could probably hear it next door. But Beckett was also breathing roughly, his breath hot on Donovan's hand, his eyes also *hot*. Hazy with liquid desire.

"All better now," he murmured, lifting his head but keeping a firm hold on Donovan's hand.

Jesus Christ. It was *not* better now. Not even close. Because now he knew how it felt to have Beckett's mouth on his skin and Donovan wanted more. He sure as shit wanted Beckett's lips on his lips. Hell, Donovan had never wanted to kiss anyone as badly as he wanted to kiss Beckett in this moment.

His tongue flicked out to wet his lips, and the flare of Beckett's nostrils bucked through Donovan's already turgid cock like a bolt of lightning.

Fuck. How many minutes left?

And then, blessedly, a horn sounded. How Donovan heard it over the thrum of his own heartbeat—the urgency of his own *need*—he didn't know, but he grabbed it like a lifeline. Pulling his hand away, he stepped back. "That must be your Uber." He sounded like he'd just chain-smoked an entire packet of cigarettes.

Beckett smiled one of his tender smiles, nodding slowly. "Thank you for rescuing me from the rain."

Donovan shrugged, his shoulders stiff. "I'd do the same for anyone."

The grooves of his dimples deepened. "See you at the game on Saturday," he said as he brushed past, not waiting for a reply.

Donovan, his back to the door, didn't turn around and watch Beckett go. He heard it opening, then the drumbeat of the rain, then the door closing again. He didn't say goodbye. He certainly didn't acknowledge Beckett's parting statement.

See you at the game on Saturday.

Not if he could help it.

Chapter Four

"*What the fuck*, Dono?" Tanner Stone, the team captain demanded, his voice strident enough to be heard over the cheers from the opposition supporters in the crowd.

Clearly his legendary patience was at an end as Donovan barely got his fingers to the stray ball he'd have normally intercepted with both eyes shut. It sailed straight into the arms of the opposition winger, who was currently running it down the field. Sure, mistakes happened—fumbles and missteps weren't unusual in any game. But Donovan's play had been riddled with them tonight, so he didn't blame Tanner for his exasperation.

His head just wasn't in the game, his mind constantly wandering to that slight brush of mouth against knuckles as it had ever since it'd happened. How could something so light and barely there feel so significant?

And really fucking hot?

For crying out loud, the guy's dick had been practically pornographic in its display of arousal, but the hand-kissing was what was distracting him?

The Smoke supporters clearly didn't care about the cataclysmic experience and were letting him know about it in the stands. Griff, who always ran a tight ship and relied on Donovan's usually safe hands, was practically apoplectic as he stalked the sidelines.

Yep. As far as games went, Donovan was having a shocker, but knowing the man who'd *kissed his hand* on Wednesday night was up there in the Smoke corporate box with the WAGs and *Harry the cute waiter*, watching him? That was really fucking with his head.

It might have been fanciful thinking, but Donovan swore he could feel the other man's eyes on him, in the same way he could still feel the brush of Beckett's mouth against his knuckles.

And he wanted to impress. He wanted to take Beckett's breath away. He wanted Harry the cute waiter to pale into insignificance. He wanted Beckett to be as turned on watching him kill it on the field as Donovan had been from Beckett's seemingly innocent knuckle-kissing.

But he *wasn't* killing it on the field. In fact, he was barely holding his own. They were losing, and he doubted that even with fifteen minutes to go, they could turn it around. He needed to give it a red-hot try, though. If not for the team than for Suit Guy in the corporate box.

So, *enough with the moony teenage bullshit, dude.*

It was time to play ball.

• • •

There was general grimacing and surprised intakes of breath in the box as Donovan missed the intercept. "Bloody hell," Matilda Kent, Tanner's wife, said. "What's up with Dono tonight?"

"Yeah, he's really off his game, isn't he?" Eleanor replied.

She was Bodie Webb's fiancée and Ryder Davis's little sister.

Several furrowed brows and enthusiastic nods appeared to agree. Beck, who was standing between Val and Harper, might not be a huge rugby aficionado, but even he could see Donovan was not having a good game. He'd come prepared for some breathtaking action, but it hadn't eventuated.

Which was surprising. But also not.

Donovan had clearly been discombobulated the other night. He'd made some big revelations, and the way he'd looked at Beck as he'd pressed his mouth to Donovan's knuckles had been...

Well, Beck was still trying to find a word for the depth of *longing* in his eyes. It had been almost painful to witness. Big and wide and hungry.

Desperate, almost.

And that could still be weighing on his mind. Hell, Beck hadn't been able to stop thinking about it, stop turning it over in his head, either. The taste of his skin, the roughness of it, the slow, hard bob of Donovan's Adam's apple that had made him want to press a kiss to that heavily whiskered part of his throat.

Was it weighing on his mind? And, if so, then *Beck* had to take partial responsibility for Donovan's bad form tonight.

"Another beer, sir?"

Beck glanced to his side where Harry—who was indeed *very* cute—stood with a loaded drinks tray. For the last ten minutes, Beck had been standing sandwiched between Val and Harper, who were about as close to the glass as was possible without squashing their noses against it. All the WAGs had risen to their collective feet about ten minutes ago when Lincoln Quinn had made a dash for the try line, and they hadn't sat down since.

"No thanks," Beck declined, smiling politely at Harry, careful to keep his natural inner flirt under wraps. Prior to

Monday, Beck would have picked up what Harry was putting down without thinking twice. But it just didn't appeal tonight.

And besides, he'd already had two beers and was driving home later.

Harry gave him a disappointed but still very cute smile before offering the tray to the nearby WAGs. Harper nudged Beck as she picked up a glass of champagne. "I told you he was a cutie," she whispered. "And into you."

He bestowed another polite smile, on Harper this time. Both things were true, but neither were of interest to Beck. He only had eyes for the big guy with the brown skin in the tight jersey and shorts that were positively indecent. His thick, crinkly hair was tied back in a man-bun and, even from all the way up in the box, thanks to the powerful lights situated around the grounds, he could make out the shine of sweat beading on Donovan's forehead.

Beck's nostrils flared involuntarily. What would Donovan smell like after a game? That potent mix of earthiness from the grass covering the field, the leather of the ball, the sweetness of Gatorade on his breath.

And the intoxicating bouquet of healthy male sweat—salt and pheromones.

"Well," Val demanded. "Can you see it? Have we managed to convert you yet?"

Harper snorted. "Tonight hasn't exactly been the best example."

Beck shrugged. "It's quite the spectator sport," he said, injecting just the right amount of sexual innuendo to be humorous. After all, sweaty athletic guys *were* in his lane. But he was careful to ensure his gaze took in the whole field and wasn't linked to one man.

"Yep." Em, Lincoln Quinn's fiancée, sighed. Then there was collective sighing as she said, "Not really a hardship to watch big, buff men run around a field in tight jerseys, is it?"

He laughed as the WAGs' gazes all seemed to focus suddenly on the field. "No argument from me," he agreed, and then, while the women were all distracted, ogling their own men, he ogled the fuck out of Donovan, whose frame had taken on an alertness that caused a prickle down his spine.

Every muscle in Donovan's body seemed to coil tight as a spring, ready to unload. It made him seem suddenly more… *compact*, and for such a big man, it was a visible change. But it wasn't for long, his laser-like gaze tracking the ball, which had been kicked high and was currently being eyed off by an opponent.

What happened next left Beck breathless. The spring *sprang*, and Donovan intercepted the ball with a burst of speed and skill that made Beck as hard as the steel of the goalpost. All the women in the box screamed their lungs out, banging the glass, yelling, "*Go, Dono, go!*" as the TV commentators excitedly narrated the play from the small screen mounted high in the corner behind them.

With the ball tucked securely under his arm, he ran with it, zigging and zagging down the field as if he was being hunted by lions, which, given the size and the closeness of the pack behind him, wasn't far from wrong. Beck doubted he'd get to the try line before they caught him up, but he had no support there yet, either, to pass it safely, so he kept on running.

When two of the pack finally caught him up, they leaped at his body, one around an ankle, the other grabbing his shoulder. But Donovan refused to be deterred, shrugging them away, the player only managing to grasp hold of his jersey as Donovan kicked out of the foot hold with a slight stumble.

And still he kept powering forward, dragging the player still attached to his jersey behind him like a matador's cape.

The crowd was roaring. A commentator was going nuts, his voice high and fast as he called the play. Beck's pulse was in a similar condition as he watched Donovan still running, hampered and slowed but still making ground as another opposition player made a swipe, grabbing him momentarily, slowing Donovan's momentum further but failing to drag him to the ground.

It was *electric* stuff, and Beck was riveted, his heart taking it in turns to accelerate for several seconds then stop for several seconds more. Sure, Donovan was a big guy, but how much longer could he keep upright, could he keep *going*, as dude after dude came at him, trying to bring him down?

He would have to succumb soon, surely?

And goddamn it, watching them on him, watching him evade those clutching hands, was all kinds of erotic.

But then, suddenly, just as Donovan was starting to pitch forward, Ronan Dempsey, the Smoke's new American import, as blond and apple pie as Donovan was bronzed and fucking *warrior*, was there beside him. Donovan passed the ball as he succumbed to the mauling. Entirely engulfed by the pack now, he finally allowed himself to be taken to the ground with the kind of crunch that had Beck wincing and wondering if anything had been damaged.

And if Donovan would let him kiss that better as well.

Christ, he had it *bad*, but that display of sheer potent masculinity, of *grunt*, had him so fucking hot, Beck didn't know what to do with it. He'd sure as hell never thought he'd be this turned on in the presence of a dozen women. But thoughts of how close he might be to actual orgasm were overridden as the noise reached a crescendo, dragging his attention away from a felled Donovan.

The Smoke supporters both inside and outside the box were all on their feet now, going absolutely wild as Ronan ran the ball over the try line. The WAGs erupted in cheers, hugging and high-fiving each other, mimicking the players on the field running to congratulate Ronan, who'd already made a beeline for Donovan. Several of the team members helped pull the big guy up off the ground, and Ronan launched himself at Donovan as soon as he was upright.

And then everyone else piled on.

Beck tried valiantly not to make it something it wasn't, but *man*...all that sweaty male flesh pressed together was prolonging a hard-on that was already in imminent danger of losing its load. He knew it wasn't supposed to be homoerotic, but Christ—all that hugging and patting each other in the thrill of the moment was only adding to his condition.

He'd seen porn that was nowhere near as good.

"Wasn't that amazing?" Val demanded, her hand gripping his sleeve, her cheeks flushed, her eyes flashing with pride and excitement. "Now do you see it?"

Oh yeah. He definitely saw it. "Yeah." He grinned. "Now I see it."

Pretending to polish her fingernails on her T-shirt, she blew on them and murmured, "Then my work here is done."

$$\cdots$$

When the hooter sounded ten minutes later, they'd lost by six points, but at least Donovan felt like he'd redeemed himself with that try he'd set up. If he was being honest, it had probably been one of his best ever. Hell, it might be one of the best this year across the whole national competition. Which was just as well, given nothing else about his game had been redeemable. And all because Beckett—a man whose surname he *still* didn't know—was watching him from the corporate box.

"Donovan, my man," Linc said, slapping him on the back as they all trooped into the locker room, sombre from their defeat, cleats clacking against the floor. "I don't know how you pulled that off, but it was brilliant."

"Come on, Linc," Ryder said with his slow country drawl as he sat on the bench in front of his locker, grabbed a cold beer from the nearby iced-filled cooler and popped the top. "If anyone knows how to pull things off, it's you."

The locker room cracked up despite the loss hanging over them.

"That's true," Ronan chipped in as he took his jersey off, his American accent standing out like a pimple on a pumpkin amidst all the Australians. "Even all the way back home in Denver, he's known for being the king at pulling things off."

Since joining the team at the beginning of the season, the young American had quickly slipped into the smack-talking banter that Donovan loved so much about the locker room.

Linc snorted. "King? I am a freaking ninja Jedi at pulling things off." To demonstrate, he grabbed his crotch and thrust his pelvis twice in lewd suggestion.

"Jesus, Linc." Dexter Blake laughed as he opened his locker and wiped the sweat off his brow with a towel he had stashed there. "Wanking's supposed to be a dirty secret, not something to brag about."

Donovan, who was removing his shoes, thought about how many times he'd jacked off this week to the memory of Beckett's teeth digging into his knuckles and the lap of his hot tongue as it soothed the sting. Twice that night in bed. And the two nights after despite the quickie wanks he'd had in the shower upon returning from training each day. And this morning when he'd woken with wood that could bang in nails and no training to distract him from his desires.

It felt like a *very* dirty secret. And not because he was hiding his sexuality from a bunch of guys he considered his closest friends. Or not *just* because of that, anyway. It was more how...vanilla the fantasy was. It was hardly a gay orgy or sucking random anonymous dicks through a glory hole.

Bodie Webb, Spidey to his teammates, made a dismissive kind of *pfft* noise. "It's something to brag about if you go to private school. Hell, it's practically a sport."

"I'd have thought constant wanking was the only way to get through private school," Kyle Leighton quipped. He was Val's husband—and the baby daddy of Griffin King's grandson—and had grown up in western Sydney in a place where no one went to private school.

Laughter filled the locker room. "That explains the early onset arthritis in his right wrist," Ryder said.

There was more laughter, which was interrupted by Griffin King entering the room. Silence fell as everyone sat a little straighter. He was not only one of the best coaches in the country, but in the entire world of elite rugby. An ex-player himself, he'd switched to coaching upon his retirement and had been at the Smoke from the get-go. He was a formidable presence with his great mane of ginger hair, full ginger beard, a body that had not softened one iota in his post-player life, and a reputation for not suffering fools gladly.

A family tragedy had toughened the man in ways that went beyond the discipline of rugby. It had made him a hard taskmaster, not the kind of man who believed in gently, gently or excuses or any of that *touch-feely crap*—his words.

He was old school through and through. He loved his team, though, he loved his players. He just showed it through toughness and gruffness and hard-won compliments. But he was fair and never asked of his players what he wasn't prepared to give.

And there wasn't a man in the locker room who wouldn't go to the mat for him.

He'd mellowed significantly since the arrival of little Griff last year and the slowly healing chasm he'd created between himself and Val. Still, he was a long way from quitting rugby to volunteer as a school crossing supervisor.

"So," he said, shoving big hands on hips, his voice a deep rumble. "We lost. Someone's got to."

The words weren't surprising. Griff didn't believe in niceties and preferred to cut to the chase. Why use a couple of dozen words when a few would suffice? As a man of few words himself, Donovan concurred.

"I think we all know that wasn't our best performance out there." That was an understatement, but Griff wasn't the kind of coach who yelled and berated when they lost—only when his men didn't give a hundred percent.

Donovan's cheeks heated. Sure, his contribution to the game hadn't been the only lacklustre one, but several of his missteps in particular had cost them dearly.

"We'll look at the tapes tomorrow," he continued. "See you all here at eight sharp."

Griff's post-game speech was as succinct and pragmatic as usual. *Game over. We lost. Moving on.* Which wasn't that different from his winning speech. *Well done. Moving on. See you tomorrow.* The pride in his eyes, though, that was always golden. That's what they all played for. And tonight they'd fallen short.

A disappointed Griff was harder to take then a pissed-off Griff.

He departed then, but not before he said, "Dono, my office."

The men watched their coach depart in heavy silence. Dex, who was sitting beside Donovan, handed over the beer he'd cracked just prior to Griff entering. "This might help," he said.

Donovan doubted it, but he took the beer anyway, downing three long, cold mouthfuls before handing the can back to Dex. "Thanks."

Tanner stood as Donovan moved toward the exit,

meeting him at the door. He held up his arm, his elbow bent, and they locked their hands together as if they were about to arm wrestle but held in solidarity instead. "We can all have an off night," he said.

"Yeah." Didn't make it suck any less, though.

Donovan didn't bother with his shoes as he padded barefoot to Griff's office, which wasn't far from the locker room, his body hurting in that familiar way it always did after a game of rugby that involved being regularly slammed into the ground. But it was nothing on the way he felt at having let the team down. He wasn't concerned that he'd lose his place in the team or that Griff would rip him a new one—although he may well be benched if he didn't get his shit together.

He just hated letting the man down. Letting the team down.

The door was shut, and steeling himself for a beat or two, he knocked. "Come."

Donovan opened the door to find Griff already behind his desk. It was as messy as usual, crammed with papers, notebooks, several large ring-binder folders, and god only knew what else. There were two empty coffee mugs—three, if the disposable one was counted—and the resultant brown rings on the table surface beneath, as well as a mug with several large cracks that had obviously been broken and glued back together that was stuffed full of pens.

Next to the PC monitor was a framed picture of Val with little Griff.

"Coach."

"Shhh." Griff had a remote in hand and was already watching the TV situated on the wall opposite his desk— muted. As far as wall-mounted TVs went, it wasn't large, but it was big enough to see all the errors Donovan had made tonight, that was for damn sure.

Hell, *they* were big enough to drive a Mack truck through.

After several beats, Griff paused the play, freezing the

frame on the missed intercept. Glancing at Donovan, he demanded, "What in hell is going on with you lately?"

He didn't yell. Hell, he barely raised his voice. He wasn't spitting fire and fury like he did when someone wasn't giving their all during training, but he was clearly at a loss for what had gone wrong.

If Donovan was being honest, he knew exactly what had gone wrong and why. He was slightly less clear over what in the fuck he was going to do about it. "I'm sorry," he apologised.

"Don't be goddamn sorry," Griff growled. "Fix it."

"Yes." Donovan nodded. "Absolutely." Easy. *Not.*

"You're my most dependable player. And it's not just me who depends on you—the entire team does. You play textbook rugby and you're focused. You have a job to do out there, and you do it every time. *Every* time. Until this week."

Donovan opened his mouth to apologise once more then snapped it shut. Griff hadn't wanted to hear sorry the first time. He sure as hell wouldn't want to hear it again. "I'll work it out."

He had to.

If only the thought didn't fill him with despair. He didn't know *how* to work it out. Unless he did the one thing he'd decided to put off until *after*. But he doubted Griff would thank him for the three-ring circus that would evolve from the first pro rugby player in the country to come out of the closet.

Griff hated it when his players lost focus—tonight being a good case in point. He especially hated it when the loss of focus came from *private shit* playing out in the press and the public. Having been at the centre of intense media and public speculation when he'd accidentally run over and killed his own child—Val's twin sister—two decades ago, Griff knew that playbook well.

And while the secret of Donovan's sexuality couldn't be compared to the tragedy of a child's death, it would still consume them all, not just Donovan. It'd engulf the whole team. Their *combined* focus would be fucked.

He could only imagine the state of Griff's temper should that occur.

The coach nodded grimly. "Good." Obviously satisfied with the pep talk and that his message had been received loud and clear, Griff picked up the remote. "See you tomorrow." He un-paused the screen and turned his attention to the play.

Donovan left the office, wishing he was as confident as Griff that all would now be well. Meeting Beckett had been like opening Pandora's Box, and it seemed he was forever destined to be tortured by the things inside he *couldn't* have.

It was ludicrous, really. He'd been denying himself for a long time—what was a few more years? But suddenly they yawned in front of him like a gaping hole in the earth's crust.

Big and deep and *impossible* to ignore.

• • •

Beck sat in his parked car, peering over at Donovan's house, summoning the courage to go and knock on his door. It seemed bigger on the outside than it had on Wednesday night, now it wasn't shrouded in the heavy cloak of torrential rain. He hadn't planned on coming here when he finally got back to his car after the game had finished, but he hadn't been able to stop thinking about Donovan's brilliant setup, the way he kept powering forward, dragging grown men behind him in his determination to keep going.

And so here he was, watching Donovan's house like some…weirdo stalker.

And it wasn't because he was horny, although God knew he was seriously fucking horny after all that testosterone and frank display of male dominance. But he could get sex anywhere if he just wanted to slake a thirst and that was his thing. It was because Donovan had been utterly *riveting.*

Captivating. And he just *had* to see him again. Tell the man how amazing he was. Bestow his admiration.

It had seemed reasonable at the time—necessary, even—but now that he was here, his impulsivity felt ridiculous. The guy was probably out clubbing somewhere with his teammates. Wasn't that what footballers did after games? Hit the town. Paint it red. Dance with nubile women, pose for selfies with them, sign their breasts? Or was that only when they won?

But…there was a light on inside.

Of course, there could always be a light on inside at night whenever he wasn't home—that was only security conscious, after all. It was probably on a timer.

Christ. His hands were actually sweating. What was he doing?

If he went in there, what was he expecting? Where would it lead? What did he want? Was it conversation? Just two dudes hanging out, shooting the breeze about footy? Was it friendship? Or was he hoping for more?

Hoping for Donovan to want more?

He'd seen the bright burn of the other man's desire on Wednesday night. Had felt the connection like a jolt as he'd sat at that table with him on Monday. He *knew* Donovan wanted him. But the man's *can't* from the other night rang clear as a bell through his head.

Did Beck really want to get into something that was thorny and complicated? Because it was. Donovan was at a stage where what he wanted and what he felt he could have were in mortal combat. That was heavy going and not a situation Beck wanted to put himself in the middle of.

But if the man was open to something sexual only? He *could* do that.

He wasn't up for investing any feelings in a guy who wasn't being honest about his life. Not again. Not when what Beck ultimately wanted was someone to love. And someone to love him back. And he'd be a fool to think that could be Donovan, a guy who was so clearly *not* on the same page he wasn't even reading the same book.

Which just left sex.

Beck shut his eyes. Was he here on some booty call the other party hadn't even asked for? He didn't know. All he knew was that he wanted to see Donovan. So enough with the second guessing and the incessant bloody analysis. He was just going to go up there and take it as it came.

Opening his door, Beck stepped out then shut it behind him and headed for the house. When he got there, he knocked quickly, feeling even less sure in the handful of seconds it had taken him to arrive. But it was done now. No backing out.

He heard immediate noises inside, but it felt like an age before Donovan answered the door, and Beck's heart thumped louder with each tick of the clock. Did he know it was Beck standing out here, waiting? Was he deciding whether to answer or to barricade the door?

When it finally opened, Beck almost sagged in relief. That was a positive sign, surely? "Hi," he said, his voice high.

Bloody hell. He sounded like he'd been mainlining coke *and* helium. But his adrenaline was surging, and Donovan in a white tank top that barely covered his chest and shorts that rode high on his thighs was a sight to behold. The sharp tang of something hot and pleasantly pungent wafted out on a wave of heat. The black of his half-sleeve tattoos was fully exposed, and Beck wanted to trace them with his tongue.

Hell, he wanted to trace them with his *dick*.

"Oh." Donovan swallowed, his eyes widening. "Hi," he said as one big hand came up to absently massage the muscles that connected his neck to his shoulder.

Beck's eyes followed the movement of those thick fingers, realising as he ogled the action that the aroma he could smell was some kind of liniment. "Are you hurt?"

He shook his head, dropped his hand. "No more than usual." Silence descended then for long moments, their gazes locking, and Beck held his breath.

"How was Harry?"

The question was gruff, and Beck blinked in surprise. He hadn't been expecting *that* and was momentarily lost for words. Had Beck spending some time in the company of a gay man been weighing on Donovan's mind? A slow smile spread across his mouth. Was Donovan…jealous? The thought was more pleasing than it should have been.

"He *was* cute," Beckett said, rolling his lips together so he wouldn't laugh at Donovan's quick, dismissive snort. "But apparently I'm now into big, buff rugby dudes who crack their knuckles and have never been kissed."

The sudden flaring of Donovan's nostrils coincided with the sharp internal rebuke Beck meted out. So much for taking it as it came. This was outright leading, damn it.

"Have you come for your bike?"

Beck shook his head slowly, the *thud* of his heart like a gong in his chest. Tonight's game and his urge to see Donovan had completely obliterated the bike from his memory.

"No." He hadn't meant for it to sound so low and rough, but it did.

He watched as Donovan swallowed, the bob of his throat thick and apparently painful if his grimace was any indication. His large hands clenched and unclenched by his side, his jaw blanched almost white through the cover of his whiskers. It was as if he was standing on some kind of precipice, deciding whether or not to take a chance and leap.

"It's okay…I can go," Beck offered. *Hell, he shouldn't have come.*

But then Donovan stood aside, a clear invitation. "It's fine," he said, and Beck brushed past him and into the house.

Chapter Five

Apparently I'm now into big, buff rugby dudes who crack their knuckles and have never been kissed.

Fucking hell. Donovan had no idea what to do with that. Or even why he'd let Beckett in. But he hadn't wanted him to go, either.

"You want a beer?" he asked, still clutching the doorknob, wanting Beckett to say no. Wanting him to say yes.

"Yes. Please."

Fuck. Shutting the door, Donovan was grateful for the opportunity to move as far away from the guy as was possible, even if he was playing Susie fucking Homemaker. His pulse was hammering and his breathing had got all backed up in his lungs and he didn't feel like he was getting enough air. At least doing something far away from the temptation of Beckett bought him time.

Breathing space. *Thinking* space.

Why in hell hadn't he just sent the guy away? Got his bike, loaded it into his vehicle, and waved him goodbye. Especially with Beckett looking all casually sexy in his faded Levi's and navy button-down shirt that fit snug across his chest and abs.

He'd seen the guy looking corporate hot in a suit and tie, sporty hot in soaking wet Lycra, every part of him moulded to perfection, and now relaxed hot, and Donovan couldn't decide which hot he liked more. He was pretty sure naked hot would outrank them all.

For fuck's sake, it wasn't like naked guys were a rarity for him—they were a goddamn occupational hazard. He'd lost count of the number of bare asses he'd seen and showers he'd taken with other dudes in locker rooms over the years.

But he hadn't wanted to check them out. To stare and ogle. That was work. Not play.

Not…whatever this was with Beck.

Donovan twisted the lids off the long-necked bottles of beer, and then, steeling himself, he wandered back to Beckett, who had moved away from the door to stand near the couch.

"Cheers," he said as he handed the beer over, taking care to stay just outside of reaching distance. He probably should offer him a seat, but standing felt safer.

Felt temporary.

"Cheers," Beckett returned before pressing the bottle to his lips and taking a deep pull of the ale.

Donovan was temporarily transfixed by the bob of the other man's throat, his cleanly shaven face and neck allowing an unencumbered view. He wished he didn't have the urge to nuzzle the hard ridge of his windpipe—to *sniff* him.

"You were great tonight," Beckett said.

Donovan blinked then laughed. It felt good to laugh. Felt good that his lungs were expanding fully again, felt good knowing he wasn't in any imminent danger of the hypoxia that had threatened the second he'd opened his door. "You really *don't* know much about rugby, do you?"

He grinned. "Okay, yeah…I could see you didn't exactly have your best game, but the way you set up that try for

Ronan, running along with three guys attached to you like cling-ons trying to pull you down, and you just kept forging on, refusing to be stopped?" Beckett shook his head. "That was…something else."

Donovan was used to accolades. He was used to people telling him he was brilliant and relaying a try or a tackle, play by play. Those compliments didn't usually go to his dick—Beckett's did. Because there was such blatant admiration in his tone. From a guy who'd confessed to *not* being a rugby groupie. And because there was definitely an edge of sexual appreciation that was fucking *electric*.

"Had to get something right," he dismissed, trying not to let that edge go to his head—either of them.

They both drank then, and when he was done, Beckett glanced around, his eyes settling on the television which Donovan had paused. "You're re-watching the game?"

"Force of habit."

"I figured you'd be out…partying or something?"

"I do sometimes, with the others, if we've won. We used to do it more, but with three quarters of the team all partnered up, we don't tend to go out as a group anymore, and if we do, it's usually to Tanner's." Donovan grimaced at how boring he must sound. "Sorry, it's not very rock and roll, is it?"

Sure, he did attend some swanky events from time to time, and he was more than aware his celebrity opened doors, but he preferred to stay out of the spotlight. For him, in particular, recognition was a double-edged sword. Hard to fly under the radar when too many people knew who you were in the age of phone cameras and social media.

Beckett shrugged. "You're a homebody. I get that."

Yeah, that descriptor was spot on. Mostly because he was a family man. He might not be married anymore, but he still had Miri to think about, and any bad press could blow back on her. As well as her mother. And then, there were his parents and grandparents, who were proud of his accomplishments. He didn't want to jeopardise that by going out and making the kind of headlines football players too often did.

Apart from training, games, team social gatherings, the odd official awards night or fundraiser/galas necessitating a tuxedo, and his regular Wednesday night poker game with the guys, he was pretty much a hermit. Which suited just fine, because outside the door lurked temptation.

The kind that would bring a whole host of different headlines.

"Still, I'm surprised you're watching the game."

Donovan frowned. "What else would I be watching?" He would probably watch this game, remote in hand, another half dozen times before next week's game.

It's what he did.

Beckett gave a laugh. "I don't know. You're a guy who just dragged three men down a field, got crunched and crunched back countless times, and ran your ass off for eighty solid minutes. Even losing, you got to be jacked up on some kind of testosterone high and you're alone in your house with a big-screen TV. I would have thought porn was a go-to?"

Porn. The word and the open way Beckett bandied it about hit Donovan straight in the chest. Men—himself included—watched porn. He knew that. So did women. And it was apparently perfectly au fait these days to be out and proud about it. But it felt different admitting the practise to another gay man.

And loaded.

Like talking about this with Beckett was another step toward something he told himself he couldn't have. Another step onto the slippery slope.

Also, he actually wasn't a regular consumer of porn—not the kind Beckett was referring to anyway—not least of all because his fourteen-year-old daughter stayed at his place a half dozen times a year. When he did succumb to the allure of, it was in his bedroom on his laptop. Not out here on the TV.

If Miri was anywhere near as good with cyber snooping as she was at sniffing out where he hid her Christmas presents, he didn't need to leave any breadcrumbs on the smart television for her to follow. The only thing Annie had ever asked of him was that Miri at least be out of high school before Donovan came out publicly. Neither of them had wanted their daughter subjected to any schoolyard slurs, and as Donovan had no intention of revealing his sexuality until after he'd retired, that worked out well.

He certainly didn't want to ruin that plan by her stumbling across a stash of his gay porn.

"Oh God," Beckett said, shaking his head as Donovan chose to have another mouthful of beer rather than respond to the question.

Why did he open his damn door again?

"You *don't* watch porn? You've never been with a guy and you have all that—" He paused and ran his eyes over Donovan's body, which, although brief, was as sexually cataclysmic as a blowjob. "Excess testosterone. You have to be out of your *mind* with horniness. You're going to blow a nut if you're not careful."

Donovan almost laughed at the abject horror in Beckett's voice. He waggled his right hand instead. "Don't worry. I'm not in any imminent danger of nut blowout."

A slow smile broke over the other man's face, his dimples deepening into grooves, his eyes going all soft and flirty. His face went from achingly good-looking to impossibly sexy in the space of a heartbeat. "I'm sure they're grateful for that."

His voice was warm and rich with innuendo, making Donovan a little dizzy.

"So if you're not watching porn to get off, you must have

a very…active imagination." Beckett waggled his eyebrows and lowered his voice a notch. "What kind of dirty things go on in that brain of yours, Donovan Bane?"

Donovan's grip on his beer bottle tightened as he shifted his weight from one foot to the next. He was both discomforted by this topic and utterly turned on. It wasn't like he hadn't been part of many conversations over the course of his teenage/adult life with other guys about porn and masturbation and who had what in their spank banks.

But mostly that was just dudes talking shit. This was much more risqué. Its potential to become *something else* hovered just out of reach if he had the cahoonas to snatch it up.

"Do you really just say anything that pops into your head?" he sidestepped, because there was no way he was admitting to how the brush of Beckett's lips on his knuckles, the slight scrape of his teeth, had caused him to lose his load several times since Wednesday.

He'd bet Beckett was into more hardcore stuff—orgies and BDSM shit. Handcuffs and paddles and…gimp masks.

"Yeah, sorry, terrible habit," he apologised with a grin that said he wasn't even remotely sorry before continuing. "I think my next *masturbatory aid*"—the words rolled off Beck's tongue like he said them all the damn time—"will be recording rugby games and watching all the good bits on slow-mo. Particularly if you're in them."

Had Donovan not already been painfully turned on, that admission would have done the trick. The tantalising thought of Beckett sitting at home, jacking off to *him* running down the field or mauling or tackling insinuated itself into his head.

And his cock.

"So…" Beckett said as the silence stretched, because Donovan couldn't *word* right now. Not with the image of Beckett, hand on his cock, playing through his head.

Donovan watched as he lifted the bottle to his mouth and

tipped his head back slightly. Their gazes held briefly before Donovan's drifted south to the other man's throat. Beckett swallowed—once, twice, three times—real slow, clearly aware of Donovan's interest.

Pornographic drinking of his beer done, he continued. "If you're not going to tell me what you think about when you"— he leaned in a little and whispered—"*touch yourself...*" Then he straightened, a small, sexy smile playing on those full, sexy lips. "I'm going to have to guess."

Just barely suppressing his snort, Donovan said, "Oh yeah?" *Good luck with that, buddy.*

"Let me see." He rubbed his jaw, pretending to think, that hovering smile, small but utterly biteable. "Threesome? Or maybe you fantasise about doing it with some military dude? No, wait—" He wagged his finger at Donovan. "I reckon you're more of a fetish guy. You're into feet. Or food. Or...giant tentacle dildos?"

Donovan couldn't help it, he laughed out loud. He knew Beckett was being deliberately outrageous to dispel the awkwardness, but he was going to have to get a lot more vanilla if he hoped to hit anywhere near Donovan's proclivities.

"Not into giant tentacle porn?" Beckett clutched his chest and faked being crestfallen.

Blowing out a breath, Donovan gave a half laugh. "No." And he almost left it there. He *should* leave it there. But what was wrong with talking about this stuff with Beckett? He'd have smack-talked his way through this conversation in the locker room like a pro. Why did he want to avoid it here? With someone who understood him far more than any of his teammates ever would.

Because it felt illicit. *Good* illicit. And that was terrifying. Also hot as fuck.

Slowly, Donovan took a step toward the slippery slope. "I know I should be all about the ass, right? I'm this big, hard,

Maori rugby dude with tats and a rep for ploughing through a pack, right? I should be all about the domination. About… being daddy. Or however it goes." His cheeks grew hot at his lack of knowledge where gay *sex stuff* was concerned. "But, honestly, I just like to watch guys…" He hesitated, wanting to say it but unsure.

"You like to watch guys *what*?"

"I'm into…kissing."

Beckett's lips parted slightly, his brow wrinkled. "Kissing?"

The guy seemed perplexed, and Donovan immediately wished he'd kept his mouth shut. Beckett's open, nonjudgmental demeanour had lulled him into a false sense of security. For crazy moments he'd thought he might not sound…sad. Shaking his head, he said, "It doesn't matter," before turning away, heading to the kitchen to dump his empty beer bottle and grab another.

"Donovan."

The quiet entreaty in Beckett's voice reached across the room, but he ignored it. "You want another beer?" he asked, his head in the fridge. Although *leave* would probably have been a better thing to say.

"Donovan, kissing was a good answer. I just…didn't expect it."

Donovan straightened as he pulled out two more beers. "Of course you didn't, because it's…pathetic." Jesus, he couldn't even pick the right gay porn.

"No." Beckett crossed to the kitchen. "It's not. It's sweet, actually."

He winced at the *S* word. No one had ever called Donovan Bane sweet. Screwing the top off his bottle, he said, "I rest my case," then drank half his beer in one go. He could feel Beckett's eyes on him the whole time and fought the urge to turn and run.

"Is there something kissing-specific you like to watch?"

Donovan pushed the other beer across the countertop. "It doesn't matter," he repeated.

"I'm not here to judge you." Beckett picked up the bottle and took a drink before meeting his eyes. "I *want* to know."

Beckett's tone ached with sincerity, and Donovan swallowed, feeling that ache in his lungs and his bones and his *balls*. He sighed, dropping his eyes to his beer. "It's just…a reel someone put up on YouTube. It's like nine minutes… an amateur thing that's all individual footage that has been edited together so there's one couple after the other just… kissing."

"*Hot* kissing?"

Donovan glanced up at the timbre of Beckett's voice, huskier now. Their gazes met. Heat enveloped him—so much heat. He swallowed. "Yes." *Hell yes.*

"How?"

It didn't occur to Donovan to ask for clarification of the how. How hot? How long? How much? The gravelly tone of the other man's voice left no doubt he wanted a blow-by-blow description. "Deep, wet, open-mouthed. Lots of tongue. The kind of kiss that goes on and on and you can barely see where one person stops and the other one starts."

Beckett nodded, holding his gaze. "And that's how you fantasise about being kissed?"

He swallowed again. "Yes." To share that kind of passion with another man? To be able to kiss so deeply and so freely? His gut twisted at the thought. The muscles between his hips looped and dipped, sliding over each other with a languid heat.

"I bet there's more than one of those types of reels around."

"Sure." Donovan nodded. There were a lot. "I like this one the best, though."

"Oh?" He quirked an eyebrow as he held Donovan's gaze. "Why?"

"Most of them have music edited over the top. This one is just the raw sound and the..." Donovan faltered, licked lips that were suddenly tinder dry as the nonsensical sounds made by two guys lost to each other—eyes closed, moaning and panting, clinging and rutting—echoed through his head. "Noises," he continued. "The heavy breathing and the—"

"Groaning?" Beckett supplied. When Donovan nodded, he asked, "You like it when they groan?"

He nodded again, wetting his lips, feeling exposed and vulnerable beneath the intensity of Beckett's eyes. He dropped his gaze to the counter. "And their breathing. It's ragged...heavy..."

"Out of control?"

Donovan wet his lips again. "Yeah." Out of control. That was the best part.

A soft *tink* of a glass bottle meeting granite cracked across the divide of the bench, dragging Donovan's gaze up again, meshing with Beckett's. "Show me."

A brief battle ensued between wisdom and want. He should say no. Take the damn beer off Beckett and send him on his way. Why had he given him a second beer?

But *want* won out. Donovan's body was burning from the fever in his blood. He knew there was a line he shouldn't cross, and he *would not do that*, but Beckett was giving him a glimpse of what could be. Accepting him as he was, letting him be who he was—the person he couldn't share with anyone else.

It was a relief. It was a blessing. It was a fucking revelation.

With his pulse loud in his ears and on legs that were far from steady, Donovan crossed to the television. He wouldn't normally, but watching it on the big screen appealed. And there was *a bed* in his bedroom, which they should definitely go nowhere fucking near.

He just needed to remember to scrub his history afterward.

Donovan sat on the couch, conscious of Beckett moving closer as he navigated to YouTube. Conscious of him standing directly behind the couch as he pulled up the reel. Grateful for the couch, too, for having temptation firmly behind as the frozen main image, a close-up of two guys kissing, made Donovan even harder.

Thirty-two years as a dude and he wouldn't have thought that possible.

Maybe it was just how *big* it all was on the TV screen compared to the laptop, but between the size, the anticipation, and the warm, solid presence of Beckett behind him, his arousal was at DEFCON 5.

He didn't bother to check if the other man was ready to watch it, he just clicked play, and the image sprang to life, the guys on screen suddenly going for it, a needy male groan, low and sonorous, breaking the silence in the room, the couple's heavy breathing infecting Donovan's own lungs with a similar affliction.

Then Beckett came around and sat beside him, and every muscle in Donovan's body tightened. Donovan refused to look at him, but the heat pouring off his body and his peripheral vision told him Beckett was close. A hand's breadth between them.

A space fraught with possibilities.

He should move, or ask Beckett to, and yet, conversely— *perversely*—he didn't want to move. Not at all. It felt right being this close even if *right* just happened to feel like a heart attack.

The couple on the screen changed to different people. A threesome. Three shirtless guys, taking turns to kiss each other, hands ploughed into hair and grasping at shoulders.

The brief glimpses of tongue and the hungry, almost dazed way the third guy watched the other two kiss before they swapped again, squeezed hard at Donovan's balls.

A hand slid slowly, tentatively, onto Donovan's thigh, and his quad turned to granite, his heart skipping several beats as the air in his lungs stuttered to a halt. He swallowed, dropping his gaze to see Beckett's hand right there, looking so damn *good* on his thigh Donovan felt dizzy.

Blowing out a pent-up breath, he glanced into the other man's eyes and asked, "What are you doing?" It was too husky to be either demand or accusation.

Beckett smiled one of his gentle smiles. "Touching you." Which was also ridiculously husky. "Is that okay?" With their gazes locked and to the soundtrack of moaning, gasping dudes, Beckett's hand slowly moved higher, giving Donovan ample opportunity to call a halt. "God…you smell good," he murmured.

Donovan snorted, but it came out as a low kind of rumble. "I stink of liniment."

Beckett's nostrils flared as he leaned in, and Donovan held his breath as he nuzzled the spot behind Donovan's ear. "I like it," he whispered, his breath hot. "Makes me dizzy."

Yeah, Donovan knew all about dizzy. "That's the eucalyptus."

A low, sexy laugh puffed warm air down Donovan's neck as Beckett nuzzled lower. "It's *not* the eucalyptus." Then his fingers grazed Donovan's erection.

It was the lightest of touches, but it slammed into his groin like a fireball. The next touch, which cupped the massive bulge in Donovan's shorts, slammed into it like the asteroid that killed the fucking dinosaurs. Hissing out a breath, he closed his eyes, sliding his hand over top of Beckett's, fighting a battle between grinding into it and pushing it away.

Jesus. What was he doing? Was it not enough that he

was sitting on the couch with a guy watching sexy footage of dudes kissing without letting himself be fondled?

He'd told himself he wouldn't do this. He *wouldn't* cross that line.

Dragging in a breath that felt as dry and ragged as tumbleweed, he opened his eyes. Gently but firmly he removed Beckett's hand and placed it back on his knee, the other man raising an eyebrow. Donovan, ignoring the belt of his heart and the screaming of his libido, simply said, "No," then returned his attention to the screen where a Black guy and a White dude with bright red hair and a lumberjack beard were trying to eat each other's faces off.

Conscious of Beckett also turning his attention back to the TV, Donovan watched the parade of familiar images, his dick at the point of strangulation as his chest filled with familiar yearning. He wanted that. To be able to kiss a guy— kiss *Beckett*—like that. Hot and frenzied.

"Turn it up," Beckett said.

Donovan, who had kept the sound low, but always listened to it as loud as his laptop would let him, didn't argue. He picked up the remote and hit the up button on the volume until the noise of aroused men seemed to bounce off all the walls in stereo. And just in time for the moment when the ranga bit at the Black guy's bottom lip, and the groan that spilled from his mouth was so fucking *unholy* Donovan had often lost his load at that point.

But the volume wasn't loud enough to cover the noise of a zipper being lowered. Hell, that echoed around the room loud as a gunshot.

Before he could check himself, Donovan glanced down to discover Beckett's hand fisted around himself, around his fully exposed cock. His long, beautiful, *smooth* cock. Perfectly cut and proportioned, beautifully veined, sprouting hard and proud from a thatch of light brown hair.

It was the supermodel of dicks.

Fuck.

Dragging his gaze upward, he met Beckett's, locking tight. His breathing felt like razor blades now, his exhalations cutting the air. Beckett's sounded the same. In fact, he didn't know whose breathing was louder—theirs or the dudes on the TV—in this suspended moment when neither of them did anything other than breathe.

He looked down again, at Beckett's hand wrapped firmly around his cock, and there went that dizziness again. He swallowed. His hands shook, and his heart beat double time.

"You want me to stop?" he asked, his voice gravelly.

God no. Donovan did *not* want him to stop. Would it be wise? *Yes*. But… He swallowed. "No."

"You too," Beckett said.

The statement was husky, a request more than a demand, but when Donovan lifted his eyes once more, he saw both dare and challenge. Eyes that seemed to say, if you won't let me touch you, then touch yourself.

You. Know. You. Want. To.

And hell fucking yes, he did. It should be awkward, but right now with his heart in his mouth and his dick begging for release and grown men heavily panting their lust all around, it didn't feel like that. It felt sexy and edgy and just what he needed.

But could he? More to the point, *should* he?

Fuck *no*, he should not. And yet…this *wasn't* crossing that line he told himself he wouldn't cross. He wasn't touching Beckett. Nor was he being touched. They hadn't kissed. Weren't going to, either. This was each of them doing their own thing. Next to each other but completely separate. Just…two guys watching porn together.

Masturbating together… Natural, right?

Christ…even this far gone on sexual anticipation,

Donovan knew that was a bunch of bullshit, but he had pure tunnel vision at the moment as Beckett deliberately broke eye contact to glance at the TV, and Donovan dropped *his* eyes to the other man's lap. To the hold he had around his dick and the slow movement of his hand and the shiny bead of fluid coming from the tip of the full, flushed crown.

Fuck. He wanted to lean over and lick it right off. To taste Beckett's desire on his tongue. To savour it. To know it was *for* him. *Because* of him. But that *would* be stepping over the line. So really, taking his cock out was tame in comparison.

In fact, it was probably the better option…

With a shaking hand, Donovan breeched the elastic of his shorts and his underwear, sucking in a short, sharp breath, his eyes closing, as his fingers brushed the taut, aching flesh of his shaft. A current of hot, white heat shot all the way down to his balls and, for a horrifying moment, he thought he was going to lose his load right there and then, and he had to squeeze his dick *hard* to interrupt the jolt of sensation before he could pull it free of his clothes.

When he opened his eyes, they met Beckett's, and for long moments they just stared at each other, the sound of heavy breathing like jungle drums around them. Until Beckett broke contact again, his eyes dropping to Donovan's lap, his pupils dilating, his nostrils flaring. His tongue came out, flicking along his bottom lip, and his throat bobbed as he swallowed, and Donovan couldn't breathe for the *wanting.*

When his gaze lifted, Donovan was in no doubt Beckett also *wanted* to do some tasting, but he glanced back at the screen after a beat, allowing Donovan to find his breath and his sanity—or his purpose at least—as he turned his attention to the screen.

Ostensibly, anyway.

His eyes might have been on the parade of men on the screen hot-kissing—licking and sucking and panting and *devouring* like it was their last day on earth—but his peripheral vision was full of the movement of Beckett's hand, slow and sure. And his brain was racing ahead, tumbling over and over, running in circles, exhausting itself, questioning the wisdom of what was happening, weighing the consequences.

Then his hand, almost of its own volition, stroked up the length of his shaft, and nothing else existed. He hissed loudly as the flesh of his cock practically blistered it was so excruciatingly, painfully *good*, and Beckett's attention was drawn temporarily back to Donovan's hand, lingering for long moments before he lifted his gaze and their eyes met. "That's how I'm going to kiss you," Beckett whispered. "Exactly like that."

Then he turned back to the TV, leaving Donovan to ponder whether it was threat or promise and fucking *when* exactly that might be? Leaving him hot and hungry and panting, his heart pounding, his lungs tight, his cock straining for more, weeping for a tongue to swipe away the glistening bead of arousal.

Squeezing his eyes shut for a brief moment, Donovan drew in a steadying breath before opening them again and forcing himself to focus on the screen as he worked his dick. Focus on the strangers he knew so damn intimately after years of watching. On the guy with the baseball hat on backward open-mouthed kissing down a whiskery throat. On two dudes with one behind, his hand on the other guy's jaw helping him crane his neck as far as possible so their lips could meet in a messy, sloppy tangle of tongues. On the buff gym junkie type who moaned *loud* when his skinny, nerdy partner pushed him up against a wall and fucking *owned* his mouth.

The images fed the already thundering river of Donovan's desire, but not as much as the man sitting next to him on the couch, so clearly at home with this utter...*debauchery*. That was the most arousing thing of all. Beckett's hand was moving faster now, and his breathing was growing huskier, becoming shallower, and Donovan found himself keeping pace, gritting his teeth against the hot spike of lust, the tight clench of his balls, and the driving need to just let it all go and fly.

He held himself in check, though, refusing to look at Beckett or the way his hand picked up the pace again and his breathing got rougher and rougher. Donovan kept his eyes to the front. If he didn't, all would be lost. He concentrated instead on keeping every muscle between his belly button and his thighs coiled tight. Keeping his arousal leashed. He didn't want Beckett to think he couldn't go the distance. He was about as exposed and vulnerable now as he'd ever been, but he still had his fucking pride.

He was an elite rugby player—he could *go* all goddamn night.

But then Beckett really started to pant like he was finding it hard to stay in check, and Donovan felt each one like a mantra rising in his blood. "Are you…waiting me…out, Donovan Bane?" he asked, a strangled kind of amusement lacing his words. But then a low groan slid from his lips, and he muttered, "*Fuck*," under his breath.

It was so *rough* it squeezed Donovan's balls, and he swivelled his head, his gaze meshing with Beckett's. He didn't know what to say about the flush staining the other man's cheekbones, about the dig of his teeth into that full bottom lip, about the flash of what almost looked like physical pain in those blue eyes.

All he knew was that Beckett was in this state because of *him*.

Sure, he might have started this whole thing, but Donovan daring to go there as well had pushed Beckett to this point of almost delirious arousal. *He* had the man teetering on the edge, and fuck if that wasn't like a lightning bolt to his dick. Donovan's balls pulled even tighter as his hand moved faster, his hips thrusting of their own accord, sliding his cock in and out of the firm hold he had on himself.

And he couldn't look away from the tight grimace of building pleasure on Beckett's face while the surround sound of other men lost to their delirium formed a cacophony of male rutting that spiked the air with a heavy fog of lust.

"You want me to come?" Beckett asked, a sharpness to his gaze now, an edge to his voice that spoke of barely leashed control.

Donovan nodded, too far gone to go back, to realise that this one time was never ever going to be enough, but not yet ready to say the word.

Not yet. Not *out loud*.

Beckett grunted then said, "Look what you're doing to me." His eyes blazed, demanding *everything*. "You're making me come."

He cried out then, his hips bucking, and Donovan couldn't *not* look. Wild fucking horses couldn't have stopped him from looking as a jet of ejaculate pulsed from the tip of Beckett's cock, his cries turning almost feral as another one followed, then another.

It was all the stimulus Donovan needed, his own climax boiling out of him in hot jets of ecstasy as all those taut muscle fibres uncoiled, unravelling heat and pleasure *everywhere*, lighting up his erogenous zones like New Year's Eve fireworks, wrenching cries from his throat and the breath from his lungs.

The fact that Beckett was watching it all happen— his mouth parted, his hot eyes firmly fixed on the blur of Donovan's hand—even in the midst of his own rapture, only prolonged the orgasm. It was so fucking *carnal* having an audience of one.

This audience of one.

Knowing that Beckett was experiencing the same level of

pleasure, that they were doing this together even if they were apart, kept Donovan in such a heightened state of arousal he didn't think the climax was ever going to end. Given how long he'd waited for this experience, a never-ending orgasm seemed like a fitting reward.

But it did slow and then ebb, the climax waning deliciously, oozing out of his cells and his system in a far gentler way than it had arrived. Which was the opposite of the abrupt ending to his *alone time* orgasms that always left him feeling achingly lonely. He wasn't feeling lonely now as Beckett's gasping and panting seemed to settle in time with his.

Donovan wondered if the other man felt as if the whole world had shifted off his axis or did he regularly mutually masturbate with other guys to soft porn? It was a sobering thought as they both collapsed back against the couch. The YouTube video had ended, the screen black now apart from the usual static advertisements for other videos and, as real life intruded, it just felt a little...sordid.

He glanced down at himself, at his hand still around his cock, which hadn't yet fully deflated. At the state of his hands, his clothes. The state of Beckett, his dick and clothes similarly dishevelled. Christ, what a *mess*. Splashes of spunk soaked into the fabric of his shirt and sat in cloudy puddles on his shorts. There was some on his arm, and he wasn't sure if it was his or Beckett's.

The thought turned him on even as he fought against the illicit pull of it.

Donovan didn't know whether to feel embarrassed, ashamed, or king of the fucking world over their appearance. But reality was a bitch, and he knew he couldn't deal with what had happened now, the liberties he'd allowed himself. Just because they hadn't touched or kissed didn't mean Donovan hadn't stomped all over that mental line he'd put in place. In his giant fucking size fourteen rugby boots.

And he didn't know what to do now. Because nothing would ever again be the same, and yet nothing had changed.

Christ, his heart rate, which had started to settle post orgasm, suddenly sped up to the point where Donovan thought cardiac arrest was imminent. And how would that look to the ambos coming to his aid? With his hand on his exposed dick, splattered in cum, gay porn on the TV?

Fuck.

Springing from the couch, Donovan ignored the mess and tucked himself away. "I'll get you something to clean up," he said, not looking at Beckett as he fled.

Not that distance from Beckett helped. Not the way his pulse was still hammering and his brain was somersaulting over and over like a malfunctioning ride at a theme park. What he needed was for Beckett to leave. There was no hope for any clarity while the man who was responsible—or at least the catalyst, anyway—for the war raging inside Donovan was sitting on his couch.

The war between what Donovan wanted and what he could realistically have.

Entering the laundry, he shucked out of his clothes and blindly grabbed for fresh ones, throwing them on before grabbing a towel and a clean shirt for Beckett. If he kept turning up here requiring changes of clothes, the man would have a whole bloody collection soon.

But he didn't want to think about Beckett turning up here again. Nothing could come of this, so there was no point getting used to him being around.

Returning to the living room, he tossed the towel at Beckett, who was still sitting but had also tucked himself away. He barely looked at the other man as he headed for the kitchen and pulled another beer out of the fridge, drinking half of it down immediately. He didn't really want it, but it gave him something to do while Beckett cleaned up and changed his shirt.

"Donovan?"

The soft entreaty reached across the room and right inside, cupping Donovan's heart. He closed his eyes. How could one word be imbued with such gentle understanding?

"Don't be ashamed of what happened just now."

He wasn't ashamed. He was…terrified. Of the door it had opened. And how the fuck he was ever going to shut it again. "Please just go."

"What we did is perfectly okay."

He opened his eyes and took a steadying breath before slowly turning. The sight of Beckett all earnest but also clearly tousled from their session on the couch and in *his* shirt hit him hard in the chest. *Christ*, he wanted this man. And therein lay the problem. Donovan couldn't afford to want *any* man.

"It's not. Not in my world. It's *not* okay to be gay." He needed Beckett to heed what he was saying.

"And you think me not kissing you or touching your dick makes you *not* gay?"

God, if *only* it was that easy. "It makes being gay more bearable." Because if he kissed Beckett, he wouldn't want to stop, and then where would he be? Better to not get a taste for those lips. "Can you please just go?"

"No."

He shook his head, but there was still no rebuke in his eyes or his tone, just that quiet patience and understanding that made Donovan yearn for something he knew was impossible.

For now.

"Not if you're going to self-flagellate all night thinking you did something wrong."

"I don't think I did anything wrong." Donovan could see that what two consenting men did in the privacy of his house wasn't *wrong.* But for him, it was problematic. "I won't be self-flagellating, I promise. I just need to…think." To figure out how to put the genie back in the bottle.

If it could be put back in the bottle.

"Okay." Beckett nodded. "That's good. You think." He crossed to the door, touching the handle. "I'll be thinking, too. About how good it was watching you work your cock. And hearing that groan as you came. And about how you came for *me*." He turned the handle and opened the door. "You can bet I'll be wanking to that before the end of the night."

Donovan swallowed as Beckett slipped out the door, the soft *click* as it shut barely registering. Yeah…he was probably going to be doing that, too.

Chapter Six

The next morning, Beck's finger hovered over the send button on the text he'd just composed—his fifth attempt. Last night had been…well, it had been a *night*, that was for sure. Between the rush of the rugby game and the even bigger rush of what happened on that couch, he was utterly obsessed with Donovan Bane. Even better, he was pretty sure the pro rugby star was similarly obsessed.

But…it was complicated. Beck appreciated that.

Gay relationships often were when a lot of society still wasn't okay with same-sex couples. And, after going back and forth all night on whether he really wanted to put himself into that position again, Beck still wasn't sure. The one and only closeted guy he'd been with had been a total disaster. Dieter had been so dazzlingly good-looking it had taken Beck too many months to see how ugly his self-hate and loathing made him on the inside.

And then there were the potential professional ramifications—if any—to being with a player from the club he worked for. Was that frowned upon? Would it land him in hot water if the truth came out? Was there some kind of conflict of interest because he was, ultimately, as Harper had pointed out, the guy who *paid* Donovan?

If it all went to shit and their relationship became public knowledge, would *he* be the one forced to pack his bags and go? From a job that had already been more fulfilling than *any* previous job?

Beck shook his head to stop the escalation of his thoughts. *Relationship?* Get a grip, dude. He was sending a text, not a love letter.

Calm the freaking farm.

Quickly, before he could change his mind, Beck tapped the button. The phone made a whooshing noise as the text went out into the ether.

Can I drop in and pick up my bike today? Whenever suits.

There, neutral and to the point, but man…he'd agonised for far too long over each word and had tried several different approaches. From *great night last night* to *are you okay* to *I wish you were here so I could suck your dick*.

Bloody hell, the number of times he'd thought about Donovan's cock last night was *in*decent. Beck wasn't exactly a peewee in that department himself—in fact, they were probably the same length—but fucking hell, Donovan was *thick*. So thick his hand had itched to knock Donovan's aside and wrap firmly around the girth just to see *how* thick. To squeeze it, feel the smooth solidity of the shaft as Donovan thrust his hips and pushed all that glorious hardness through the tight ring of Beck's clenched fingers.

To bend and suck it so deep inside his mouth he could taste it at the back of his throat. The mere thought making him salivate, and thinking about it sinking into his ass? Stretching so damn good, pounding so damn good…that made him shiver.

His phone dinged, and Beck jumped on it. He hadn't

expected Donovan to answer so promptly. In fact, he wouldn't have been surprised had the big guy not answered at all.

Out all day. Will leave against back wall. Go through side gate. It's not locked.

Beck stared; it wasn't what he'd hoped for. There was no banter, no innuendo, no chattiness. Which wasn't that surprising given the man wasn't exactly the chatty type. It was succinct and to the point.

But he *had* answered, and that was something.

• • •

On Monday, Beck, whose office had a good view over the pitch at Henley, found it exceedingly hard to concentrate knowing Donovan was down there getting all hot and sweaty despite the cold day. When he could deny himself no longer, he stood at his tinted window and watched the team running through their drills.

Watched *Donovan* running though his drills.

The man really was a machine. Someone that big could be forgiven for being slow and unwieldly, but not Donovan. Sure, he wasn't the fastest runner on the team, but for a guy of his size, he was surprisingly nimble.

After about a minute, Donovan glanced up in his direction, and Beck knew that he was looking straight at him. He might not have been able to see the other man's eyes from this distance, but he could *feel* them through the tinted, double-glazed glass and over the few hundred metres that separated them. Until Griff yelled something at him, anyway, and Donovan dragged his attention back to the training session.

Not wanting to be a distraction, Beck headed back to his desk then picked up his phone and tapped out a text. *Looking good down there.* And he sent it before his better angels talked him out of it.

It was just another quick, friendly, neutral text, for crying out loud. Nothing sexual, nothing pushy. Just a statement of fact then moving on. Donovan could reply in an equally friendly tone or he didn't have to answer it at all. The ball was in his court. And if he didn't return the serve, then Beck would let it drop.

But he did return it. Two hours later and with the team now gone from the field, Beck's phone dinged. His hand actually trembled a little as he picked it up and tapped in the code to unlock the phone.

Aren't you supposed to be working?

Beck smiled. Was Donovan annoyed or was he…flirting? Only one way to find out. *I am. Getting to stare at buff sweaty rugby dudes is a perk.* He added the zany face emoji to indicate he was in jest. In case Donovan thought Beck was standing at the window every hour of the working day checking him out.

Christ…no guy had ever tied him in such knots. He had good text game, even better flirty text game—having to tread so carefully was entirely foreign.

Beck drummed his fingers on his desk, waiting for the reply. Waiting for the bubble that indicated Donovan was typing. It wasn't forthcoming, but he had been communicating, and that was enough to keep the smile on his face for the rest of the day.

When he got home from work that evening, he took a picture of his bottle of beer next to his meal, which had just been delivered from Uber Eats. It was a gourmet burger and hand-cut fries that had cost a stupid amount of money. Attaching the image, he tapped out another short, non-flirty text.

What's on the menu at yours tonight?

He wanted to add *I volunteer as tribute* but sent it instead—quickly, to avoid the temptation.

The response came fifteen minutes later. A picture of a healthy salad with a side of what looked like fish and a glass of some kind of milkshake. *Steamed coral trout. Bean sprout salad (no dressing). Kale protein thick shake.*

Beck was impressed. He supposed that Donovan had all kinds of nutritionists and team doctors that monitored his diet to within an inch of its life, and his burger and chips felt rather slovenly by comparison.

Do you make all that or does someone do it for you?

The reply was swift. *I made it.*

Oh dear God, a man who could cook. Beck wasn't great in the kitchen—unless it was using food and/or kitchen implements as weapons of erotic torment.

You cook? Be still, my heart.

Beck held his breath for the reply. He'd let some flirt creep in there—would it send Donovan scurrying? Apparently not, as the texting bubble appeared on the screen.

My mother is a great believer in equal division of household labour. She taught all four of us to cook and considering how useless my father apparently was in the kitchen and with other domestic chores when they were first together, she was determined to raise a boy who could cook, clean, and sew on a button. She said I'd thank her for it one day.

Beck smiled at the small glimpse into Donovan's early life. Considering how little he'd talked when they'd been together, this text was practically chatty. It certainly felt like he'd opened the door a crack. In fact, sharing this tiny detail, strangely, felt more intimate than their mutual masty session on the couch.

You can sew on a button?

The response was almost immediate. *And darn a sock.*

There was no earthly reason why any of this should be turning Beck on, but fucking hell, it was. Something about a big, tough pro baller darning a sock made him hotter than the hottest chilli on the Scoville Scale. He sent off his text. *She sounds awesome.*

The bubble appeared again briefly before the words flashed on the screen. *She is.*

Beck ate his burger and chips, his eyes glued to his phone, waiting and hoping Donovan would prolong the conversation. After fifteen minutes and an empty plate, it became obvious he wasn't, and Beck turned his phone over and headed for the shower.

• • •

On Tuesday, Beck sent a similar text as the day before, knowing it would be waiting for Donovan when training was done. He replied, but it was brief and not particularly encouraging. That night, Beck snapped a picture of the *salad he had made* and texted it to Donovan along with a *you inspired me* message. Donovan's image was of a delicious-looking vege pasta stack, which could have come from the kitchen of a Michelin-star restaurant.

But no message.

The same happened on Wednesday. Another *good training session* text from Beck followed by a quick *that's what they pay me for* response. Wednesday night was different, however. He sent a picture of his acai bowl freshly delivered to his door and added a message.

Yum. Breakfast for dinner. Then he added the licking lips emoji.

The picture that came back was unexpected. A giant slice of loaded pizza complete with an empty pizza box in the background. Beck blinked at the image. Had he eaten the whole thing?

And why the fuck was *that* a turn-on?

Was he regressing? Was he going back to his fifteen-year-old self where *any*thing could give him a boner? Doughnuts. White socks. The sound of the air dryer in the school bathrooms.

Freaking pizza boxes?

Donovan's text arriving interrupted Beck's confusion. *Poker night.*

Poker night. So he probably hadn't eaten all the pizza, then. News that was far too late for his poor, suffering dick, which had seen more ups and downs these past ten days than a freaking flagpole but was fascinating nonetheless. Donovan played poker. Regularly, too, by the sound of it. He hadn't said *playing poker*, he'd said *poker night*.

Tapping on the keys, Beck sent his reply. *Is poker night a regular thing?*

Several minutes passed before it was answered, during which Beck stared obsessively at the screen. *Yes. Most Wednesday nights.*

The information didn't surprise Beck at all. In fact, long, boozy poker nights with footy teammates was just the rock-and-roll lifestyle he'd pictured Donovan living. Assuming it was his teammates he played with. Beck almost asked him who was there, but he didn't want Donovan to think he had any interest in anyone else on the team.

Because he didn't. He wasn't a Smoke groupie. He was a Donovan Bane groupie. He settled for something less nosy instead and potentially flirtier. *Are you any good?*

The response was swifter this time. *I suck at poker.*

Beck laughed out loud, not least because his erection reacted like it'd been hit with a lightning rod. Bloody hell—he was going to stroke out and die through lack of blood supply to his brain if he kept this up. With a giant freaking boner.

Mostly he laughed because he hadn't expected such a frank admission. Too many guys considered it a blow to their egos to admit any kind of deficiency, especially when it came to macho bullshit like poker. But Donovan apparently had no such problem. And it added to the measure of the man that he could cop to it so openly.

It was a tragedy he felt unable to be so open about his sexuality.

I bet there's a lot you don't suck at.

Beck's finger hovered over the send button. It was stepping it up a notch and digressing, but he didn't think for a second Donovan would misunderstand that Beck had moved on to an entirely different kind of sucking now.

The best kind.

But would Donovan pick up what he was putting down? He hit send and held his breath, his eyes glued to the screen. There was nothing for ten minutes, then the typing symbol flashed up, and Beck stared at it hard, his pulse skipping like crazy.

I wouldn't know. There's a lot I haven't done.

Hmm. Interesting… He wasn't exactly picking it up, but he wasn't leaving it the hell alone, either. It wasn't information Beck didn't already know—Donovan had confessed to never having been with a guy—but he could have slammed the door shut by changing the subject. Or not answered at all.

Hell, if Beck chose to look on the positive side of things— and he usually did—Donovan's reply could be optimistically described as fishing. Bloody hell. His hand actually shook a little as he tapped a reply and sent it off.

You just need a good teacher.

Education was everything, right?

An age passed before Donovan responded. The big bang happened. Creatures crawled out of the primordial swamp. Dinosaurs died. Ice ages came and went. He was probably just involved in the poker game, but every second felt like an eon. And then a reply zipped onto the screen.

I'm used to being coached.

Beck stared at those five words, reading them over and over. Did that mean what he thought it meant? Was Donovan also just pushing the boundaries? Testing the water? Or was he leaping in? Maybe he'd been drinking and he'd regret it in the morning. God knew Beck had been there before...

Or maybe he was hoping Beck would meet him halfway?

Nervously, he typed and sent his response. *I am at your disposal.*

He shouldn't be. He should so *not* be up for this. Being someone's first gay sexual experience could be a disaster. It sounded exciting, *initiating a virgin* and all that, but in reality, it was like being rebound guy and gigolo all in one with a shit tonne more expectation and often even more baggage.

But Beck sure as hell didn't want it to be anyone else, either. Donovan Bane was a drumbeat in his blood—no freaking way could he *not* volunteer. And he could do casual sex. He'd been king of casual a few years back. He sure as shit could do it again.

For Donovan.

As long as he remembered it was just sex. Even if he hadn't been burned by the disaster that had been Dieter, Beck knew it would be dumb to get emotionally involved with a recently out—*privately* out—dude. At some stage, Donovan was going to want to enjoy his new life. Experiment. He was going to want to see who else was out there. He was going to want to date other guys, *fuck* other guys.

First *boyfriends* never lasted, and Beck was not lining up for that. He was totally up for initiating Donovan into the wonderful world of guy-on-guy, but he was keeping his heart firmly out of the equation.

Another text arrived, and Beck dragged his attention to the screen. *Gotta deal now. Talk tomorrow.*

Talk. Tomorrow.

It was the first time Donovan had signed off with a tacit promise of continuing their conversations, and Beck beamed at the phone. He might be blowing him off to play cards with a group of his guy friends, but there was always tomorrow.

· · ·

There was no way, the next day, Beck could sit in his chair and ignore the fact that Donovan was outside running around on the field, and he thanked god for the luxury of his own office. Getting up a dozen times in a few hours may well have been noticed had his work area been outside in the more open-plan section.

The power and muscle of Donovan's physique was breathtaking even from this distance, and Beck simply couldn't keep his eyes off him. He was a magnificent beast of a man, and he couldn't wait to have all that hard muscle and heft between his thighs.

Hell, just the thought of it was making Beck restless. Desire burned bright in his gut and his groin, his blood thickening as Donovan's solid quads and calves of steel lifted, twisted, and dodged through a zigzag course of tyres laid on the ground. Every step pulled the strings of Beck's arousal tighter and tighter, his cock hard enough to smash the glass separating his world from Donovan's.

Reaching into his pocket, he pulled out his phone and opened the text stream to the guy sweating his ass off down on the field. Things had ended on a promising note last night, but this was the cold light of day. Did Donovan regret what he'd said? Was he suffering from some kind of morning-after remorse?

Would he try and walk it back?

He guessed there was only one way to find out, and the time for subtlety was over. And maybe Donovan had been waiting for a more forthright opening? Beck's fingers quickly typed out the message and let it fly.

How is it possible you can get me hot from the other side of the stadium?

It wasn't full-on *meet me out the back so we can fuck* pornographic, but it was giving Donovan a more obvious come on. If he was having any kind of morning-after regrets, he'd run a mile. But if he was still in the same frame of mind as last night, then they had a ballgame.

Unfortunately, the answer had to wait, because the Smoke still had an hour of training to go. But when that was done, Beck would know one way or the other whether Donovan wanted to go further.

Surprisingly, Beck settled to work. Now the text was sent and he knew there couldn't be any communication for a while, he got stuck into the pile of things that had been mounting on his desk. It was only the little *ding* on his phone alerting him to an incoming text that dragged him away from the computer a couple of hours later.

It was Donovan. *I don't know. But knowing you're watching me from up there gets me hot, too.*

Beck's heart stopped for a full two beats as a lightning fork of desire streaked through his body, earthing in his *balls*. This was big. *Really* big. He might not have known Donovan for long, but his conflict, the struggle between the rugby player and the man, was real.

And Beck knew *he'd* been the catalyst.

The part of him ruled by his testosterone revelled in that knowledge, but given its potential consequences—for them both—he knew better than to let it go to his head. Beck thought of, then mentally discarded, multiple replies before he settled on one and sent it off.

So...what are we going to do about it?

He liked it. It put the ball in Donovan's court, but by

using *we*, he also made it clear that he was in for some action, too. He wanted what might happen between them to be Donovan's choice, but he didn't want to put all the pressure on him, either. He wanted him to know that he could meet him halfway.

It was a full twenty minutes before the reply landed. *I don't know. I'm sorry. Need more time?*

Beck tamped down the surge of disappointment. His expectations had been galloping in time with his pulse. But of course, Donovan was wary. He was thirty-two years old and not officially out yet. It was a long time to keep something that close, a long time to be in his head about it. Considering how high the stakes—perceived or actual—were for Donovan, he'd come a long way in a short time.

He responded. *Of course. No pressure.* And then after a beat or two, he added some more. *If you want to just be friends, we can do that, too.*

It would kill him for sure, but he'd manage. Beck wanted more than just friendship with the rugby pro, but he had to accept that it might be the only thing the other man was willing to give. Donovan was putting a tentative foot on the road to being the person he was born to be, and that could be fraught at the best of times without potentially doing it under a national media spotlight.

Which was why it was a bad idea to be even contemplating getting involved with a guy in the closet. *Any* guy, really, but this one in particular.

For crying out loud, there were plenty of dudes out there fully embracing their gayness. Hot, smart, kind ones. Deep, interesting, introspective ones. Ones that could hold conversations and exist in social situations without hiding who they were. He could hit up several guys right now and have himself a date tonight, which would, for damn sure, end up in sexy times.

Because God knew, he wanted sexy times very fucking badly. Unfortunately, he wanted them with Donovan Bane.

And it wasn't like anyone actually ever died from pent-up lust.

He could hear his gay buddies laughing hysterically at that one, but it was true. Beck was thirty-one, not thirteen, and if nothing else, his hand could always take the edge off.

Thank you, opposable thumbs.

I don't want to just be friends.

The text pinged onto the screen, interrupting Beck's ruminations, which evaporated in an instant. Donovan Bane didn't want to be *just* friends. He smiled a big, goofy smile as a well of relief, cool as a mountain stream, washed through his system.

Well, alrighty, then—game on.

Phew. Beck added the sweaty brow emoji and sent the text, following it quickly with another. *I'll give you some space. Let me know when you're ready to talk.*

Donovan had indicated he wanted some time, so it was Beck's job now to give the man what he needed. He just hoped like hell Donovan didn't talk himself out of it while psyching himself into it.

• • •

Nine o'clock Sunday night, Donovan was lying on his couch, watching yesterday afternoon's game for the third time. Or at least he was trying to. It was hard to concentrate when he remembered what had happened on this couch, which he did all the fucking time, his mind constantly wandering to it, wandering to Beckett. Wondering what he was doing and if he was out with any of his mates again. He'd seen the image Beckett had posted to Instagram this morning of him and three other guys out at a bar somewhere in Kings Cross last night, all grinning at the camera like they didn't have a care in the world.

Beckett's dimples had taunted him as had the way his sandy hair was just starting to curl a little on top. A hot rush of envy had almost swallowed Donovan whole as he'd stared at the picture. He wasn't jealous of the other men—well, not really—but he was envious of their freedom.

And then, because his life wasn't fucking sad enough, he'd tormented himself a little more by looking at all of Beckett's Instagram pictures and wondering why the hell Beckett was even interested in getting involved. After their texting session the other day, his hopes had been so high. Beckett—he still didn't know his last name—wanted to be with him, that had been clear. And Donovan had actually been able to see the possibilities.

He'd even promised himself last night he'd contact Beckett this morning and take the first step. Then he'd looked at Instagram, and the doubts returned. He and Beckett wouldn't be able to go out on the town like that. They wouldn't be able to go out *anywhere* in public.

Together. As a couple.

And sure, that would be fine for a while as they burned off this insane chemistry that hissed and bubbled between them. But Beckett was a social guy. How long would it be before he tired of living in Donovan's closet?

If the universe was good to him, he had another five years, maybe more, left in his career—would Beckett really want to be off the social scene for that long? Or maybe he'd go out anyway. Without Donovan. Because of course, he should.

But how would *that* feel?

There was no alternative, though, was there? They couldn't even socialise with friends in private, because sooner or later, someone would talk—either an accidental slip or because they wanted to make a quick buck.

And then *bam!*

He and Beckett would be the story all over the papers, and nobody in the Smoke would be able to play decent rugby with the tabloids knocking on their doors and shoving cameras in their faces. Asking dumb questions about how long each player had known and had it disrupted team unity and had Donovan ever checked out anyone's junk.

He'd be the distraction the team didn't need, and that could be catastrophic if it came out at the worst time, like, say, just before a final or a vital, must-win game.

None of it boded well for either of them, which took Donovan back to the beginning. Maybe it was better to just keep the status quo. Beckett had left the ball in his court, so it was his decision, and he got the impression that the other man would respect whatever conclusion he reached.

He didn't know if they could be *just* friends, but it might be good to have someone to talk to at least. Someone who understood.

Fuck. His head was just going around and around and around. Chopping and changing between the conviction he could make it work to the conviction it was going to be a total fucking disaster to utter conviction Beckett deserved better than a boyfriend in the closet.

It was almost a relief when there was a knock on the door. A distraction from the whirlpool of his contradictory thoughts. For a moment, anyway. Before reality intruded and he realised who was at the door. That it could only be one person. Actually, it *could* be anybody, but Donovan knew in his gut who it was, and it twisted in anticipation.

Within three beats of his heart, his pulse was pounding loud through his ears.

Taking a steadying breath, Donovan walked to the door and opened it to Beckett. They didn't say anything for long, long moments, just stared at each other, their gazes eating each other up. He was in jeans and a navy, long-sleeve T-shirt that hugged his broad chest and flat abs. It was pushed up to the elbows to expose the sandy-blond hairs on his forearms, which were so fucking sexy. A three-day growth peppered his jawline and his hair was tousled on top.

Donovan wanted to push his hand into it, feel the glide of it against his fingers. "Hey," he said instead, his voice already husky.

"I'm sorry." Beckett raked a hand through his hair. Maybe that's why it looked so tousled. "I...don't know why I'm here."

Donovan's heart rate slowed at the genuine note of confusion in his voice. His blood thickened to sludge, adding to the heat in his system. "Okay."

"I told myself I'd stay away." His brow furrowed, his eyes earnest in appeal as if needing Donovan to understand something he didn't understand himself. "To give you space."

"Okay."

"I even went out last night with some friends so I wouldn't come here. But tonight I just...found myself in my car and then I was...here."

Donovan swallowed against the parchment-dry tissues of his throat. "Okay." The loud buzz in his ears was clearly rendering him incapable of *wording* right now.

Their eyes locked. "You should send me away."

Probably. But seeing the usually calm and reasoned Beckett so...undone was sparking little fires in his belly and his thighs and his ass. His breath stuttered to a halt at the twin flares of desire he saw burning in the other man's eyes. "Okay."

But he made absolutely no move to do so.

Another beat passed. Two. Then, "*Fuck it*," Beckett swore under his breath as he took two steps forward, slid a hand onto Donovan's nape, and kissed him *hard*.

It took a couple of seconds for Donovan to respond, for all the parts of him to come together, to register the firm mouth, the delicious minty breath, the hot spice of cologne. To realise he was being kissed.

By a man. By *Beckett.*

It was a busy couple of seconds. But in one pure beat of the heart, it all clicked, and he ceded to the probing of Beckett's tongue against his closed lips, opening to him, every cell straining to the feel of his mouth, to the taste of him, to the smell of him. It filled up Donovan's senses until he was drowning in sensations.

So this was how it felt to be kissed by a man. Harder, deeper, earthier. Scratchier, bulkier, hairier. Double the testosterone. Triple the hit. Like being part of those YouTube videos, not just an onlooker.

This was what he'd been waiting for. *This* moment. Nothing had ever felt this right. This natural. This innate. *Nothing.* Not even rugby.

And it consumed him. *Beckett* consumed him.

He moaned then. Hell, he *groaned.* A low, rumbly noise that would barely register on a decibel meter but would blow the top off a seismograph. That spoke of desperation and fulfilment all at once. That spoke of lust and hope after denial and darkness. Of blood pumping and veins pulsing and sparks igniting.

And then Donovan was falling back as Beckett advanced, their mouths still fused. And then somehow they pivoted, and Beckett, whose hand was still at Donovan's nape, was pushing him against the door. He only just registered his ass and shoulder blades hitting wood and the clicking noise as it shut under the combined force of their weight as Beckett's body pushed hard against his, pinning him to the door and *grinding.*

Donovan gasped at the potent contact and muttered,

"*Fuck*," against Beckett's mouth, his hands sinking into the other man's hair as his hips responded out of some kind of primitive instinct, grinding back.

Beckett groaned then, deep in his throat, as he continued to rub and grind his patently aroused dick along the length of Donovan's patently aroused dick while *going to town* on his mouth. His lips demanding *more*, almost blistering in their intensity. His whiskers pricking and spiking despite the thicker cover of Donovan's growth. His tongue thrusting hot and hard in time to the grind of his hips.

Donovan twisted his fingers into Beckett's hair, trying to keep pace and breathe and not dissolve into a boneless mess. Or have a stroke, his heart thundering so fast and loud against his rib cage he was amazed he couldn't hear it knocking on the door behind. Not that he could hear anything over the roar of testosterone inside his head bellowing like a fucking grizzly bear, like they were two wild animals rutting instead of dry humping against a door like teenagers.

But what it looked like didn't matter as Donovan drowned in the thrust of Beckett's tongue and revelled in the grind of his hips. Luxuriated in the soft glide of his hair through his fingers and wallowed in the rigid contours of his chest, keeping him caged against the door.

It only mattered what it *felt* like. And it felt amazing. It felt *right*. Like a homecoming after a million years in the wilderness.

He felt like a fucking *God*.

Donovan was vaguely aware of Beckett's hand sliding from his nape but too consumed by the twist of their mouths, the tangle of their tongues, the loud suck of their breathing to protest the removal of what had felt oddly more intimate than the deep-throat kisses. But when it brushed against his dick, the jolt to Donovan's groin was hot and fast, and his hips jerked to a halt as he broke off the kiss.

Panting hard, his gaze dropped between them to find Beckett's hand fumbling with the zipper of his jeans. When he glanced up again, Beckett was watching him.

"You want me to stop?" he asked, his breathing just as erratic, his voice husky, his eyes intent, searching.

"No." Donovan did *not* want Beckett to stop. Not when he was looking at Donovan like that, with his lips full and wet from their kisses, a feverish glint in his eyes, and a dull flush staining his cheeks.

"Then watch," he said, the hand that had been on Donovan's nape sliding back there again, warm and firm as the other reefed down his zipper.

Donovan couldn't *not* watch as Beckett reached into his own jeans and pulled out his cock. His long, beautiful cock. He couldn't *not* watch when he yanked on the elastic waistband of Donovan's shorts and pulled out *his* cock, which bucked almost violently at the touch. And when Beckett sandwiched them together, his fingers clamping firmly around their combined girth, it tore Donovan's breath from his lungs it looked so fucking good.

So fucking *right*.

Beckett's long and fleshy pink, lightly veined and perfectly proportioned. His just a little longer, a little thicker. Blunter, darker. More heavily veined.

He moved his hand then from the base of their shafts to the tips of their dual flushed crowns, twin beads of liquid pearling at the slits. Donovan hissed out a breath and grabbed hold of Beckett's hips as every muscle in his body clenched tight and a bolt of white-hot heat lanced his balls in a searing flash that almost brought him to his knees. The hand at the back of his neck tightened convulsively as if Beckett was also having problems staying upright despite the counterbalance provided by the closeness of their bodies.

It didn't stop him doing it again, though, despite the

limited room between their bodies to manoeuvre. Up and down. Up and down. Over and over. With his forehead pressed to Beckett's, Donovan had a bird's-eye view.

They both did. And neither of them looked away.

Beckett was as seemingly mesmerized as Donovan as he worked their cocks, from base to head, two engorged crowns, pushing though the tight band of long fingers. Friction built from every angle. From the rub of Beckett's hand on the outside to the grind of cock-on-cock where they were wedged together.

Donovan's hips started to rock, leaning into the action a little. He couldn't help it, his body was calling the play, and he was a slave to its dictates. Beckett's rocked as well, and Donovan grunted as their dicks slid against each other, the friction increasing tenfold. His heart was a hammer in his chest now as they rutted, their pants and groans an erotic opera building in the debauched bubble they'd created, Beckett's hand still at his nape.

Nerve endings deep behind Donovan's belly button started to flare then contract. Muscle fibres buried between his hip bones started to unravel from the tight coil they'd wound into from the moment Beckett had kissed him. His balls pulled taut as walnuts.

"Oh God," he panted, his tone a low, rumbly warning as the seductive stroke of pleasure started to lick over nerves and unfurl through veins. "I'm almost there."

Beckett's hand clamped and unclamped on Donovan's neck as his other hand kept up at the pace on their cocks. "Good," he muttered. "You first this time."

Donovan didn't need any further instruction, mentally opening the gates, allowing the rush of sensation to swamp his pelvis as he surrendered to the crescendo of pleasure. "*Beckett*!" he cried out as ropes of hot, white cum spurted from his cock, splattering against his shirt and arm and spilling over Beckett's fingers.

Not that Beckett seemed to care as his hand jerked to a halt and his face twisted into a grimace and he stopped breathing for a beat before he bellowed out something completely unintelligible and came *hard*. It was such a guttural sound that Donovan slid one of his hands onto Beckett's nape. For comfort or connection or grounding, who knew?

It just felt right.

And they clung to each other like that, hands on napes and foreheads pressed together as they shuddered through their climaxes, watching their dicks rub together until they'd unloaded their last drop and the waves receded and they were spent.

Donovan's hand fell away, his head thudding back against the door as he gasped for breath. "Fuck," he said, when he'd regained enough puff.

Beckett, whose forehead was now pressed into Donovan's throat, laughed, warm air caressing the demarcation line between where his bare skin stopped and the heavier growth of whiskers began. "I couldn't have put it better myself," he murmured.

Goose bumps broke out down Donovan's neck at the way Beckett's lips brushed his skin. They travelled all the way down to his nipples, prickling at the tips. Lifting his head off the door with great difficulty, he glanced down as Beckett glanced up, his eyelids fluttering at half mast, his mouth utterly and thoroughly kissed.

He looked as relaxed as it was possible for a person to look, like he'd taken some kind of illicit substance. But drugs hadn't been responsible for Beckett's super-chilled state—*he'd* done that.

Tentatively, Beckett smiled at him. A slow, easy smile. A smile between lovers.

And Donovan smiled back.

Chapter Seven

Donovan took his time cleaning up in the laundry before he faced Beckett again, waiting for his higher functioning to come back online. He was going to need it so he could do the things that would be required now.

Like talk. And think.

What had happened against the door had rocked his world—more than that first time with Beckett. Because this time they'd kissed. He'd let Beckett touch him. It hadn't been a solo endeavour to get off. It had been very much a team effort.

Christ. He shut his eyes as a delayed shudder undulated through his belly. He didn't even have words for how incredible it had been. Every fantasy he'd ever had about kissing a guy— and he'd had many—had been blown out of the water. That video he watched? He wouldn't need it anymore. All he had to do was think about Beckett's kisses, *about tonight*, and he'd be set.

It had been beyond his wildest dreams, and Donovan wanted nothing more than to keep doing it, but...they needed to *talk* first.

Not dance around via SMS. *Talk*.

Beckett needed to understand what he was up for. They both did. It was tempting in the aftermath of great...whatever it was they'd just done—dry humping, frottage, *sex*?—to think they'd just keep on this track and everything would come easily now. But Donovan was a realist. More than that, he was a pragmatist. His life wasn't normal, so it was best to lay all their cards on the table *now*.

He'd asked Beckett for time so he could think, and now he'd decided. Best to get on with discussing how—*if*—this thing could work. And that included both of them talking about their doubts and fears.

He found Beckett in the kitchen. He was *shirtless*, having cleaned up at the sink, and it was Donovan's first instinct to look away. Not to ogle. But then he remembered he *could* ogle this man. He could ogle *the fuck* out of this man. And that made him smile as his eyes devoured the puckered contours of his abs, the slight curve of his pecs sprinkled lightly with sandy brown hair, and the flatness of nipples. The bony framework of his ribs and the prominence of his collarbone.

Good Christ, he was sexy.

Beckett's left eyebrow kicked up at Donovan's blatant perving. "I thought you must have been freaking out somewhere. Obviously not."

"No." Donovan dragged his eyes off Beckett's chest. "More like waiting for my ability to form coherent sentences to return."

He laughed. "Nothing like the power of a good orgasm."

Donovan couldn't agree more, as his gaze drifted again, his body stirring again. "Christ." He shook his head. "Put this on." He tossed the shirt he'd brought with him at Beckett's chest. "We should talk."

Beckett grinned. "I can talk with my shirt off."

"Yeah, but apparently where you're concerned, I can talk or ogle. Not both."

"I'm okay with the ogling."

Donovan smiled at the twinkle in the other man's eyes. Was this what a *relationship* with Beckett would be like? Fun and flirty and…happy? His smile slipped as an ache took up residence in his chest. He wanted that.

But could he have it and rugby *and* keep them completely separate? Could he compartmentalise them? And was that even fair?

"Okay, okay. You win. I'll put it on." Beckett grinned then shoved his arms in the shirt. "But I think I'm going to need to start bringing my own change of clothes whenever I come here."

Donovan's smile slipped even further as Beckett ducked into the head hole. That was one thing they had to talk about.

Beckett *couldn't* come here if they decided to start something.

People in his neighbourhood were pretty cool with him. They knew who he was and would wave and call him by name if he was passing or out the front. Some would even stop for a bit of Monday morning quarterbacking. There were also several families in the street with kids Miri's age who all played together whenever his daughter was over from NZ.

But largely they left him alone.

It was a close-knit street, though, with an active Neighbourhood Watch programme—Beckett's car parked outside regularly would be noted. Mrs. Connor, the head of the programme, would notice for sure. She might be in her eighties, but she had eagle eyes and a *lot* of time on her hands. And whilst he didn't think she'd give a damn about Donovan's sexuality—she'd proudly hung a rainbow flag in her window and voted yes in the national plebiscite on same-sex marriage—it didn't mean she wouldn't tell someone, and that someone might use the information for ill.

"I'm getting quite the collection now." Beckett's voice was muffled as he continued, oblivious to the doubt demons chasing one another around Donovan's head. "I've been stashing them under my pillow to dream sweet dreams about you."

Beckett emerged from the head hole, still grinning, but it faded slowly as he regarded Donovan. "I was just joking."

Donovan gave a half smile. "Yeah. I know."

Straightening the shirt, Beckett cocked one hip, leaning it into the benchtop. "Look...I know I shouldn't have come tonight. I told you I'd give you space. I told you to get in touch when you were ready. And I know I should say sorry, but I can't be sorry about what just happened. It was too damn good, I won't—"

Raising his hands in the universal signal of *enough now*, Donovan cut Beckett off. "I know, it's okay. I'm glad you did." The other man narrowed his eyes, obviously not convinced, and Donovan sighed. "Honestly, I don't know if I'd have ever made the first move. I...overthink things."

Beckett laughed like that was the biggest understatement he'd ever heard. "Well..." He shrugged. "I guess that's what comes from having to keep secrets."

"Yeah."

"So—" Beckett pushed away from the benchtop and walked slowly toward Donovan, not stopping until he was close. Close enough to touch if Donovan wanted, and God help him, he *did* want. "Why are you giving yourself early wrinkles?" He lifted his hand then, smoothing a finger along the furrows in Donovan's forehead.

It was such a light touch, yet Donovan felt it *everywhere*. Just as he felt the spicy accents of Beckett's cologne wafting over him on a warm pillow of pheromone-laden air.

"Because...I don't know how to...do this."

"This?" Beckett's hand fell to his side.

"I don't know how to do *gay*."

"Donovan…" Beckett's warm chuckle, the way he always called him by his full name, set up home inside Donovan's belly and lit a fire. "Being gay isn't something you *do*. It's something you *are*." Beckett tapped his chest lightly, right above his heart. "So, however you *do* your life is fine. Really."

"*Fine?*" Donovan stared at him. "I've been ignoring this"—he tapped his chest in the exact spot Beckett had tapped—"since I was fifteen."

"Yeah, but not anymore, right? So you start from today."

"How? When I have to stay in this damn closet?"

"Hey." He lifted his hand and cupped Donovan's jaw, and the tangle of emotions that were threatening to overwhelm him hushed at the touch. "The first step is always the hardest. Finally accepting who you are, saying it out loud, often takes place in the closet. You're not on your lonesome there. Don't underestimate how far you've come."

Donovan wished Beckett's hand didn't feel so fucking good cradling him like that. Wished his voice wasn't so soothing and his words so damn sensible. Wished he didn't want to shut his eyes and just lean into all that calm rationality. It made him believe everything could be all right, that he could actually step out of the closet with this man and everything would be okay.

But it *wouldn't* be.

"And now you get to choose what you want to do." Beckett waggled his eyebrows suggestively as his hand slid down to rest against a bicep decorated in swirls of dark ink. "What *do* you want to do, Donovan Bane?" he asked, a smile hovering on lips that had introduced him to a whole new world.

One that was *still* frustratingly out of reach.

Donovan shook his head as the weight of the unknown threatened to crush him. He backed up a step or two, and

Beckett's hand slid from his arm. He turned and paced into the living area. It was easy for Beckett—he'd been living a full life as a gay man for a lot longer. He knew all the rules. All the do's and don'ts. The...conventions.

Donovan was utterly clueless.

Standing near the couch, he turned and faced the other man. "I don't know. That's the thing...I don't know how it works with two gay men."

Beckett gave a crooked smile. "Pretty much the same as two straight people."

"No, I mean..." *Fuck.* Absently, he started cracking his knuckles. What *did* he mean?

"Donovan," Beckett said quietly, his smile gentle. "Is this about the sex stuff?"

"No. Yes." Donovan stopped cracking his knuckles. "Maybe." He started to pace from the couch to the bean bag and back again. "I mean...I don't even know how to do the sex stuff."

A low chuckle slid from Beckett's lips. "Oh, trust me, you *know* how to do the sex stuff."

Donovan stopped pacing and glanced at Beckett. "What? That thing just now? That's what it is?"

"Sure." He shrugged. "Sometimes."

"See, I don't know any of this. I'm just a...big...gay... virgin. In every sense of the word. This *is* my first rodeo."

Beckett laughed, full and throaty. "A gay virgin?"

"Well, I don't know, do I?" He started to pace again, cracking his knuckles in time with the falls of his feet. "I mean, is there such a thing? Because I have *had* sex before, so I'm technically not a virgin? Does sex with a woman count in—" Christ, he didn't know...some mental ledger?

"The land of the gays?"

Donovan shot Beckett—who was clearly enjoying himself a little too much—an exasperated glare. He just grinned bigger as Donovan paced.

"Do gay men consider other gay men who haven't had sex with a man a virgin?" he continued.

"Wow, you really do overthink things, don't you?"

Another thought occurred to Donovan then, and he stopped abruptly. "*Am* I still a gay virgin after what happened before? Did you just…pop my gay cherry?"

Beckett burst out laughing, throwing his head back. Donovan shoved his hands on his hips and waited for the hilarity to die down. "I'm sorry," Beckett said, trying to suppress his laughter and catch his breath. "I know these are genuine questions. It's just…you're too damn cute."

Donovan rolled his eyes. He'd been called a lot of things in his life—cute wasn't one of them. He went back to pacing. "And what about…I don't even know if I'm a…top or a bottom or—"

"A *top* or a *bottom*?" Beckett interrupted, his eyebrows rising on his forehead.

"I watch TV," Donovan said as he trod his path from the couch to the coffee table.

"Okay."

"And what if we're both the same? Is that incompatible? Or do some guys go both ways? Is there a name for that?" He glanced at Beckett, who'd come around to the other side of the centre island, looking cool as a fucking cucumber, leaning his butt against the counter, his hands gripping the bench behind, elbows bent, his feet crossed at the ankles. While Donovan felt like he was being plunged into boiling hot water.

"Vers," Beckett said.

"*Vers?*"

"Versatile."

"Oh God." Donovan shoved a hand through his hair. "See…I don't even know the terminology."

Beckett laughed again. "I don't think they kick you out or take away your gay card for not knowing the terminology."

But Donovan wasn't finished. "I don't know if I want to… if I want you to…" His face grew hot as his words petered out, because he wasn't sure he could admit that out loud.

Wasn't he supposed to want the ultimate intimacy with a man?

Beckett's sigh was loud in the silence that followed. "Donovan."

He pushed off the bench and headed toward Donovan, who stopped pacing as Beckett drew near. When he was close enough, he slid his hand onto Donovan's arm all the way up to his shoulder. It was instantly soothing, and the panic started to recede. Beckett's aura from the day they'd first met had been imbued with calm and serenity, and Donovan envied the man's composure.

"It's okay," he murmured, giving the shoulder a squeeze. "You don't have to know any of that stuff yet. You can take your time figuring it out."

"But *you* have a preference, right?" Wasn't that important to know?

"Yeah." He nodded. "I prefer to take rather than give."

Which meant he'd expect Donovan to…? The thought put a skip in his pulse. "But you've done both?"

"Yes."

"And not having a preference is…okay?" Wasn't knowing how you liked it supposed to be innate?

"Of course." Another squeeze to the shoulder and then a soft smile, which warmed his eyes and made Donovan just want to dive in and stay there. "Look…" he continued. "I think you're getting way too ahead of yourself. Let's just… take this one day at a time. See if we actually like each other first before we worry about the sex stuff."

"I like you," Donovan responded quickly, because it was

an absolute no-brainer for him and he wanted Beckett to know that whatever other questions and doubts he had, he didn't question or doubt that he really, *really* liked the man.

"Yeah?" There was a tease in his voice as Beckett's hand moved to the side of Donovan's neck, his fingers stroking lightly. "I like you, too."

A frown crinkled Donovan's brow. He couldn't fathom why the other man could be bothered. "Why? Why not be with someone who's…easy? Who's out and knows what they're doing? Who at least knows the *terminology*, anyway?" He barked out a self-deprecating laugh. "Who isn't so… messed up?"

The other man shook his head slowly. The soft, indulgent smile touching his mouth belied the flare of heat in his eyes. The slow stroke of his fingers was causing an outbreak of goose bumps up and down Donovan's throat, prickling through his beard and along his scalp. "You think being out gives you some kind of get-out-of-messed-up-jail-free card? I've been with guys who were out and still didn't have their shit together. My straight friends could tell you the same. Everyone carries a little bit of baggage. It's part of the human condition."

"Yeah." Donovan nodded. He was right.

"Okay, how about this?" Beckett dropped his hand to Donovan's chest as their gazes met and held. "Let's spend the next few weeks getting to know each other. And I don't meant sex. As much as that pains me." He grinned as he waggled his eyebrows. "I mean talking. Face to face. Casual, PG, get-togethers, in the evenings. Get used to being with another guy as a gay man but without the sexual pressure. Like dating, but we don't go anywhere. Just here or at my place."

"It has to be your place," Donovan said, quickly jumping in. He hated doing it. He felt like a fucking heel already erecting the boundaries within which they had to operate. "Everyone knows one another in this neighbourhood. They notice things like a new car in the street. And they like to... talk."

"Okay." He nodded, no hesitation. No sign that such a stricture was irksome. "My place it is. It'll work well, actually. I live in a large apartment block where pretty much nobody knows anybody and there's basement parking."

"Sounds good."

It sounded more than good. It sounded cosy and fucking *wonderful*. The no-sex thing didn't even faze Donovan—he'd gone this long without it. He could last a few more weeks. Besides, there were different levels of intimacy, right? Sharing nights with Beckett in his home, talking and laughing and eating together, sounded great. Just being able to be *himself* around another guy—a guy like him. Not having to hide who he was...

Standing close while they cooked, sitting close on the couch. A kiss hello, a kiss goodbye. The mere thought of spending that time together heated his loins.

Who knew something so...domesticated could be such a fucking turn-on?

"It does. And we can reassess after a few weeks. Decide if you want to take it further."

Further. That would be the *sex stuff*. Christ alive, his curiosity, his yearning for *that* level of intimacy, seemed to grow by the minute. But...he needed Beckett to be sure.

"Are you *sure* this is what *you* want?"

"Yes."

"To be a...secret?"

"It's a few weeks."

"Could be more."

"Let's just..." Beckett shrugged. "Take it a day at a time, okay?"

Donovan could see Beckett was trying to slow him down, but he needed him to know all the pitfalls. "We won't be able to be seen out together in public. We can't go out to a restaurant or see a movie."

"I know."

"We can't socialise together with any of our friends."

"My friends will understand."

Donovan wished he could say the same, but he didn't know that for sure. Football teams weren't exactly known for their tolerance, and he'd certainly heard his fair share of homophobic slurs being tossed around, both during play and in locker rooms, over the years.

Hell, given his *brown*-ness, he'd been the brunt of several on-field racial slurs, too.

And yes, Tanner ran a tight ship, with zero tolerance for disrespecting anyone's differences, but would one of their own coming out as gay expose deeper prejudices?

Hand on his heart, Donovan would say that the guys he was closest to on the team wouldn't give a shit. They'd be surprised for sure, but for a bunch of macho footballers, they were all fairly woke. Everyone had reported they'd voted yes in the same-sex marriage plebiscite, and when John's brother had come out as gay five years ago, everybody had been very supportive.

He thought—he hoped—they'd do the same for him.

But…given he wasn't coming out to anyone else any time soon, the point was moot, so he ignored it and moved on. "You won't be able to go to the corporate box anymore."

"It's fine. It's much easier to masturbate when I'm at home, anyway."

Then he grinned completely unabashed while Donovan's brain temporarily fritzed out. *Fuck*. Now all he was going to think about when he was playing was Beckett watching him at home with his hand on his cock.

Refusing to be side-tracked by such blatant—and deliberate, he suspected—sexual imagery, Donovan pushed on. "You *can* come to a game. You'll just have to…sit in the stands." He shoved a hand through his hair. Beckett was being so fucking *decent* about this. Cracking jokes and trying to put him at ease. It wasn't fair. "This sucks, I'm so sorry."

"It's fine."

"It's not." It really wasn't. He hated that they were stuck between a rock and a hard place because of him.

"I'm a big boy. I'm capable of making my own decisions, and I say it's fine."

"Beckett." Donovan shook his head. "I'm trying to give you an out."

"I don't want an out."

Hell, if that didn't do things to Donovan's equilibrium. "You said you only want real."

"I did?" He frowned. "When did I say that?"

"On your Grindr profile."

The frown cleared as Beckett laughed. "You checked me out." Then he frowned again. "Wait, you're on Grindr?"

"I made an anonymous profile years ago because I got curious. But I never used it and deactivated it after a week. I reactivated it briefly a couple of days after I met you to see if you were there."

"And what did you think?"

"I thought you looked hot and fun and interesting and so comfortable in your skin it made me ache all over. And I envied every one of your friends in those pictures because they knew you and I didn't."

"Yeah?" He smiled soft and slow. "I'm flattered."

The tenderness in that smile made Donovan ache all over again. Beckett's obvious pleasure in the compliment bubbled like champagne through his veins. But that wasn't the point of this conversation, and he gave himself a mental shake, clearing his throat. "I can't do real, Beckett."

"I know."

"Then how is this fine by you?"

"Because what kind of a person would I be if I didn't take your personal circumstances into account? You're not some guy who's trying to have it both ways. Who jumps in and out of the closet whenever it suits him. This is your career, Donovan, I get that, I understand why you're not out. But…"

Donovan watched as Beckett took a deep breath. "That sounds ominous?"

He shrugged. "You're laying your cards on the table, so it's only fair that I do, too."

"Okay?" Jesus…*what?*

Beckett's gaze dropped to his hands. "I was…involved with a guy for a while who wasn't out, and it was a…shitty relationship, and I swore I'd never do that again." He glanced up again, his eyes meeting Donovan's, the shadow of old wounds lurking deep in the blue depths. "But the thing is, I just can't stop thinking about you, either." A self-deprecating smile pulled at the corners of Beckett's mouth. "So, I'm fine with fitting into the confines of your life—for a while. I'm up for spending time together, up for helping you navigate this whole new world, and I'm definitely up for some sexy times, but I don't see this as a long-term thing, and I'm definitely not looking for a *boyfriend*."

The news rocked Donovan back on his feet a little. He'd clearly been getting way ahead of where Beckett was emotionally. He'd been cantering along, thinking *future*, because he wasn't going to take such a huge step with just anyone—not when so much was at risk. Beckett, on the other hand, was being more guarded. He was thinking…fuck buddy?

And Donovan didn't know how to feel about that right now.

But he'd be some kind of prick if he didn't try to understand where Beckett was coming from, particularly when he'd been so understanding of Donovan's situation. Beckett had clearly been hurt by someone in his past. So it was hardly surprising he wasn't keen to line up for an emotional involvement with another guy who wasn't coming out of the closet any time soon.

That only made sense.

It made sense for him, too, he realised—to not think long term. Not get too far ahead of himself. Because that's what Donovan did. He was a father and a career rugby player, both of which required long-term strategy and goals. But what did he really know about any of *this*?

Being with a guy?

It was his first time. And just because he and Beckett had chemistry and there was a strong attraction didn't mean it would last. It would pay Donovan to be a little more tempered, too.

"Okay." He nodded. "Fair enough. I can do short term."

Maybe a *dalliance* like this—even a short one—could get Donovan through the next five or six years remaining in his career? He hoped so—he really did. Because now he'd had a glimpse of what could be, that time stretched ahead in a long, lonely corridor.

And hell…didn't he deserve a little something after all this time ignoring his true desires, telling himself that his career was paramount? That it came first and his personal life had to take a back seat?

That he'd get to it *after*?

Beckett was offering him *before*. He was offering him *now*. Even if only the two of them knew it. Even if it was only for a little while.

"You sure?" Beckett asked, lifting his hand to cup Donovan's cheek.

"Yeah," Donovan agreed. Then he turned his face into the warmth of Beckett's hand, closing his eyes as he nuzzled at the palm. He dropped a kiss in the centre, and the low, needy noise—like a whimper—that slipped from Beckett's throat caused an answering flutter in Donovan's belly.

He opened his eyes to find Beckett staring at him intently, and the air between them grew thick and fat for long, still moments.

"Well," Beckett said, loosening his fingers, his hand falling away as he cleared his throat of the huskiness. "I'm going to go now before things get out of hand and someone in the neighbourhood takes down my number plate."

Donovan grimaced. "I'm sorry."

"It's fine," he assured. "I'll see you tomorrow night at my place?"

"Yeah. Text me the address."

"Okay." He didn't move for a beat or two, and that thickness bloomed between them again until Beckett reached across, grabbed two handfuls of Donovan's shirt, jerked him closer, and gave him a brief, hard kiss on the mouth. It lasted mere seconds but was like a sledgehammer to Donovan's equilibrium.

As abruptly as Beckett had grabbed him, he broke away, unhanding his shirt and taking a step back. Donovan blinked then smiled as they both stared at each other, clearly dazed. Beckett shook his head. "Keeping my hands off you these next few weeks is not going to be easy."

Ditto. That was the only thing about this of which Donovan was sure.

"Okay. Goodbye, then."

Donovan smiled as Beckett stayed rooted to the spot. "Goodbye."

He sighed but moved, heading for the door, getting all the way there when Donovan called his name. "Beckett?"

"Yeah?" He turned.

"What's your last name?" If they were really doing this, then Donovan should know the man's full name.

He laughed. "It's Stanton."

"Okay, then. See you tomorrow, Beckett Stanton."

"Looking forward to it, Donovan Bane."

Then he slipped out the door, and Donovan broke into a giant grin. Holy fuck. They were *really* doing this.

• • •

Beck's phone rang during his lunch break on Monday. He was sitting at the café by himself, trying not to think about tonight too much, because that only resulted in a massive erection no matter how much he mentally berated his dick for getting excited *at work*. And about something that was going to be PG only.

A picture of himself and Pete—one of his oldest friends—flashed on the screen, and Beck contemplated letting it go to voicemail. He knew what it was going to be about, since he'd texted Pete and cancelled their regular Monday night Netflix hangout. Pete hated it when Beck cancelled, not least of all because their current watch was *The Witcher* and Pete had always had a hard-on for Henry Cavil.

He was more a Matthew McConaughey guy himself—until Donovan, anyway.

But Beck knew that Pete would just keep ringing until he picked up, so it was better to get it over with now. "What could possibly be more important than Henry Cavil in body armour, wielding a sword?"

Beck laughed. He'd met Pete at a university gay pride march, and they'd been firm friends ever since. It helped that neither had fancied the other. "It's a...work thing."

Which, strictly speaking, wasn't true, but if he hadn't

started working at Henley Stadium, then he'd have never met Donovan, so it was work…adjacent. He'd tell Donovan tonight that Mondays going forward wouldn't work. As, he presumed, Wednesdays wouldn't work for Donovan because of his regular poker game.

It didn't stop the spike of guilt lancing Beck's belly, though. He'd never had to conceal who he was seeing from his friends. Not even Dieter, who'd socialised happily with Beck's friends even while denying he was gay to everybody else—sometimes even himself. But he was going to have to get used to it if he and Donovan decided to pursue something sexual for a while.

This would be his life. Clandestine meetings with Donovan in between their various commitments while pretending he was still single-and-looking for his friends. Or they'd know something was up for sure. Last night, being with Donovan in the aftermath of their incredibly heady petting session against the door, it had seemed anything was possible. Talking to Pete, he realised just what a challenge it would be.

"Fine, but this is the second time in as many weeks you've blown me off."

That was true. Beck had been scheduled to see Pete and the rest of his guy group the night he'd spent at Henley in the corporate box, watching Donovan run around that field. There had been a flurry of confused texts from his *hilarious* friends when he'd revealed he was going to a rugby game.

"We saw each other on Saturday night." Beck had leaped at that invitation, desperately needing a distraction from ending up at Donovan's. Like he had the next night.

"Please, you were so distracted you might as well not have been there. Looking at your phone all the time. What's going on with you?"

Beck rolled his eyes, but Pete could sniff out a secret

better than anyone he knew, so it was best to be on guard. "Nothing. I've just started a new job. I've got a lot on my plate, that's all."

"Hmm, okay. But we're still on for this Saturday, right?"

"Yep." The guys were going to the Beresford, where they hung out most Saturday afternoons, weather and schedules permitting. The Smoke were playing an away match in Canberra on the weekend, so Donovan wouldn't be around. "I'll be there."

But in the meantime, he had five nights with Donovan, and he couldn't wait. All he had to do was remember that it was about setting Donovan at ease. Talking. Getting to know each other. Platonically. *Not* carnally. He was to use his mouth for good—not evil.

And keep his damn hands to himself.

Chapter Eight

It took Beck less than one minute to realise keeping his hands to himself was going to be just as challenging as keeping this whole thing a secret. Donovan arrived on his doorstep encased in a dark gray hoodie, which he unzipped and shrugged out of the second he walked inside. Beneath was a plain white T-shirt and dark blue jeans, both of which sat snug against the hard wall of his physique. Neither were tight. They just cupped and hugged in all the right places.

The white of his shirt was a stark contrast to the brown of his skin and the swirling dark lines of his tattoo. His hair, which he'd always worn tied back, was loose tonight and still damp, hinting he'd not long been out of the shower. He wore it pushed back off his forehead, the rest falling loose around his neck and shoulders, the moisture giving it a slight crinkle.

He'd trimmed his beard, and for the first time since they met like this, he didn't smell like liniment. He smelled like he'd just climbed out of the shower. Like soap and shampoo and his freshly laundered clothes with their sweet, milky fragrance. For someone who owned about a dozen different expensive brands of cologne, it was a surprise to Beck to discover that inexpensive, everyday aromas of liniment and Lux flakes could do it for him.

He'd desperately wanted to kiss him—a quick peck hello was all—when he'd arrived on the doorstep, but he hadn't. Donovan had appeared awkward and nervous standing on the doorstep huddled in the hood of his jacket, so Beck had just ushered him in and made a mental note to get a spare key cut so he could let himself in.

"Beer?" Beck asked as he watched Donovan prowl around his small living room like a caged animal. The sixth-floor apartment wasn't huge—two bedrooms with a shared bathroom between, a living room, and a kitchen.

"Thanks, yeah."

Beck had taken note of the beer Donovan drank and had bought a six-pack of it on his way home from work. He grabbed one out of the fridge, cracked it open, and walked it over, the glass of wine he'd been drinking when Donovan arrived in the other hand.

"Cheers." He held up his glass of red, and they clinked, the *tink*ing noise like the ringing of a bell.

Round one!

It didn't feel like a boxing match, though; as their eyes met, it felt like a slow dance. One of those old-fashioned ones where the couples swirl around each other, barely touching. Like something out of Jane Austen or *The Sound of Music*. For two people who had already shared certain intimacies it seemed comical, but it didn't feel like that.

It felt *genteel*.

When Donovan had downed three mouthfuls, he dragged his gaze away and glanced around the room, saying, "This is nice."

"It's okay for now. It was hard to find good rentals over this neck of the woods, and I needed something quickly. I'm hoping to find a townhouse somewhere in suburbia. It's close to everything here, but it's kinda loud with all the traffic noise coming up from the main drag all hours of the day and night."

He indicated the glass sliding doors that led to the outdoor area, and Donovan said, "You have a balcony?"

"Yes." Beck strode toward the doors. They were shut both for the noise and to keep the cold night air at bay. "With a glorious view of the road and the apartments opposite."

Opening them, he stepped out onto the generous tiled area he'd wasted no time in turning into a mini jungle and headed for the rail. Right on cue, a screaming siren zipped past as cold air nipped at Beck's face and pushed icy fingers through the thin material of his shirt. Warm air slipped from his lungs on a foggy cloud.

"It's a decent size," Donovan murmured from somewhere behind.

Beck turned, resting his ass against the rail. "It's bigger than the bathroom," he joked.

"How many apartments?" Donovan asked as he stepped out and sauntered over to Beck, coming to a halt at the railing a good few feet to the left. He leaned his forearms on the railing, cradling the beer in his hands as he peered down at the road.

Beck turned back again, mimicking Donovan's stance, aware of the sheer bulk of the man in his peripheral vision and of the heat pumping from his body. Suddenly it didn't feel as cold out here. "There's two more floors above this and three apartments that way." He pointed to his right. Then, pointing in the other direction, he said, "Four that way."

There was a knock at the door, and Donovan turned his head, capturing Beck's gaze, a query in his eyes. "That'll be dinner," Beck said with a grin before pushing off the railing and hurrying inside.

By the time Donovan came in and closed the door after him, shutting out the cold, Beck had unpacked the brown paper bag and was taking lids off ecologically sound cartons. "I hope you don't mind I ordered the beef cheeks in red wine jus on a bed of mash with steamed vegetables from this great place in Harris Park. They do massive serves and also the most amazing sticky date pudding, which is the best thing you'll ever put in your mouth."

Beck probably shouldn't have put that out there, especially when the thought of Donovan putting things in his mouth—Beck's dick in particular—was making him weak.

Not *PG, Beckett, not PG*. Move on.

"Unless you're not a fan of dessert?" *Oh shut up, already.*

Donovan's gaze settled on Beck as he came to a stop on the other side of the bench, where four stools sat tucked beneath the overhang. "I love dessert."

Which did not help Beck's resolve to keep things PG. He held up the carton containing the hallowed dessert. "Trust me, you're going to want it every day."

Ugh. Seriously, dude, enough *with the head job innuendo.*

Donovan broke eye contact, glancing at the carton. "Do you always get your food delivered?"

"Pretty much."

"Okay, well…" He shook his head. "I'm cooking tomorrow."

And he would get no argument from Beck. There was only one thing better than a man who could cook, and that was a hot rugby dude who could cook and was volunteering to do it in *his* kitchen. Beck grinned. "Do you wear an apron?"

Donovan shot him a sardonic look, the eyebrow that was bisected by the small white scar lifted. "No."

Beck laughed at the flat no. "Not even if I asked?" And he smiled that smile he knew went straight to his eyes and made his dimples deep as ditches.

"Not even if you begged."

Aaaand the weakness was back. Deciding to leave that well alone, Beck asked, "You want another beer?"

"Yeah, thanks. But I gotta drive later, so I'll stop there."

"Can you grab it while I plate these up?"

He nodded, making his way around to the fridge. Beck heard it open then some kind of muttered expletive. "This is your fridge?"

"Yeah." Beck looked over his shoulder to find a disparaging expression on Donovan's face as he stared into the sparse shelves.

"I'm going to need to bring some groceries with me tomorrow," he muttered before grabbing a beer and shutting the door like an empty fridge was an insult to his eyes. "You want more wine?"

The question glowed warm and pleasant in Beck's belly. Despite Donovan's reserve, it felt so damn domesticated. He'd lived with two men over the last decade—one for seven months, one for five—both of whom he'd been in a relationship with for at least six months before deciding to finally move in together. Because it had felt like the next step.

This felt nothing like that.

He and Donovan were only officially on their first stay-at-home, PG *date* and already Beck was impatient to have this man to himself twenty-four seven. To share meals and conversation and showers. To go to sleep together, to wake up together. Not because it *felt* like the next step, but because it *was* the next step.

Already.

With a man who couldn't come out of the closet. Possibly for years. Which was *ludicrous*. This was short term only, damn it.

Beck smiled. "Yes, please."

They sat opposite each other at the countertop, Beck on the kitchen side, Donovan on the other. When he was alone, Beck ate in front of the TV, and when he entertained, he used the deck, but it was too damn cold and noisy out there. And it was way too warm and cosy in here to even think about moving, the downlights in the kitchen cocooning them in a golden glow.

Beck was grateful to have the counter between them as the meal progressed. It put Donovan well out of lunging range, because watching him slowly relax and let his guard down as he talked about his day and laughed and made appreciative noises about his food was so freaking sexy the urge to jump his bones was never far from the surface.

He'd not seen this Donovan before and he liked it, very much.

Chatter throughout the meal had stayed to safe topics—their day, their jobs, where they lived. The Sydney traffic. As Beck was dishing out the sticky date pudding, Donovan grew quiet again, a palpable tension radiating from suddenly tighter shoulders, and he wondered what the man was thinking. The urge to ask, to probe, to assure him he could say or ask whatever he pleased, grabbed at Beck's throat, because he was a guy who believed in tackling things head on, getting everything out in the open.

But Donovan was living the very definition of a closed life, and he was beginning to understand that the man in his kitchen needed a slow hand.

"Can I ask you a personal question?"

Beck glanced up from the plates to find Donovan watching him. "Of course." Absently, he licked some stray butterscotch sauce off his fingers, which caused a little flare of Donovan's nostrils and a big surge of blood to Beck's dick. He dropped his hand, but Donovan's gaze was still hot on his mouth. "Anything," he assured, a husky catch to his voice.

"How old were you when you knew you were gay?"

Beck rubbed his hands together. "I think I always knew. Even before I could articulate it. But probably in grade two when every boy in the class was wild about a girl called Molly Gates and I was deeply fascinated with a boy called Jackson

Fish, who was cool and popular and didn't even know my name." He smiled at the memory. Jackson Fish had a yoyo and knew how to use it.

"How old were you when you came out?"

Beck bent slightly, leaning his elbows on the bench, propping his hands under his chin. "I told my mother when I was eleven. She said, 'Yeah, we know.' Then she hugged me and said some people in life wouldn't understand me, some wouldn't like me, and worst of all some people would hate me, but that *they* loved me and all that I was, and that I was to tell her immediately if anyone was being mean and she and my grandmother would eviscerate them."

Donovan blinked, then he barked out a laugh. "Eviscerate?"

"Yeah." Beck grinned. "I asked her what that meant, and she told me to go look it up in the dictionary. She's an English teacher."

He laughed again. "Well…she sounds cool."

"She is. My dad is, too, but he's an accountant who approaches things more methodically than emotionally. He prefers to write letters to politicians and newspaper editors and rally the troops for things that need protesting. That's how he got involved in PFLAG. This year he's been put in charge of their float for Mardi Gras. He's chosen the Mamas and the Papas as the theme." Beck gave a rueful smile. "God help us all."

Donovan smiled, too, but not for long. "You were lucky. Having that support."

"Yeah, I was. I am. You don't think your parents will support you?"

"No…I think they will." His brow furrowed. "They're both socially progressive. My sisters are all pretty cool, too. I mean…it'll be a surprise, an adjustment, but I don't think there'll be any tantrums or disownings."

"That's good." Beck had too many gay and lesbian friends

who, even in these supposedly enlightened times, had been disowned by the people who were supposed to love them the most. He pushed the plate with the pudding and a dollop of cream across the counter. "What about you? How old were you?"

He gave a half laugh, half snort as he sliced through the sauce-drenched pudding with his spoon. "Way older than that. I was fifteen."

"That's fairly common, actually. With the dawning of adolescence and all those hormones *yada yada.*"

Donovan glanced up as he slipped the spoon between his lips. His hair, almost dry now, slid against his shoulders, and a lock fell forward to obscure his face a little, and Beck's fingers itched to push into it, push it back, feel the cool glide of it and inhale its fresh, clean fragrance. But then Donovan's face morphed into an expression of ecstasy, and Beck lost his place in the conversation.

He groaned a little and shut his eyes as his cheeks moved and his mouth pressed together and his tongue slicked out to swipe along his bottom lip. Freaking hell. The next time he saw that look on Donovan's face, Beck hoped he was responsible for putting it there.

"Oh my god," he muttered as his eyelids fluttered open, his gaze locking with Beck's. "You were right. This *is* the best thing I've ever had in my mouth."

Beck laughed. Donovan was teasing, which was a huge accomplishment considering how awkward he'd been on his arrival almost an hour ago. It made his heart skip a beat and tiny little bubbles of joy to float through his veins even as a lewd comment—*that's because you've never had* my cock *in your mouth*—clawed at his throat to get out.

But he wasn't going to say it, because he would keep it PG if it killed him, and he didn't want to get side-tracked from the conversation Donovan had started. Beck had finally been given an opening to talk about the things that must have been weighing on Donovan's mind for a long time, and he wouldn't be derailed by thoughts of blowjobs.

"You didn't have any inklings before then?" Beck asked.

"I guess I did feel different but not in any way I could articulate. Like…" He paused to load some more pudding in his mouth, chewing and swallowing, before continuing again. "There was no Jackson Fish moment when I was younger. I guess I just didn't really feel romantic about *anybody*. Which probably should have been a head's up. My friends were always obsessed with one girl or another. I was just… obsessed with footy."

"Until?"

"Mr. Ramsay. My tenth grade PE teacher."

"Ah." Beck shot Donovan a teasing smile. "Chalk another one up for the Phys-Ed teachers."

Donovan returned the smile. "Yeah."

"He was gay?"

"No. He was happily married."

"Was he hot?" Beck asked as he took his first bite of the sticky toffee pudding.

"Not really. I mean, he was fit—he'd been a long-distance runner for over a decade—and not objectionable to look at, but he had charisma and confidence. He was approachable, and he spoke to you like you were an adult and had interesting things to contribute. He loved rugby, so we used to often talk about it. And I just…my heart sped up whenever he looked at me, and I knew almost straight away it wasn't because I *admired* him but because I *fancied* him. That's when I started cracking my knuckles." He drew in a long breath. "I dreamed about kissing him in a thousand different ways. I'm surprised my dick didn't drop off from all the self-abuse."

Beck laughed. Yeah, he remembered those fevered teenaged nights when hormones raged and burning them off in any way possible became not merely a choice but a biological imperative. "If only there was some way to harness all that heat produced from teenage fantasies and channel it into the grid. They'd power the planet for all eternity."

Donovan chuckled as he scraped the bottom of his empty bowl. "Carbon neutral, too."

They laughed together this time, and that ramped up the cosy intimacy that had been building between them. "And you've not had *any* gay experiences in all this time?" Beck asked once their laughter had settled.

He sighed. "Well...yes. Once." Standing, he grabbed his plates and came around to Beck's side of the bench, walking to the sink and dumping the dishes into the bowl.

Beck swivelled on his stool, admiring Donovan's back view, supressing the urge to walk over and slide his arms around the other man's waist and press his cheek between those solid shoulder blades. "It wasn't a success?"

"It was a disaster."

"Do you want to talk about it?"

For a beat or two, Donovan's entire body tensed, but just as quickly everything relaxed, and he turned, leaning his ass against the bench and crossing his arms over his chest as the warm glow from above set an aura around his hair and spotlighted the ink on his arm.

Lordy...the man was sexy.

"It doesn't exactly colour me in glory."

The regret in his voice was palpable. "Why?" It wasn't uncommon for early sexual encounters to be viewed through a prism of shame or guilt, often for no reason. But that was true whether gay or straight.

"I was eighteen. Engaged to Annie at the time. Miri was six months old."

Ah, so his infidelity was the basis of his statement. "Okay."

"I'd just got my big break and been signed to a national

team in the NZ rugby comp, and the local team I was playing with at the time had just come off a win in an away game in a town a few hours south of Auckland. There was a lot to celebrate, and we'd been out drinking. I wasn't drunk, but I'd had a few. We'd all just arrived back at our hotel when I realised I'd left my wallet behind, so I got back in the taxi and went back to the bar."

"Was it still there?"

"Yeah. It took me a while to find it, but it was still there," Donovan confirmed. "While I was waiting for another taxi outside, I heard someone call to me, and I turned to find this guy just inside the alley entrance behind me. He was good-looking, a few years older than me, and had been at the bar earlier. I'd noticed because he'd been checking me out. His interest had worried me at the time. I mean, *how* did he know? And did anyone else? But it didn't worry me then, with him smiling at me and tipping his head toward the alley and I…God…" He shook his head. "My heart was belting like a train. I was excited and terrified and…conflicted. And tempted. So fucking tempted. Just to…see, you know?" His gaze turned intent as it bored into Beck's looking for understanding. "Just to…try."

"Yeah, I know." Beck had indulged in a couple of quick and frantic alley episodes in his life. They'd been wild and fun. Also stupid and potentially dangerous, and an oily knot formed in his belly thinking about all the shit that could have gone wrong in that alley for Donovan.

Clearly something had.

"So, I went. I followed him in. I wasn't thinking about Annie or Miri. Just me. And it was past midnight and there was no one around and no one knew me in town. The alley hooked a left, which he took presumably so no passersby would be able to spot us out on the street. He stopped a couple of paces in, leaned against the wall, yanked down his zip, and pulled out his cock. It was dark but not pitch black, there was a streetlight toward the end, and I could see his cock well enough. It was hard as the fucking bricks behind his back. He didn't speak, he didn't ask me to suck it. I just…" Donovan blew out a breath. "I just really fucking wanted to."

"Of course you did," Beck said softly. Donovan didn't have to justify anything to him.

"So I did. I got on my knees in that alley and I took a man's dick, a *stranger's* dick, in my mouth, and it felt so fucking *right* in that moment, right in a way that being with Annie had never been, and I had to shut my eyes to stop the tears from welling."

If Beck hadn't been so sure this was going to end in Donovan being set upon by homophobes in an alley, he might have been a little turned on by the retelling, but the knot of worry just got oilier. And the conflict in his voice was heartbreaking. Even now it sounded like Donovan was still torn between the exhilaration of his first gay sexual experience and the shame of cheating on Annie.

"I didn't know what I was doing, but I must have been doing something right because he was groaning and grunting and saying, 'Yes, yes,' and, 'Suck me good.' Stuff like that. And then he said, 'Look at me, look at me while I fuck your mouth,' and I opened my eyes and looked up and he was filming me with his phone."

"Oh, Jesus." That was not what Beck had been expecting. Donovan *hadn't* been beaten. Not physically, anyway. "What an asshole. What did you do?"

"Let's just say he didn't get his happy ending."

Beck laughed. Donovan's face had been so grim telling the story Beck wouldn't have thought him capable of levity in this situation.

"I *freaked* out. Everything that was at stake flashed before my eyes. Hurting Annie and jeopardising my relationship with Miri, not to mention my football career if he'd figured out who I was and he tried to blackmail me with it or something. I was so…ashamed of myself. So disgusted by how selfish and *weak* I'd been. I pushed him away, snatched the phone, and stomped on it. He was yelling at me to stop and that I was crazy, but I didn't stop until it was a pile of pulverised metal and glass dust. And then I got the hell out of there."

God…no wonder he'd stayed closeted after that experience. He'd obviously been seriously burned and had decided it was best to do nothing than risk everything.

"I'm sorry," Beck murmured, sliding off the chair and slowly covering the few metres between them, Donovan watching him intently as he drew nearer.

He stopped close enough to feel the heat radiating from his chest and smell the beer on his breath. Tentatively, their gazes locked, and he slid his palms onto Donovan's chest, the rounded contours of well-formed pecs filling his hands. He half expected the other man to flinch or to side step, but he just stood there, his dark, brooding gaze holding Beck's.

It felt good to be this close. Good to be the one to whom Donovan had confided. "I'm sorry that happened to you."

Two big shoulders moved in a silent shrug. "It wasn't your fault," he dismissed, his voice a low burr in the air.

"Doesn't mean I can't be sorry it happened to you. Doesn't mean I don't want to kiss it all better."

Slowly then, his eyes never leaving Donovan's, Beck leaned in, their chests coming into contact, angling his head as his mouth inched closer to Donovan's. He paused when he was so close he could feel the ruffle of warm air slipping from between Donovan's slightly parted lips, could almost taste the butterscotch on his breath. The moment hung in time for long seconds, both of them just breathing, their torsos pressed together, the *thud* of their hearts intermingling to become one.

"I'm so, *so* sorry," Beck murmured, his fingers curling

into the fabric of the white T-shirt as he gently pressed his lips to Donovan's.

It was soft and closed-mouthed and fleeting—he didn't dare linger for fear of not being able to stop—but it reached a fist inside his gut and squeezed, and when he pulled back, his breathing was rough. So was Donovan's.

Mustering strength from God knew where, Beck pushed away and took a step back. Absently he noted the twin marks on Donovan's shirt where his fingers had curled and gripped the fabric. "How about we watch TV for a while?" Clearly, they were going to need a distraction.

Donovan shoved a hand through his hair. "As long as it's not YouTube videos of dudes kissing."

Beck smiled. Hell no. He was not in any state to be further sexually titillated right now. Not if he wanted to stick to his PG pledge. "How about rugby?"

The eyebrow with that little white scar quirked. "Isn't that the same thing for you?"

Beck grinned. God…he freaking loved it when Donovan *teased*. It warmed him right through to his middle. "Only when you're playing," he quipped and loved it when Donovan's nostrils flared in response. "I need a rugby tutor. I figure I should probably know more about it than I do."

"Oh, you do, huh?"

More teasing, with a smile this time that set Beck's heart a'flutter. "Well, I mean, I do work for the Sydney Smoke, so…"

He rolled his eyes. "Yeah, yeah, okay. Rugby it is."

. . .

Donovan prepared salmon with crispy skin and a mound of steamed vegetables the next night. He'd made an online order for groceries as soon as he'd arrived back at his place last night, and they'd been delivered to Beckett's apartment shortly before he'd arrived on the doorstep.

"I'm going to need a bigger fridge," Beckett had muttered as Donovan had helped him put things away, but he was an enthusiastic kitchen helper, and it had felt a hundred times less awkward than last night.

He'd still arrived—and departed last night—in a hoodie just in case there were any rabid rugby fans in the apartment block, because the law of averages told him there would be. But Beckett had greeted him with a key, and that had felt… well, *good*. And not because it meant he didn't have to hang at the door waiting to be let in, but because it felt like Beckett wasn't just in it for a bunch of booty calls.

He'd billed these next few weeks as casual, getting-to-know-you nights. As preliminary matches. Decider rounds. But that kiss from last night definitely hadn't been casual. It may have only lasted a second or two, but it had touched him everywhere and *not* sexually. Its sincerity had touched his heart.

I'm sorry that happened to you.

The alley experience had played on his mind so much these past years, acting as a salient warning against any slip to the mask he hid behind. And the anger he still felt over that night, over the position he'd put himself and his family in, was never far from the surface. But, with the reassurance of that kiss, of that expression of sorrow, perspective was granted.

He'd been young and stupid and confused and… desperate. It was time to stop giving it power. It was time to forgive himself.

"So, your mother, she's Maori, right?" Beck asked, placing his utensils down on his empty plate. "Your dad's an Australian?"

Donovan pulled his head out of last night and back to the present. "You been doing a little stalking of me, huh?" He liked teasing Beckett. He liked the way it softened his eyes and parted his mouth and brought out his dimples. It looked good on him.

"I have a fairly good Google game."

"Apparently."

"Is that where the tattoo comes from?"

Donovan glanced down at his right arm, running his palm over the swirls of his *tā moko*, pushing up the sleeve to reveal all of it. "Yeah. It represents my lineage and cultural heritage. My great-grandfather had similar patterns on his head, and the artist incorporated it into the design, along with symbols for athletic prowess."

"How long have you had it for?"

"I got it when I turned eighteen."

"Looks like it took quite a few sittings."

"It did."

"Well...it suits you. Makes you look like a...warrior. Especially out there on the field."

Yeah, that didn't exactly hurt. "Good." Donovan grinned as he dropped his sleeve. "What else did you find out about me?"

"You were born in Australia and stayed until you were twelve when your family moved back to New Zealand."

"Correct."

"I'm assuming that's why you don't have much of a Kiwi accent."

"Correct. Although I sound way more Kiwi when I'm in New Zealand."

"And that's where you met Annie?"

"Also correct."

It was tempting just to leave it there. In fact, had it been anyone else he probably would have, but he wanted to tell Beckett about Annie. About his marriage. About Miri.

He wanted to tell this man *everything*. That was the whole point of this time together, right?

Pushing his almost-empty plate aside, Donovan, leaned

his elbows onto the counter. "I met her on the first day at my new school. She's really arty, and she was doing these chalk drawings on the cement pathway near where I was eating lunch and some older guys were hassling me about my accent. I was handling it because even as a twelve-year-old I was a big fucker, but Annie, all five-foot-two-inches of her, told them to piss off." Donovan laughed at the memory. "We kinda clicked after that."

"When did you start dating?"

"After Mr. Ramsay came on the scene."

Beckett nodded. "Ah."

"Yeah." Not his proudest moment there, either. "I was confused and petrified. I did *not* want to be gay. I wanted to be an elite rugby player. Elite rugby players were not gay. And I adored Annie. I loved her; she was my best friend. She still is. I just didn't like her like *that.* But I asked her on a date and she said yes and suddenly we were a couple."

"How long before you had sex?"

"Two years."

"*Two years?*"

Donovan smiled at the incredulity in Beckett's voice. "We both had strict parents and Annie wanted to wait until she was older, and that suited me. We did…other stuff, but we didn't get a lot of alone time together. And then in our senior year she started pushing for more, wanting to go further, wanting to go all the way. And one day I was with my guy friends and they were all taking about sex, I admitted that I was still a virgin and they looked at me like there was something wrong with me, and I desperately *did not* want there to be something wrong with me, so…"

"You succumbed."

"Yes. We had sex about half a dozen times over a period of about three months and then Annie got pregnant."

"And you were…stuck?"

"No." Donovan shook his head. He'd never felt stuck. "It felt like a lifeline. Sure, we were young, but I could throw myself into family life and forget all about the side of me I didn't want to be. I could be *normal*."

"How long have you been divorced?"

"Eight years." He picked up his forgotten beer and took a swig. "We moved to Australia when Miri was two, when I first signed with the Smoke. But Annie moved back to NZ with her two years later because she missed home and her family, and we decided we'd do a long-distance thing." Donovan shrugged. "It's only a three-hour flight to Auckland, and Annie really wasn't happy away from her family and the art scene she'd been so much a part of. I missed them, of course, but Annie was much happier, and my family got to see so much more of Miri. We both came and went as often as we could. Annie probably spent two long weekends a month here during the season and came across for any special events. I spent as much of the off-season as possible back in New Zealand."

"Sounds like there's a but?"

"Yeah." Donovan sighed. "When I came home for that last off-season before we split, Annie asked me if I was having an affair."

Beckett whistled. "Did she have a reason for her suspicions?"

"No. But...yeah. I guess. I was a young, fit guy in my prime who was spending long periods of time away from my wife but was always too tired to have sex when we were together."

"Ah." Beckett nodded. "She thought you didn't want to have sex because you were getting it elsewhere?"

"Yes. I mean, we'd never had much sex anyway, what with Annie getting pregnant and her crippling morning sickness, which seemed to last the entire pregnancy, and then Miri came along and she was a crying, demanding, clingy baby with reflux, who was in our bed more often than not and seemed to thrive on the barest minimum of sleep." Donovan shuddered at those early years and how amazingly Annie—a teenager—had coped. "Honestly, sex was the last thing on either of our minds for a long time."

"So you were able to hide in plain sight?"

Donovan gave a half laugh. That was one way of putting it. "Yeah. And just as Miri was finally sleeping through the night, she and Annie moved back to New Zealand."

"Which took the pressure off even more."

"Right." Donovan was pleased he didn't have to spell anything out for Beck. "But soon after that, Miri seemed to turn a corner with her reflux, and Annie, who'd been breastfeeding all that time, mostly overnight, because it was the only thing that seemed to help with Miri's night-time reflux, was coming out of the fog of hormones and sleep deprivation and was, well…kinda horny."

"And she noticed that you weren't."

"Yes. When I denied having an affair, she assumed the only other thing it could be was that I didn't fancy her anymore, that I didn't find her attractive after watching her push a baby out of her vagina and constantly spray milk from her boobs, and she was so damn distraught and distressed that I assured her she was beautiful and I loved her, which she was and I did, and I pulled myself together and we had sex most times we saw each other. The sex wasn't bad, she certainly always seemed to have a good time, it just…"

"Wasn't what you craved."

"Yep." Donovan nodded. It had felt like a point on a list he was checking off. "And she could clearly tell I was just going through the motions, because one night we were lying in the dark after and she asked me what was wrong. She said that she knew me, that she'd known me since I was twelve and that something was bothering me. She believed that I wasn't having an affair, but she was convinced something was wrong and that she loved me and I could tell her anything."

"So you told her?"

"No, I told her I was just tired from the backing and forthing, but Annie is like a bulldog when she wants to be, and she wouldn't let it go. She persisted for the next few weeks until I finally cracked and told her."

"How was that?"

"The most difficult conversation I've ever had."

Beck reached across the counter, splaying his hand on Donovan's forearm and squeezing, and it was...nice. *So* nice.

"Was she angry?"

"A little, sure. But mostly she was...hurt that I'd kept something like that from her for so long. She was also relieved, because suddenly a bunch of stuff she'd never really understood made sense. And she felt vindicated. Despite my assurances, she'd been worrying that my poor libido was something to do with her and had been blaming herself for my lack of interest, and my confession freed her from the emotional pinball of those thoughts."

Just as it had freed him from the prison of secrecy. The fact that he could finally be who he was with the woman who was his best friend and the mother of his child had loosened the chains around his chest.

"She asked me if I'd ever been with a man. I confessed about the guy in the alley and told her it was wrong and I was sorry, and she just...understood. Hell, she thanked me for being honest."

"That was very mature of her."

"Yes." It could have gone very differently. "Then she asked me for a divorce."

Chapter Nine

Donovan watched as Beck's eyebrows practically hit his hairline. "Bloody hell," he muttered.

"Yeah." He nodded. It had been unexpected. "I told her that if that was what she wanted, she could have it, but I'd be happy to stay married and raise Miri together."

"That obviously didn't fly?" Beckett asked, removing his hand from Donovan's forearm to pick up his wineglass and take a sip.

"No." Donovan gave a half smile and shook his head. "She said she loved me, she'd always loved me and that we'd always be best friends, but she needed a man who loved and wanted her as a woman, not just as a friend. Which of course she did, because she's amazing and she deserves to live a rich and full life, and it was selfish to have even asked her."

"When did she remarry?"

"Three years later. They have two boys together."

"Does he know? Her husband?"

"No. She's always said my sexuality is nobody's business, but she also reiterated that night I told her what I already knew—that I *couldn't* come out. Not because of her or Miri, but because of rugby. She'd been in the professional rugby world, too, for as long as I had, and she understood the impact it would have on my career."

Taking another sip of wine, Beck regarded him for long moments, and Donovan had to pinch himself. Would he ever get used to the way this man stared, so frank and unapologetic? He'd spent a lot of his life *not* meeting men's gazes, being extra careful to not linger, to not betray any kind of attraction he might be feeling. Beck obviously felt no such compunction, and to be able to return that interest was something he was still getting used to.

"How do you think your daughter will take it?"

Now *that* was a good question. One Donovan had worried about obsessively over the years. "I think for most teenagers today, a person's sexuality is no big deal. LGBTQIA communities and issues are fairly prominent in media, and being raised in a biracial family she seems more accepting of difference than some. Still, I guess it'll come as a surprise, and Annie and I would like her to be older before any conversation has to take place."

"You don't think she can handle it at fourteen?"

"I think she can. I just would rather she didn't *have* to. Finding out at this age would mean my hand was being forced, and it wouldn't be any *normal* dad-coming-out scenario that'll titillate the neighbourhood and cause a few raised eyebrows in polite company. It'll be splashed all over the papers and the internet. Trolls on social media will tell her I deserve to burn in hell. They'll question whether I'm her father and disparage her upbringing. There'll be shitty kids at school doing what shitty kids do. And she'll spend a lot of time trying to defend me instead of being young and carefree, which is all you want for your kid."

"Yeah." He sighed. "I really wish that wasn't true."

Donovan wished it, too, but sadly, the internet had given voice to a dark underbelly emboldened by anonymity. "But if I come out after my career's over, with no fanfare, it'll be different. Sure, it might cause a mild stir for a few days, but it'll be a flash in the pan story about some rugby has-been, and then something else will come along and it'll be over. And she'll be older, more anonymous, away from the schoolyard, and hopefully better equipped to deal with any crap."

He nodded slowly. "I'm sorry." Beckett's hand slid across the bench again to rest on top of Donovan's. "I wish it was different for you. You shouldn't have to hide who you are."

Donovan gave a dismissive shake of his head. "It is what it is."

"I know. It just—" He huffed out a breath. "Sucks."

Yeah, Donovan supposed for someone like Beckett, it would suck. For him, though, living a life of concealment wasn't new, and while he hated that being gay was still an *issue* for some people, he was resigned to this life—for now. But for Beckett? Who lived openly and to the fullest? It had to chafe.

He placed his other hand over top of Beckett's. "Look… if it's too much, I'd get it if you wanted to walk away now." He'd be gutted, but he'd understand.

Beckett's shoulders, which had tensed a little, slumped as he let out a breath. "What?" he asked, a smile softening his mouth. "Before my rugby education is complete?"

Relief flowed like cool water through Donovan's veins as he barked out a laugh. How had he gotten so lucky to have found a guy who was so damn understanding and knew when to push, when to back off, and when to tease? "You want more?"

He waggled his eyebrows. "Always."

Another laugh as he shook his head at Beckett. "I thought I was boring you last night."

They'd watched an old rerun of a game from a few years back when Australia played New Zealand in the Bledisloe Cup. The remote had been given a good workout as Donovan had paused and rewound and fast-forwarded, explaining all the various plays and moves and positions. A game went for eighty minutes, but it had taken well over two hours to get through to the end.

"What?" He laughed. "I wasn't bored."

Donovan cocked an eyebrow. "Miri could sit stiller than you did when she was two."

"*That* wasn't from boredom."

"Oh? Did you have ants in your pants?"

"No. Not ants." He grinned, his dimples deepening and elongating. "But every time you said *ruck* my dick got hard, and you were being all teacherly and *instructional*—which, by the way, is hot as fuck—and my dick was going up and down so frequently I'm amazed I didn't stroke out. By the time you left my balls were bluer than that woman from Avatar."

The frank statement stopped Donovan in his tracks. Locked away in this apartment, the strictures of the world shut out, he'd become more relaxed in Beckett's company. But the ease with which Beckett flirted and spoke about his biological reactions, about his wants and desires was a revelation. He just…said whatever he was thinking, without any filter.

Dare he do the same? Could he say something risqué, something flirty, something a little…dirty and not sound like an idiot? It felt weird even contemplating it, but there was just the two of them and Beckett had opened the door.

Donovan cleared his throat. "Did you…" He let his gaze drop, even though the height of the bench hid what he really wanted to see. "Do something about it? After I left."

Beckett raised an eyebrow, a flicker of surprise in his eyes soon replaced by a gleam of something hot and dark. "I did."

Oh, Christ—suddenly the air was practically steaming between them. "What?"

"I went into my room, took my clothes off, turned out the light, lay on the bed, and stroked myself to images of you all hot and sweaty after kicking ass on the field, fucking me in your locker room."

Donovan swallowed. *Oh Jesus.* So much for PG. "Okay."

"Did you wank when you got home?"

"Yes." Just like he would tonight. Except now he had a whole other fantasy in his spank bank.

"Did you watch the kissing video again?"

"No." Hell, he wasn't going to need that ever again.

"Really?" Beckett's slow smile only added to the sudden dirty in his eyes. "What *did* you think about?"

Oh no. *Nope.* No way could Donovan admit to what he'd thought about as he'd touched himself last night. How could he justify that he'd reimagined that night in the alley? But with Beckett as the stranger and no douche nonconsensual video move. How could he find sexual pleasure from an event that had hung over him like a cloud ever since?

What did that say about the messed-up state of his mind?

"I thought about that night we"—Donovan swallowed, his throat suddenly dry as dust—"wanked in front of the TV." It wasn't like he *hadn't* masturbated to that plenty.

"Well." His smiled morphed into a grin. "That was pretty hot."

Donovan gave a half laugh at the understatement. "Yeah."

They didn't say anything for long moments. They didn't need to; their hungry gazes said it all. Donovan ate up every inch of Beckett, who returned the favour, eye-fucking him with a thoroughness that stole Donovan's breath.

"Okay, well…" Beckett withdrew his hands from Donovan's clasp and stood, picking up his plate. "Now we got that off our chests. We should…"

He drifted off, and Donovan wondered if it was because Beckett was as discombobulated as he was or if he was giving Donovan the opportunity to fill in the blank. A choose-your-own-sex-adventure option. "Yeah." Donovan pulled himself together, also standing with his plate. *PG, dude,* PG. "Rugby lesson number two awaits."

He couldn't be sure if somewhere in the lusty quagmire of his brain that he hadn't deliberately chosen the word *lesson* or if it was just the most appropriate word for the occasion. But it certainly seemed to have an effect on Beckett, his nostrils flaring, his lips parting. "There's going to be more rucking, isn't there?"

Donovan laughed a husky laugh. "Count on it."

Beckett groaned. "You're trying to kill me, aren't you?"

"I'm just being…*teacherly,*" Donovan said, knowing now that Beckett had found it *hot as fuck* and revelling in a power he'd never been able to exercise.

"God, I've created a monster."

Grinning, Donovan tipped his head in the direction of the TV. "Get your ass over to the couch."

Another flare of his nostrils before Beckett's plate clattered onto the counter. "Yes, sir," he said and swaggered over to the living room like he knew exactly how hard Donovan was checking him out.

If there was a monster in this apartment, it was Beckett Stanton.

· · ·

They spent the next three nights together, Donovan arriving in his hoodie, cloaked and shackled by his straight-man guise then shedding the jacket and the weight of conformity with the shrug of his shoulders as soon as he crossed the threshold.

And it felt good. *So* good.

Being with Beckett like this. Sharing meals and talking about their days. About their lives. Chatting and laughing as they compared notes on friends and family. And there was rugby, of course, as Donovan insisted on continuing Beckett's education. They kept it PG for the most part, only occasionally slipping into innuendo and sharing looks that made Donovan's pulse treble. But it was their closeness he revelled in the most. The way their shoulders brushed as they sat on the couch, their thighs met, the easy unselfconscious way Beckett sometimes touched Donovan's arm as he spoke.

Was there a low boil of something far less innocent going on beneath the surface? Absolutely. But it was as if they were both aware that succumbing to it would lead to a different kind of getting-to-know-you, and this bit was more about Donovan getting comfortable with who he *was* than doing something about their seething attraction.

So, even when Donovan said goodbye on Friday night knowing he was going to be in Canberra for the weekend and wouldn't be seeing Beckett again until Tuesday night, he just accepted Beckett's chaste peck on the cheek. And completely ignored how much he wanted to pin him against the door and kiss the holy fuck out of him.

"Good luck for tomorrow," Beckett said.

Donovan smiled. "Will you be watching?"

"Of course. I'll be right over there on the couch." He grinned then. "With my dick out."

Donovan growled. "How am I supposed to play knowing you're…"

His gaze drifted to Beckett's crotch, and his head filled with a bunch of very unhelpful images. They might have kept things platonic this past week, but he hadn't forgotten what Beckett looked like sitting on that couch with his hand firmly wrapped around his cock.

Christ—if he lived to be one hundred, he'd never forget that.

"I think masturbating is the word you're after?" Beckett supplied, his smile turning teasing again.

Yeah, that was the word. "I suppose I should feel objectified knowing you're using me as some kind of... *wanking aid*."

An eyebrow quirked northward. "And do you?"

Donovan shook his head slowly. "Hell no."

"How *do* you feel?"

"Really, really fucking turned on."

The teasing light in Beckett's eyes turned molten as he dropped *his* gaze this time to Donovan's crotch, to the massive erection that was about to punch its way out from behind his zipper. The slow bob of Beckett's throat and the way his hands curled into fists was an even bigger turn-on. God, it was madness how much he wanted this man.

Beckett lifted his gaze, his grin slow and wicked. "Good."

Donovan gave an agonised half laugh as the ache in his groin increased. "See you on Tuesday night."

Beckett placed a hand over his heart. "I'm already counting down the hours."

It seemed like such a...sappy, romantic, almost poetic thing to admit he had to remind himself that Beckett was just teasing. That underneath that flirty façade he was guarding his heart. "So am I," he admitted.

Because he was.

• • •

Donovan kicked ass on Sunday night. He'd thought having Beckett watching him through the TV screen, knowing what he was doing to himself, would be distracting, but it was quite the opposite. It was fucking *exhilarating*. He played the best goddam game of rugby he'd played in years.

If Beckett really was watching with his dick in his hand, then he was determined to give him a show.

He committed 100 percent to every run and tackle, every ruck and maul, every lineout and scrum. He was unstoppable. The crowd roared his name, which always pushed him to do better, but tonight, his audience of one was a much more potent stimulus.

By game's end, he'd personally run the ball over the try line twice and set up four more, and the Smoke had absolutely smashed the opposition. Griff had high-fived him, his teammates carried him on their shoulders off the field, and when he got back to the locker room, they showered him in beer newly released from shaken cans.

He felt on top of the world as everyone sang "We Are The Champions"—not in the gloriously melodic way a team of Welsh rugby players might have, but definitely with heart and soul. It had been a long time since he'd felt this *good*, and he couldn't wait to get back to Sydney.

Back to Beckett.

But he still had two more nights to get through. They didn't return to Sydney until Monday, and that night Beckett had a prior engagement. Something about a regular Netflix night with friends. So he had to cool his heels until Tuesday night. How he would do that he had no idea, especially when Beckett had sent him an utterly filthy voicemail about lunchtime on Monday, which he'd obviously recorded during the game Sunday night.

Donovan could hear the commentary in the background, but it wasn't what he was focused on, not when Beckett's pants and groans filled his ear, escalating rapidly in time to the escalation of excitement in the commentator's voice. His name was called over and over in the distance as TV Donovan ran the ball over the line and over and over in his right ear as Beckett climaxed, muttering it long and low like it was the dark, dirty little secret it was.

By the time Tuesday night rolled around, Donovan was strung tight with the need to see Beckett. And not just because of that voicemail but just to *see* him again. See his face, hear his voice, his laugh. Feel the full effect of those dimples as he teased.

Christ, it had only been four days and it felt like four years. And he'd known the man for not even *four* weeks.

His hand shook—it actually *shook*—as he inserted his key in the lock of Beckett's door. Ordinarily, when he was this wound up about something, he'd have taken a breath to centre himself as taught by the yoga instructor the Smoke sometimes used, but *fuck that.*

He needed to see Beckett. He needed to see him—now.

The kitchen was empty when he stalked inside, as was the living room and dining room. He'd just tossed his hoodie over the back of the couch and was heading for the deck when Beckett came through the open doorway that led to the hall, which connected the two bedrooms. He was in jeans that rode low on his hips and no shirt, a towel partially slung around his neck, one end being rubbed over hair obviously still wet from the shower.

Donovan's mouth went dry at the same time his heart skipped several beats.

"Oh, hey," Beckett said, pulling up short when his eyes fell on Donovan. Greedy eyes that devoured face and chest and abs and thighs. That lingered at all the hotspots in between, spreading heat and spark and fire. "You're early."

Donovan's heart skipped another beat at the gravelly tone scraping against his skin, turning hotspots to raging infernos. "I couldn't wait."

In fact, he couldn't wait another fucking second.

Stalking across the room, he advanced on Beckett, who

didn't move, just watched his progress, his lips parted, the towel sliding from his shoulders to the floor. Donovan didn't stop as he got close enough to touch. He just slid his hands to either side of Beckett's neck and kept walking, pushing Beckett back, back, back until his ass and shoulder blades hit the nearest wall and, his heart thundering, swooped to claimed those deliciously parted lips in a kiss that was hard and deep from the very first touch.

And Beckett returned it, groaning as his mouth opened and his tongue snaked out and his hands clutched convulsively at Donovan's sides. He smelled and tasted so fucking wholesome—minty breath and soapy skin—yet everything else was blatantly indecent. The expert twist of his head and the relentless hunt of his tongue and his heavy, ragged breath sounding like a symphony from some dark and twisted fairy tale in Donovan's head.

The man practically pulsed in his arms, taking as much as giving, his body as hot and hard as Donovan's, his need apparently just as reckless. It was too much and not enough as, without any conscious thought, Donovan's hands went exploring, desperate to touch every inch of this man he couldn't get enough of, who had come to mean so much in so little time.

His chest bare and smooth, his abs flat and flinching, the hard bracket of his hips, the taut globes of his ass. Muscle and bone and skin stoking fire through Donovan's belly. The hard jut of his erection taunting the hard jut of Donovan's.

He grabbed for it, he couldn't *not*, needing to feel again its heavy contours even through the cloak of denim and zippers. Beckett sucked in a breath at Donovan's far-from-smooth move, breaking their lip lock, his head *thunk*ing back against the wall, his eyes fluttering open, his hazy blue gaze meeting Donovan's hot brown stare.

They were both breathing hard, and neither of them said

anything for long moments. They just stared at each other as Donovan rubbed and squeezed, his body trembling with need, screamingly taut with desire.

"Is this...okay?" he asked, feeling big and clumsy and awkward.

Letting out a shaky half laugh, Beckett said, "No, it's awful. Don't stop."

Any other time, Donovan would have laughed, too, but his lack of control was disconcerting. "I just...I'm out of my skin with needing to touch you."

"I sent you a voice message of me coming my brains out yesterday. I think a kiss is perfectly okay."

"This is more than a kiss." Donovan groaned as he replaced his hand with his cock, grinding against Beckett. "God..." He panted. "You feel so fucking good."

Beckett grunted, shutting his eyes, his teeth pressing into his bottom lip. Donovan leaned in, kissing him slower this time—softer—running his tongue over the spot where Beckett's teeth had dug, revelling in the easy moan slipping from his lips, the shudder rolling through his body.

If only it was enough. If only he didn't want more. Want *everything*. Whatever the fuck that was. *Crap.*

Pulling out of the kiss, he pressed his forehead to Beckett's, and they stood plastered together for long moments, nothing but the sound of their heavy breathing between them.

"We said we weren't going to do this," Beckett murmured eventually.

"Yeah."

But neither of them moved, and Donovan wondered if Beckett was as tempted as he was to just skip the fuck ahead. Thank God for his phone and fourteen-year-old daughter.

Miri's ring tone—"Run the World" by Beyoncé, because Miri totally ran his world—blared from his back pocket, and Donovan started guiltily. Talk about the cold slap of reality.

Beckett quirked an eyebrow. "Saved by Queen B."

"I'm sorry." Donovan took a step back as he fished around in his pocket, concentrating on that instead of Beckett's naked chest and that fascinating trail of hair heading south from his belly button. His head swam as he desperately tried to morph into dad mode from horny-making-out-like-a-fucking-teenager mode. "It's Miri. I...have to get this."

They usually had a set time they chatted each day—generally after she finished school, which was about the time he was finishing training—and it wasn't normal for her to ring outside of that time.

"Of course." Beckett smiled gently. "Why don't you use the deck?"

"I'll probably be half an hour." Miri was always chatty whether they'd already talked or not, and Donovan knew there'd come a time when she didn't want to have long chats with her old man, so he was going to lap it up while he could.

"Take as long as you want."

Twenty minutes later, he stepped back inside to the warmth and the aroma of garlic and basil. And Beckett with his shirt on, which was disappointing, but better for his sanity and ability to keep his hands to himself. "Sorry," he apologised again as he slid the glass door shut behind him, cutting off the traffic noise below.

"She's your daughter, Donovan." Beckett placed a bowl on the bench on Donovan's side. Yeah, they already had sides. "There's absolutely no need to apologise." He placed a beer down next to the bowl and said, "Sit. Eat."

"You cooked?" Something good, too, if the aromas were any indication.

"No, Tony from the local Italian restaurant did, but only

because there's no way anyone can cook risotto as good as he does."

Donovan placed his phone on the bench as he pulled out the stool, glancing into the steaming bowl of glossy rice with chunks of chicken, blistered cherry tomatoes, and an abundance of basil. His mouth watered. "Smells amazing."

"It tastes better."

He sat. "You've given me twice the amount."

"That's because you're a big guy who burns off a zillion calories every day. And anyway…" A flare of heat lit his eyes as he smiled. "I like to watch you eat. There's something about a man who appreciates food as much as you do."

Doing as he was told, Donovan picked up his fork and dug in. The first mouthful burst across his tongue, sending his tastebuds into a wild frenzy. Kind of like how the taste of Beckett had sent his body into a wild frenzy. "Oh god…" His gaze met Beckett's. "This is…"

He smiled. "Like Italy in a bowl."

Donovan did not disappoint in his appreciation, devouring half the huge bowl in the blink of an eye. He may even have groaned once or twice. Because it was that good. Also because he could feel Beckett watching and the knowledge he could turn this man on just by eating made him a little cocky.

"Everything okay with Miri?"

Looking up from his meal, Donovan paused. They hadn't talked about Miri too much. Not because he hadn't wanted to, but because he wasn't sure if Beckett wanted to listen to him burble on about how amazing she was and how lucky he was to be her father. Some people found kids boring and people talking about theirs tedious.

"Yeah. She'd just finished this painting she'd been doing for school and wanted to show me."

"Can I see?"

Donovan blinked, not surprised but…pleased in Beckett's interest. "Sure." Picking up his phone, he opened his album where he'd added in the snaps Miri had texted him. He pushed it across the bench.

He watched intently as Beckett perused the steamy geothermal landscape of Rotorua that Miri had captured so perfectly. "That's really good."

"Yeah." Donovan grinned. "She's so talented. She gets that from her mother."

Glancing up from the screen, Beckett asked, "And what does she get from you?"

"She's quite sporty."

"Football?"

"She's good at pretty much anything she tries her hand. She was a great swimmer when she was younger, but she's currently wild for cricket."

"You got any pictures of her?"

Donovan barked out a laugh. "Only about a couple thousand." He held out his hand for his phone, and when Beckett returned it, he scrolled to the album that held all his snaps of Miri and handed it back.

"Thanks," Beckett said then proceeded to scroll through them with one hand as he absently ate with the other. "She looks like you," he said, eyes not lifting from the screen.

"So people say." Donovan grimaced. "Poor girl."

Beckett's gaze flicked up. "Lucky girl," he murmured, holding Donovan's gaze for long seconds before returning his attention to the phone.

Donovan ate while Beckett scrolled, his smile warming him all over. The fact he was actually interested, not just zipping through, was heartening.

"Oh my God." Beckett glanced up with a grin. "This one is so damn *cuuute*!"

Donovan knew which photo it was even before Beckett

turned the phone around to display the one of Miri braiding his hair and decorating it with pink clips. She'd been eight and so damn proud of her handiwork she was beaming at the camera. So was he.

"Yeah." He smiled. "I have that one on the inside of my locker. The guys love it."

"The way she looks at you, like you hung the fucking moon?" Beckett pressed a hand to his chest. "That's really special."

Donovan sobered a little, his gaze meshing with Beckett's. "It is."

"You're a lucky man."

Tentatively, his heart beating a little harder, Donovan slid his hand, palm up across the bench. "I know."

Donovan was well aware that he'd lived a blessed life. He had everything he'd ever wanted—people who loved him and a dream job. And now, a chance to have something he'd never even *allowed* himself to want.

Even if just for a little while.

When Beckett smiled and reached across to slide his hand into the proffered palm, Donovan wondered if maybe it could be for a *long* while.

Chapter Ten

Beckett was fit to burst by Thursday night. They'd managed to keep their hands off each other for the rest of Tuesday night, apart from a good-night kiss that hadn't even pretended to be chaste. And then Wednesday night had been Donovan's poker night, which should have been a relief—out of sight, out of mind, right?

But apparently not, because he'd thought about Donovan nonstop. About the way he'd eaten his risotto, and that pic of him and Miri together. And then there was the voice message Donovan had left—of *him* coming this time—which had made Beckett antsier than a kid walking across hot bitumen with no shoes.

He'd already played it a dozen times, including on his ride home tonight via his earbuds, which had been a mistake—erection meeting bike seat did not make for a comfortable journey.

His aching balls hadn't exactly appreciated it, either.

He lectured himself all the way down the hallway to his apartment, wiping sweat off his forehead with his forearm, about the need to calm down. He was too overheated, and Donovan would be here in less than an hour. He needed a cold shower and a wank—which would help with the sweatiness *and* the horniness.

Except, when he let himself into his apartment, Donovan was already there, stirring the chili he'd texted he was going to cook, dominating his kitchen, looking so fucking *right* and tasty enough to eat, and his need ballooned further.

"Hey," Donovan said, turning, putting his beer down on the benchtop as he leaned his ass against it, smiling all big and sexy as his gaze took a slow and *very* thorough detour over Beckett's body, which pushed it from strung tight to excruciatingly rigid. "Man…" he muttered, his gaze hot as he trailed off. He looked like he wanted to say more but didn't.

Beckett swallowed. "What?"

He took a beat to respond then shook his head. "Nah, I really shouldn't say what I'm thinking."

Oh, *fuck that.* He should—he really fucking should. "Humour me."

"I just…wouldn't have thought *any* guy would look good in Lycra, and yet—" His gaze travelled over Beckett in another exhaustive inspection. "You look fucking incredible." His eyes finally returned to Beckett's. "I want to just peel you out of that thing and eat you like a banana."

Beckett's heart banged to a stop at the frankness of Donovan's desires. He'd been loosening up more and more over these past days, growing more comfortable with banter and expressions of need, but that admission was next level.

"See?" He smiled, but his knuckles were white, curled around the rolled edge of the bench. "I told you."

But Beckett barely heard him, his backpack sliding from his fingers and *thunk*ing to the ground. Forgetting about his sweatiness, he strode across the space that separated them under Donovan's heated gaze.

The spices from the cooking chili as heady as his lust, Beckett advanced, his pulse thrumming through his head, until finally he was close enough to touch. And he did, sliding his hands onto Donovan's chest then his neck. His body pressed into Donovan's, his hard dick rubbed against Donovan's, his mouth slid against Donovan's, his tongue duelled with Donovan's.

The other man tasted hot with spice and cool with beer as a flurry of pants and groans eddied around them. Donovan's fists curled into the front of Beckett's Lycra top as Beckett's palms curled around Donovan's ass cheeks and squeezed. They contracted at the touch, and he wanted to bite them so damn badly he squeezed them harder.

And he wasn't tight anymore, he wasn't rigid—for the most part, anyway. Everything was unravelling at a rate of knots, and he was so fucking loose he could barely stand. Hell, as Donovan's tongue danced with his, Beckett didn't want to stand. He wanted to get on his knees and blow Donovan's brain.

Dropping the delicious bulk of glutes, Beckett moved his hands to Donovan's front, grasping the steel bar of arousal that had been grinding on his since their bodies had met. Donovan grunted at the contact, his lips falling away, and as he fought and panted for breath, Beckett found and reefed down the zip of Donovan's fly.

Making a deep noise of triumph in the back of his throat, Beckett was reaching inside for Donovan's erection at the same time he was falling to his knees. He pulled it free of the confines of underwear, the loud wash of his pulse filling his ears as the engorged contours of Donovan's dick filled his hand. Jesus—he was hung. Granite hard, pleasingly long, and satisfyingly thick.

Donovan Bane, lord of the cock.

Beckett had seen it before, of course. Hell, he'd *felt* it

before. But never from this angle. From the underside looking up, it was fucking glorious.

"Beckett." Donovan's voice rumbled out, his voice deep as pitch.

"Yeah?" he asked, distracted by the taut, spongy crown flushed purple and leaking.

"What are you doing?"

Reluctantly dragging his eyes off the monster penis in his grasp, Beckett made eye contact with its owner. There was something really hot about looking up at Donovan, his dick standing out and proud between them. He pulled in a ragged breath. "I'm going to suck your cock until you come down my throat, and then I'm going to swallow every last drop."

And, just in case Donovan needed a preview of what that would be like, Beckett, his gaze locked with Donovan's, leaned in and swiped the flat of his tongue over the slit in the crown. The salt and tang of Donovan's arousal and the rough pant falling from his parted lips combined to act like rocket fuel to a system already overdosed on lust.

"That okay?" he asked, sitting back on his haunches, his voice raspy with need.

He knew he had to give Donovan an out. They'd stepped things up considerably tonight, and as much as he wanted to gobble up Donovan's dick, this was uncharted territory.

Donovan's Adam's apple bobbed convulsively, and for a moment, Beckett thought he might deny the request—deny himself. There was certainly a war being waged behind those brown eyes of his. But then he let out a breath and the whites of his knuckles returned to their normal colour. "Yeah," he said, his throat bobbing again.

Beckett's heart leaped in his chest both at the courage it had taken and the prospect of what was to come. "Good decision," he teased with a smile as he once again closed the distance between his mouth and the crown of Donovan's cock.

He went slowly, wanting Donovan to be screaming with need when his lips finally touched down on the taut, erect flesh. Beckett was excruciatingly aware of Donovan watching his progress, of the flare of the other man's nostrils and the choppy timbre of his breathing as the distance narrowed, of the shuddery release of breath as Beckett's lips brushed warm, hard steel.

Beckett's tongue slipped out to lap at the slit again, the cock bucking at the contact as Donovan sucked in a harsh breath. Salt danced along Beckett's tastebuds, and the aroma of musk filled his nostrils. "Mmm," he murmured, "you taste good." Then he sucked on the thick, spongy head, swirling his tongue around and around like a lollypop, savouring the unique tang that was all man.

"*Fuuuck.*"

Donovan's eyes shut and his knuckles whitened and he groaned a groan that seemed to rumble up from the floor. It was a *very* satisfying noise going straight to Beckett's head.

Both of them.

Knowing that *he* was Donovan's first. That *he* was the guy to introduce this man to the delights of his first ever guy-on-guy blowjob? It was utterly dizzying.

He felt like he'd *invented* fellatio. And they hadn't even got to the good bit.

Beckett opened wide then and took Donovan deeper, filling his mouth with him, taking him as far as he could, watching his face, watching the flush of his cheeks deepen and his lips part. A low, guttural, "*Beckett,*" fell from Donovan's mouth as his eyes opened and he watched Beckett hold steady. The look of awe and desire in Donovan's gaze reached inside him and yanked, flooding his system with a heady hit of sexual power.

This man. This man calling his name. This man calling

his name and looking at him with lust and wonder? This was what he wanted.

Beckett retreated then, sucking hard around the girth as he withdrew, satisfied when Donovan groaned again, and his eyes fluttered closed as he swirled his tongue three times around the tip before withdrawing completely. Satisfyingly, the flushed crown glistened with saliva—*his* saliva—and then he took him again, all the way down and all the way back.

And repeated it, over and over, his eyes shut, savouring the taste of Donovan, savouring the smell of him, savouring the sounds of his pleasure. Greedy for his release but never wanting it to end.

· · ·

Donovan could barely stand as Beckett's mouth weaved its hot, wet magic. His heart was beating wildly in his chest and the air in his lungs was thick as mud and he was gripping the damn bench so hard he was going to leave goddamn finger marks in the laminate.

It wasn't the first time Donovan had had his dick sucked. It *was* the first time he'd had it sucked by a guy. And that was *big*. The fact that it was *this* guy. This guy who was gentle and kind and patient and who had demanded nothing of him and had jolted him awake from the state of hibernation he'd forced himself into through fear and necessity?

That was bigger.

Because it was so much *more* than a physical experience. So much *more* than a blowjob. It was as if this man could see inside him, knew the makeup of every single cell. They had a *connection* that burrowed right under his skin. That went deeper than the slide of Beckett's lips down his cock— although good fucking Christ, it was making him see stars.

Hell, the wet tug of his mouth was bringing Donovan to

his fucking knees.

And when Beckett cupped his heavy, aching balls and squeezed, Donovan cried out at the hot jolt of pleasure and pain, sparks igniting along the pathway of his spine, muscles squeezing and relaxing, rippling from his belly button to his groin and back again, propelling him closer to climax.

He gasped at the sensations, his eyes opening, his gaze falling on Beckett, who was watching him, watching his face as he sucked his cock, and Donovan had to lock his legs they were trembling so damn hard. The sight of that sandy-blond head bobbing back and forth swelled in his chest. Those lips widening, stretching as he took Donovan's cock deep then narrowing on the withdrawal, his cheeks hollowing as he sucked long and hard and good, his fingers rolling and stroking his testicles, all the while his eyes never leaving Donovan's face.

That was hot as fuck.

And all Donovan needed. Beckett looking at him like that, looking at him like he was the best fucking thing he'd ever had in his mouth and, yet, precious all at once. His gaze reverent, his mouth wicked.

Like he was praying but not for anything remotely holy.

"Beckett…" Donovan groaned as the first twinge of his release undulated through muscles deep and low. And then, "*Beckett!*" his eyes widening and his heart skipping a beat as the orgasm roared out in one powerful pulse.

Panicked by the intensity, he tried to pull away, pull out of Beckett's mouth in case he was just being polite about his intentions earlier, but the other man refused to yield, clinging to Donovan, gripping his hips hard and sucking his cock *harder*, working it and working it and working it, then taking him all the way to the back at just the right moment for Donovan to spill his load right down his throat, feeling it undulate around him as Beckett swallowed all he had to give, and Donovan was gasping and panting for breath and utterly,

utterly spent.

His chest was heaving and his head was spinning and he'd never felt so goddamn weak in his life, but he reached for Beckett anyway—he had to hold him; he *needed* to hold him.

Grasping a bicep, he hauled Beckett off the floor and into his arms, and when he opened his mouth to say something, Donovan cut him off, claiming his lips in a long, sloppy kiss that was more enthusiasm than finesse. And when he tasted himself on Beckett's tongue, he *devoured* him—they devoured each other.

"God," Donovan panted when he finally came up for air, pressing his forehead against Beckett's, "that was…" He wasn't sure there were words adequate enough to describe what it was.

Beckett gave a half laugh. "Not PG?"

Donovan returned the laugh. "Definitely not."

"Are you freaking out?"

"No." Donovan shook his head. "I'm the opposite of whatever freaking out is." They might have stepped over the boundaries they'd set, but that had always been inevitable.

A loud rumble intruded into the intimacy. "Was that your belly or mine?" Beckett asked.

"Mine, I think. But it always thinks its throat's been cut."

"That's true," Beckett acknowledged. "If that chili's done, then we might as well eat. Just give me a few minutes to have a shower. I'm all sweaty from the ride and…" He glanced down at Donovan's dick sandwiched between them. "Other nefarious activities."

Donovan's nostrils flared again as a waft of fresh male sweat that he'd found so dizzying during Beckett's head job caused a warm buzz. But Beckett was easing out of his arms, saying, "Give me five," before turning and walking away, heading for the doorway and the shower.

The shower…God…he bet Beckett looked amazing in a

shower, water running in rivulets down his lean body, clinging to the trail of hair that arrowed down from his belly button, flattening the hair on his legs, clinging to the hair *between* his legs, and dripping off the end of his cock.

Donovan almost groaned out loud at the image. His dick definitely twitched. His dick that was still swinging in the breeze, sticking out of his jeans. Turning, he zipped himself away, forcing himself to concentrate on stirring the chili, but despite his best efforts, thoughts of a wet, naked Beckett kept intruding, and he turned and stared at the doorway.

Maybe Beckett needed a hand washing his back?

Drumming his fingers against the bench for a beat or two, he teetered on the edge of decorum and carnality. If Beckett had wanted Donovan to join him then he'd have asked. But curiosity and a resurgent hit of hormones needled him, and before he knew it, Donovan was pacing toward Beckett's bedroom, pacing to the ensuite, stopping in the doorway.

Donovan, his heart beating in time to the drum of the shower, sucked in a breath at the sight before him. The shower must have been cold, because there was no steam fogging the glass, which gave him a completely unobstructed view of Beckett's long, lean body, wet and glistening beneath the downlights. He had his back to the doorway, his hands up high on the tiles, his head bowed between his shoulders, the pounding spray directed at his nape.

Water cascaded south, streaming over the muscles of his back and shoulders, sheeting down his flanks and the dip of his lower back to the tight cheeks of his butt before running down the backs of his thighs and calves. Tan lines on his biceps and mid-thighs only emphasised the smooth, lily-white state of his ass, and Donovan's gaze returned to it, because fucking hell—he wanted to bite it.

Whether it was the low growl he made at the back of his throat or Beckett suddenly sensing a presence, he looked over his shoulder, his gaze finding Donovan's. His eyes widened slightly, and the muscles of his neck bunched. "Hey," he said.

Donovan leaned his shoulder in the doorframe, trying to act like it wasn't his first time watching a dude shower. Which it wasn't. But not like this. This was private.

This *mattered*.

"I'm sorry," Donovan said feeling awkward. "I…" He didn't finish. He didn't know how to express what he was thinking or what had drawn him here.

He didn't really know the etiquette.

But Beckett nodded and said, "Yeah," like he totally understood, and it suddenly felt like he'd made the right choice.

They didn't speak for a moment, just looked at each other before Donovan let his eyes go on another tour. This time, though, with Beckett's body turned slightly to look over his shoulder, he noticed the state of Beckett's cock standing hard and proud.

Fuck. His pulse accelerating crazily, he flicked his eyes up to meet Beckett's. "You going to do something about that?"

He gave a half laugh. "I've been trying to will it into submission."

"How's that working out for you?"

Grimacing, he said, "It's not. As you can see."

Oh yeah. He could see, and *fuck* if he didn't want to do something about it. Steadying a breath, he pushed off the doorframe and took a step inside. "Would you like some help? I could…" Donovan faltered, his pulse so loud in his ears now he could barely hear himself. He didn't know how to articulate it without sounding like an idiot. He still wasn't used to being frank about the sex stuff. "Return the favour."

Beckett's smile was tender as he slowly turned around to reveal the full extent of his arousal. "I didn't suck you off for some quid pro quo, Donovan."

Donovan swallowed as his own dick flushed full and hard. "I know." He nodded. "But…I want to."

"Really?"

"Yeah. I know I'm not exactly experienced at this, but…"

Beckett chuckled. "If you think I don't want big, bad Donovan Bane on his knees in front of me, sucking my dick, then you are seriously underestimating how into you I am."

He grinned again, and it twinkled in his eyes and deepened his dimples, and Donovan wondered if he'd ever stop feeling tight in the chest when Beckett smiled at him.

"But…I know your first time was traumatic, so…you don't have to do this."

"You're not hiding a camera in there anywhere, are you?"

"No. And," he added, "I would *never* do that to you. No matter what happens with us, what we're doing is private. I hope you know you can trust me on that."

The conviction in Beckett's voice was humbling, the anger at what had happened to Donovan obvious. "I do." Feeling more confident, Donovan pulled off his shirt and tossed it on the ground. Then he toed off his shoes, unzipped his pants, and peeled both his jeans and his underwear off his legs. The fact he was being watched by Beckett as he stripped was dizzying. Surprisingly, he didn't feel self-conscious standing naked in front of him.

He felt *desired*.

Beckett pushed open the shower door, the sound of running water louder now, and Donovan didn't hesitate. He entered the shower cubicle—dick first. Considering he'd come only fifteen minutes ago, he was harder than he'd ever been in his life. Beckett, his eyes not leaving Donovan's, fell back as he advanced until his ass hit the tiled side wall of the cubicle.

Lucky the shower was roomy, because, between them, they took up some space.

Donovan's eyes took another trip south, eating up

the contours of Beckett's body, his hands trembling in anticipation. He didn't even mind the cold spray of the shower hitting his thigh and running down his leg. It tempered the need roaring through his veins. Slowly, his gaze returning to Beckett's, he began to kneel.

"No."

Beckett's ragged voice was quiet but insistent, his hand warm on Donovan's shoulder. "This isn't the alley. Kiss me first."

Donovan, a warm bubble of emotion rising in his chest, could no more have denied that request than flown to the moon. Beckett was telling him this wasn't a quick blowjob from a stranger at the end of the night. This *mattered*.

He crowded Beckett against the tiles, their bodies meeting—one wet, one dry—their dicks rubbing deliciously together, his fingers burying in the other man's hair. Beckett's mouth met his halfway, and they fused on a groan that Donovan felt in his fucking *bones*.

Things heated then—real fast. Tongues and teeth and lips melding and clashing, devouring greedily, Donovan gripping Beckett's head firmly, trying to kiss him hard enough, deep enough, trying to sink beneath his skin until he was so far inside the other man, he'd never be able to find his way out again.

But when one of Beckett's hands wandered to his ass and squeezed, and the other slid between their bodies, grasping both their shafts and pumping them together, he knew he had to stop or he'd disgrace himself way too quickly, and this wasn't supposed to be about him.

Breaking their lip lock, they stared at each other for long moments, their ragged pants louder than the noise of the spray. He knelt then, slowly, his eyes never leaving Beckett's, captivated by the slack parting of his mouth, by the expression of hunger and anticipation.

The tiles were hard and cool beneath his knees, and the

spray was now on his arm and down his side, but he barely noticed as he tore his gaze from Beckett's face to his cock. Saliva flooded his mouth, and he licked his lips.

Jesus, he wanted to taste it so fucking bad.

Tentatively, he slid his hand up Beckett's thigh. It twitched beneath his palm, and he vaguely heard some kind of noise falling from Beckett's parted lips, but he was really only concentrating on what was in front of him. On the jut of his steely length, pale in comparison to his own, but nicely veined, the head plump and a darker, duskier hue. The rim perfectly delineated.

Donovan had always thought of his dick as a blunt instrument—thick and robust. Functional but not particularly pretty. Sure, it was big, he was *well hung*, but it was no oil painting. Beckett's, on the other hand, was a work of art with its intricate network of veins clearly visible beneath the surface, the perfect ruffle of tissue on the underside of the crown and the way his balls hung in absolute symmetry.

It was a magnificent specimen of manhood. It was the fucking Rolls Royce of cock.

"Just so you know," Beckett said, his voice rough, cutting in to Donovan's appreciation, "I'm clean. I always practice safe sex and have regular screening."

Donovan blinked. He hadn't given a thought to such issues, but he knew STIs could be transmitted through oral sex, and the fact that Beckett was thinking of that, thinking of *him*, when he was too far gone to think of himself, only made him want this man more. "And I've been practicing *no* sex for about a decade so…"

"Yeah." He grinned. "I wasn't worried."

"Good." Because he wanted Beckett's dick in his mouth more than he wanted to take his next breath. He slid his fingers to encircle the base, and Beckett muttered, "*Jesus*," somewhere above, but he barely heard as he got lost in how *good* his hand looked there and how good it was to be able to do this—touch, explore. Be here like *this* with *this* guy and not have to hide who he was or pretend he was a different kind of man.

"Donovan?"

It came out as a strangled kind of pant, which Donovan barely registered. "Yeah?"

A hand landed on his shoulder and slid into his hair, fingers finding his nape and pressing lightly. Donovan complied to the pressure, glancing up, their gazes meeting once more. "You don't have to swallow if you don't want to."

Ah, *yeah*. Yeah, he fucking did. He certainly *wanted* to.

But Beckett clearly needed him to know he had no expectations, so he just nodded and said, "Okay," then turned his attention back to the prettiest damn cock in the world. Leaning in, he took it into his mouth—as far as he could take it.

A loud *thunk* sounded as Beckett's head hit the tiles followed by an even louder curse. "*Holy crap.*" Beckett's hand slipped from Donovan's shoulder. "You could have warned me you were going to do that."

Donovan glanced up as he slowly withdrew, savouring each millimetre of Beckett's sweet prick, finding the man looking down at him, water droplets running from his hair to his neck to his chest. When it popped from his mouth, he said, "You don't like it like that?"

He smiled a little, trying to look innocent—with Beckett's cock an inch from his mouth. He was pretty sure he knew the answer, but it was dizzying to see that look of barely leashed lust on Beckett's face. Dizzying to know that he could put it there. Dizzying to know he could tease this man, the way Beckett liked to tease him.

Beckett gave a half laugh, his gaze intense as he slid his hand to cup Donovan's jaw, his thumb sweeping across the whiskers on his chin, brushing his bottom lip—once, twice, three times—before pressing on the corner of his mouth and slipping inside. His eyes widened as Donovan's teeth scraped the tip before his tongue soothed over the graze.

"I like it whatever way you want to give it," he said, his gaze fixed to where his thumb parted Beckett's lips. "I like your mouth on me, period."

His frank expression of desire curled Donovan's toes, and as Beckett's thumb slipped out and fell away, Donovan leaned in again, taking the neat dome of Beckett's cock into his mouth. He went slower this time, swirling his tongue around and around, savouring the salty taste at the crown before swirling on further, exploring every fucking inch of its perfection he could fit in before gagging made it impossible, then pulling back, swirling all the way off.

Then doing it all over again. And again.

The sounds that fell from Beckett's throat as he sucked his dick were deeply, *deeply* satisfying—the gasps and the pants and the groans, but particularly the nonsensical noises gurgling in the back of his throat that weren't quite words but weren't quite breathing, either.

He was the reason Beckett sounded completely undone. *He* was turning this man, with so much more experience than him, on.

Him and his *in*experienced mouth.

It was heady stuff, each of Beckett's reactions building Donovan's confidence brick by brick. From the way his hand tightened on Donovan's shoulder to the way the muscles in his thighs got harder and started to tremble to the tightening of his ass cheeks against the tiles, which thrust his cock out a little prouder. It was all so fucking *intoxicating*.

Donovan's chest was pounding and his lungs were heaving and his head was spinning and they were indulging in a clandestine affair, which could end Donovan's career and yet he'd never felt so fucking *free*.

Suddenly, Beckett's thigh muscles turned to granite and he groaned. "Fuck. *Jesus*. Donovan...I'm going to come." Then he placed his hand on Donovan's forehead, no pressure but clearly giving him an opt out.

But Donovan wasn't interested. He just locked his gaze with Beckett's and took that hand, slipping it to the back of his head, keeping his hand over the top, holding it there, both their hands holding his head exactly where it was while they stared at each other, and Beckett groaned and thrust then let go, calling out to Jesus as he spilled down Donovan's throat.

Donovan's pulse skyrocketed as the first shot of come hit the back of his tongue. He hadn't known what to expect, but the hot, salty taste wasn't a turn-off—quite the opposite. It was heady because it was Beckett, Beckett who was calling his name and muttering, "*Yes, baby, yes,*" and Donovan kept sucking because he couldn't get enough. Not of his taste or his shudders or his deep, guttural groans.

He couldn't get enough of being called *baby*.

And even when Beckett's cries settled and his quads relaxed and his glutes went lax, and his hand fell away, Donovan's head kept bobbing, because Beckett might have been spent, but he was still hard in his mouth and, coated in spunk, he tasted even better, and he didn't want to stop.

He wanted to ring every second out of it, give Beckett all that he had.

"Stop, Donovan," Beckett half laughed, half groaned, his hand back in his hair, urging him off. "God...I'm going to fall down if you don't stop."

Dazed, Donovan pulled back, Beckett's dick slipping from his mouth as he blinked up at the man who was smiling down at him with the most slumberous eyes and replete smile he'd ever seen, and he felt like a fucking *god*.

Donovan was used to being a god on the rugby field. He was used to being treated like one, lapping up the adoration from his fans as was his due. But having *this* man look at him as if he was standing in some gladiatorial ring instead of kneeling at his feet was overwhelming.

He reached for him then, sliding up Beckett's body, their skin slicked together from the spray, their breathing still erratic, his hands cradling Beckett's face as his greedy mouth landed and he kissed him, revelling in Beckett's instant response, swallowing the other man's groan even as he offered his own. As long as he lived, Donovan knew he'd never forget Beckett's kisses or the way they made him feel.

His hands shook and his legs shook and he was pretty sure they were holding each other up as he broke away to draw breath.

"Mmm," Beckett murmured, smiling at him as he lifted a hand and trailed his fingers along the line of Donovan's mouth. "I like the taste of my come on your lips."

Jesus. The bald statement slammed into his groin. Dirty and so fucking *right*. He liked it, too. Donovan smiled. "Good. Because I'd like to do that a lot more."

He laughed, his hand sliding to the side of Donovan's neck. "You won't get any arguments from me."

And then they were smiling at each other, grinning like fools, and Donovan couldn't remember a time he'd ever felt this *right*.

Until the squealing of an alarm sliced right through that feeling in one second flat.

"Fuck." Donovan pulled away, his heart rate spiking for an entirely different reason. "The chili." He hadn't turned it off, and it was probably on goddamn *fire* right now.

Turning away, he pushed open the shower door and leaped out. With his erection leading the way, he grabbed a towel on his way past the rack.

The sound of Beckett's laughter followed him all the way to the kitchen.

Chapter Eleven

The atmosphere at the game on Saturday night was way different down in the cheap seats than it had been in the glass box on high, but Beck didn't mind. The excitement was more palpable, the thunder of applause actually reverberating through his chest as the Smoke ran another one home.

They were on a roll, and Donovan was amongst it all, bringing guys down, storming the field, dragging grown men valiantly trying to stop him, in his wake. Donovan, with his tight shorts barely containing his thick thighs and snug jersey delineating the slabs of muscle making up his chest and abs.

And the way the crowd called his name whenever he had the ball...*Jesus*.

Beck was so freaking horny he was surely about to pass out from lack of blood supply to his brain. Between the visual stimuli and the reel of memories from the last two nights running through his head—there had been a lot of dick sucking—he was about as hair trigger as he'd ever been. Just picturing the way Donovan had looked up at him in the shower on Thursday night, sucking dick for the first time—

his dick—and loving it, was making him trippy.

But he was also *proud*. That was *his* guy down there on the field. *His* lover absolutely killing it. *His* man's name on everyone's lips.

It didn't matter that it couldn't last. Donovan was his for now.

"So…why the sudden interest in rugby?"

Beck half turned toward Pete, his eyes still glued to the teams on the field, interlocked heads down, asses up in a tight scrum. He picked Donovan's ass out easily from what was a very impressive collection of butts.

But then, he could have picked Donovan's ass out of a lineup.

"What?"

"This is the second game you've been to in a month. I thought you were an AFL guy."

Pete, who was not much of a sports fan, had wanted to hit the town tonight, but Beck had dissuaded him with a counter offer to the Smoke game. He hadn't been convinced initially, but Beck had won him over with the promise of hot guys in tight shorts. And he'd delivered in spades. But it was the second half now, and Pete's attention span was waning.

Not even all the guy-on-guy physical contact was holding his interest.

"I work here now," he said nonchalantly. "I get cheap tickets."

A bone-crunching tackle happened not far from where they were sitting, and Pete winced. "It's quite gladiatorial, isn't it?"

Beck nodded distractedly as he stared at Donovan's ass. "Yeah."

"He's easy on the eye." Pete tipped his chin at a young blond guy in a Smoke jersey who had made a break for it after receiving the ball. "What's his name?"

"I don't know their names," Beck said. Not really. He only knew one.

Sure, he'd Googled the team, but he hadn't had much interest in any of the other players. The crowd was chanting *Ronan, Ronan, Ronan,* which triggered a memory of the WAGs mentioning him that night in the corporate box. "Actually, I think that's the new American import."

And then Ronan was tackled, but before he hit the ground, he passed the ball to Donovan, who took off, and the crowd, including him, were on their feet. "Go, Donovan," he shouted. "*Go, go go!*"

Beck's heart was in his throat as Donovan evaded the grasping hands of the opposition and ran the ball over the line. "Yaaaas," he yelled, his voice drowned out by the rest of the crowd, his heart just about exploding in his chest now.

"You did it, man!" he yelled as Donovan was pulled from the ground by his teammates and surrounded in a group hug. Beck stayed up a beat longer than the rest of the crowd and was still grinning when he sat down. "Wasn't that amazing?" he asked, turning to Pete.

Pete raised an eyebrow, leaning in close to be heard over the excitement of the crowd. "I didn't think you knew their names."

Oh...*shit.* He shrugged to cover for his slip. Pete could sniff out sexual interest better than anyone he knew. It came from having a highly suspicious personality and an obsession with both Agatha Christie and trashy reality television dating shows. The feds should hire him as some kind of love sleuth. "Everyone was calling it."

"Oh no." Pete narrowed his gaze. "No way, Beck. Please don't tell me you have the hots for this guy."

Double shit. "Why on earth would you think that?"

Pete rolled his eyes as he spoke close to Beck's ear. "Because you've never expressed an interest in rugby before, you know his name, you're wearing a Smoke jersey, and you're looking at him like you want to suck his dick. If you haven't already."

Try as he might, Beck couldn't stop the flush of heat to his cheeks or thoughts of how he'd blown Donovan in the kitchen next to a saucepan of bubbling chili.

Triple shit. He looked away. "Now you're just being melodramatic."

"*Ha*! I knew it."

There was nothing worse than Pete when he was on the scent and knew he was right. "It's nothing," Beck denied.

"Bullshit. If it was nothing, I would have heard about it by now."

Beck couldn't fault that logic. He and Pete talked smack about guys a lot, but Beck was always closed-lipped about the ones who meant something.

"Bloody hell, Beck. Where's your head at?"

Clearly satisfied he'd sniffed it out, Pete had moved on to the admonishing part of the programme. "It's fine," Beck dismissed.

Snorting, Pete shook his head. "As far as I know, there's no gay pro rugby player here in Australia, because he'd be a freaking icon in the community by now and I'd definitely have heard of him. He's not out, is he?"

With the noise forcing them to speak close to each other's ears, Beck knew their conversation wouldn't be overheard. "No."

"Jesus…I thought you said you wouldn't ever be with a guy who wasn't out again?"

"Yeah." He'd said that.

"So?"

"It's complicated."

"It's *always* complicated."

"He's not like Dieter. He's not deceiving himself about

his sexuality." Not anymore, anyway. "He *can't* come out, Pete. He'd be putting his career on the line. And anyway, it's just…sex. He's never been with a guy before, and I'm just… teaching him the ropes."

Pete looked at him askance. "And yet here you are at his rugby game. He must be pretty damn good."

"No comment." Beck didn't kiss and tell.

"Is he worth being dragged into the closet?" Pete looked at him with a healthy dollop of pity. Then his face changed as something clearly dawned. "Oh God. You've fallen in love with him, haven't you?"

"No. *Absolutely* not." He'd been very clear with Donovan that love wasn't a part of their equation—that this was only short term. And he'd meant it.

"Beck…" Pete's voice softened. "I remember what you were like with Dieter. How miserable he made you in the end."

"That was a long time ago. And Donovan is different."

"How?"

"Because he didn't pursue me. I pursued him." Donovan had tried to dissuade him, to push him away. Dieter hadn't given a single fuck about the consequences.

"You haven't worked here that long. He can't have put up much resistance."

Beck shrugged and gave a half laugh, forcing his hitched shoulders to relax. He didn't want to argue with Pete. His best mate was just looking out for him, and they were here to watch rugby, not butt heads. "I can be pretty persuasive."

"Yeah. I've heard that about you." They smiled at each other then, and Pete sighed. "This is going to end badly."

No, it wouldn't, because he'd put in boundaries. With Dieter, he'd seen it heading for the rocks and had wanted to abandon ship every damn day, but like some junkie, he hadn't been able to stop. With Donovan, he'd been upfront from the get-go. They were a short-term thing only. There wouldn't be any feelings. He wasn't after a boyfriend.

He was Donovan's *tutor*, and that had an expiry date.

"Then you can say I told you so."

Pete's brows beetled together. "You think I want to be right more than I want you *not* to be hurt?"

Beck shut his eyes—that had been a shitty thing to say. "Sorry, no. Of course not." He opened his eyes again. "I just want to… Look, I know it's not your thing, but could we please watch the damn game already?"

"Are you kidding?" Pete perked up in his seat. "Now I know you're rucking with the big guy, I am very, *very* interested."

"There's going to be a lot of ball jokes now, aren't there?"

Pete grinned. "You can take that to the bank."

• • •

Donovan was *pumped* as he turned off the engine in Beckett's parking garage. He'd come straight from the game, hell, straight from the showers, his hair still damp, ignoring the invitations to celebrate their win because he had to see Beckett.

He swore he could *feel* him in the crowd tonight. Closer than the television, closer than the corporate box. His eyes following him all over the field, intense and…sticky, seeing through his clothes—through his *skin*—to his bones, to his muscles, to his organs.

He'd felt like he was playing the game for Beckett alone. Like they were the only two people in the whole fucking stadium. And there was no one he wanted to celebrate this win with, share this win with, more than Beckett.

Winning always put an itch in his blood, but the ratchet of adrenaline soon ceded to the happy flood of dopamine. And normally he'd hang with the team, eating pizzas and drinking beer as they dissected the game and smack-talked. But not tonight. That itch in his blood prickled like crazy, and all he wanted was Beckett.

Touching him. Kissing him. Getting on his knees for him. There was a fever in his blood only Beckett could put out. A wild sexual cocktail that held him in thrall.

Beckett was standing in front of the television, watching who-the-fuck-cared, when Donovan entered. He turned when the door opened and smiled and said, "Hey," and he was wearing a fucking *Smoke jersey* and any semblance of control Donovan had been clinging to evaporated in a hot second.

A surge of testosterone swamped him, rousing the caveman inside him, and he tossed his keys on the kitchen bench before stalking toward Beckett with the single-minded focus he usually reserved for a rugby ball flying through the air. That jersey plastered to Beckett's body had coursed urgency through his veins, roused his hunger to ravenous intensity.

Beckett's throat bobbed as he watched the advance. "You're not wearing your hoodie."

On some level Donovan recognised that had been reckless, but he just didn't care right now, because he felt utterly fucking *reckless*. "I came straight from the stadium."

"Okay."

He drew level with Beckett, their bodies only inches apart, the drum of Donovan's blood rising like a crescendo in his head as he took in every square inch of the jersey and the way it fit. His hands curled into fists as the urge to shred fabric took hold. "Christ," he half muttered, half growled. "You look hot in that jersey. I want to tear you out of it with my teeth."

The rough pant of Beckett's breath, the bob of his throat,

affected Donovan in a way that was absolutely primal.

"Now you know how I feel watching you run around in one for eighty bloody minutes."

Fuck. Donovan dragged in a breath at the frank expression of desire. It grabbed him by his heavy, aching balls and squeezed. "I could *feel* you watching me."

"Good. Because I couldn't take my eyes off you for a second."

Donovan lunged for him then, even though he was close enough to just slide his hands on over, but he wasn't capable of such finesse, such restraint. His desire was off the leash, a haze of lust taking hold, his need to touch and be touched a desperate clawing need as their mouths clashed and their heads twisted and their tongues danced.

He wanted this man. He wanted Beckett Stanton with a ferocity that was terrifying as he plucked at the jersey and yanked it up, pulling it off Beckett's head, breaking their kiss for *too many fucking seconds* before Beckett's mouth was back, harder and more desperate. The noises in the back of his throat bordered on feral.

The need to touch screamed through his veins like a fast train in a dark tunnel, and Donovan shoved his hand between them, grasping frantically, clumsily, for the hardness that had been grinding against his. Beckett cried out, his mouth breaking away on a series of ragged pants, and he stumbled a little as Donovan squeezed, like he was having trouble holding himself upright, and Donovan knew exactly how he felt.

Bracing him, Donovan walked Beckett backward. Back, back, back—never taking his hand off his cock—and then they were up against the wall and he was pulling his zipper down and sliding to his knees, because he *had* to have Beckett's cock in his mouth.

"Oh, *Jesus*," Beckett groaned as his hands slid into

Donovan's hair.

Donovan reached inside the zipper, greedily—too greedily—his hand trembling and fumbling until *finally* Beckett's cock was in his hand, long and pale and pretty, weeping for attention.

Yes. Fuck. *Yes.*

He leaned in and swallowed it up, his lips tingling at the corners as they stretched around it, the long, hard reach of it filling his mouth, pushing into the softness of his throat. All to the soundtrack of his own throbbing heart and the deep, guttural, "Oh, *Jesuuuus*," from above.

He went for it then, sucking and licking and slurping, working his mouth up and down, his tongue round and round, the convulsive gripping and ungripping of Beckett's hand in his hair, the tautness of his ass cheeks against the wall, pushing him to go faster, to take him deeper.

"God," Beckett panted. "Donovan. *Jesus.*" He clutched and unclutched his hair as his hip movements became a little discordant. "Stop. No. Wait. I want…I want…"

The word *stop* sliced through Donovan like a guillotine. He pulled away, blinking up at the man, confused at the request because he was pretty sure Beckett had been seconds away from losing his load. His face was flushed with desire, his eyes glittering with a hunger that called to the primal beast roaring inside Donovan's chest.

"What?" he panted, Beckett's dick glistening and ready only inches from his mouth. "What do you want?"

"I…" He was panting, too, as he searched Donovan's gaze intently, his chest rising and falling erratically. "I…" More searching, but then he just smiled, his hand slipping to Donovan's jaw. "Nothing." He angled his hips a little so the head of his cock brushed Donovan's lips. "As you were."

The temptation to open his mouth, to suck Beckett's dick back in and make him lose it, have those fingers twist *hard* in his hair, hear his name fall from those lips he loved to kiss so much, ticked through his blood like a time bomb, but in those seconds of searching, Donovan had seen the conflict glittering in Beckett's eyes.

He could see the guy was holding back, could sense his frustration. And *fuck that*.

Pulling his mouth away from temptation, he said, "Tell me what you want."

"God." Beckett's head *thunk*ed against the wall as his hand slid away. After a beat, he looked down. "I just...I watched you marauding around on that field, dominating every play, overwhelming everyone with your sheer physical strength, and I was so fucking horny, all I could think about was you doing that to me, too."

Oh. "You want me to...dominate you?"

Christ...Donovan didn't know what to think about that. He was a big guy, he'd always been aware of it, super conscious of it and how threatening that could look and feel to some, and sure, he was an aggressive player who liked to *win*. But he'd never throw a punch during a game—*ever*, actually—and off field he saw no place for aggression.

He wasn't sure how he felt about spanking and handcuffs and...a red room full of *toys*.

Beckett gave a half laugh. "No, I..." He shook his head. "It doesn't matter."

"It does." Donovan stood, slipped his hands to either side of Beckett's face and kissed him, slow and long and deep, until they were both clinging and needy and groaning. Donovan came up for air. "You said, *I want, I want*. What were you going to say, Beckett? Please talk to me."

He sighed. "I was going to say...I want you in my ass when I come."

Donovan's heart skipped a beat. *Anal*. Beckett wanted Donovan to fuck him up the ass? A jumble of emotion rose in his chest, tangled and twisted like a ball of string that had been attacked by a cat. Did he want to go there? A few weeks ago, he hadn't even kissed a man and now he was sucking dick like a pro, but *anal*? The thought shuddered through him, but not in a bad way. There was definitely something primal kicking to life.

Something hot and virile and *masculine* buzzing through his system.

"But I shouldn't have," Beckett said. "I got...carried away. I didn't realise I was speaking out loud. It's too soon... ignore me."

Slowly, Donovan shook his head. *No*. This was something that Beckett had obviously been wanting. What kind of a selfish prick would he be to ignore Beckett's needs when the man had been nothing but sensitive to *his* needs? Except there was just one problem. "I don't know how to do that."

He laughed again, but he sobered quickly, clearly gauging Donovan's seriousness. "I can teach you."

A surge of hot, heady desire almost brought Donovan to his knees. The care and the acceptance in those words blew him away. "Then what are we waiting for?"

He smiled as he grabbed Beckett's hand and tugged, and they stumbled into the bedroom, kissing and fumbling each other's clothes off as they went, breaking apart to finish the job until they were both naked. The bedroom was in darkness, but the en suite light was on, illuminating the room a little, and for a moment, they just stared at each other with gluttonous eyes, the only sound the noise of their ragged breathing.

"What now?" Donovan asked, his voice rough, the sight of Beckett's body, lean and smooth and long and so fucking *ready* increasing his urgency.

"We can do this face to face or...not."

"What do you want?"

"Half of me wants to watch your face as you fuck me for the first time."

Fucking hell, yes. "And the other half?"

He shoved a hand through his hair. "I've pictured you doing me doggy for so long now, I just…"

Donovan swallowed, heat blooming *everywhere* at the image. "Okay." He nodded. "Doggy it is. Get on the bed."

His voice was rough as gravel, and the bob of Beckett's throat at his command was like a charge to his testicles. But nothing prepared him for Beckett crawling across the coverlet on his hands and knees, stopping in the middle of the mattress and presenting his ass—his exceedingly fucking hot ass—to Donovan, his balls hanging low, his boner fully charged and ready to go.

Donovan's libido *roared* as he sucked in a breath and his nostrils flared, and he may have avoided thinking about this before, but he *wanted* to fuck Beckett's ass so badly now—to dominate him—his legs practically buckled.

Looking over his shoulder, Beckett said, "Condoms and lube in the drawer."

Donovan didn't need any more encouragement as he took three steps, yanked the drawer open, and grabbed the requested items. The condom was on in seconds. At ten seconds, he was on the bed and shuffling in behind Beckett, the light from the bathroom illuminating the long, pale stretch of his back.

"Lots of lube," Beckett said as their eyes met. "And go *slow*."

Donovan nodded, his hands trembling as they slid onto the hard lines of Beckett's hips. He'd go as slow as Beckett needed. He'd probably last about ten seconds before he came, so he wasn't sure how much time there'd be to make it feel good—or if he even could—but he'd go slow.

First, though, he was going to do what he'd been wanting

to do for days.

Lowering his mouth, he pressed his lips to first one ass cheek, then the other. Beckett groaned low and deep, and it roared like a stadium full of cheering fans spurring him on to more. He grazed his teeth with his next pass then bit a little with his third, encouraged by the gasped, "*Donovannnn.*"

Then he moved north, dragging his lips along the furrow of Beckett's spine, to the dip in his back and past the span of his ribs, leaning over his body the further north he travelled, until his front was pressed along the length of Beckett's back and he was at his neck, nuzzling, and Beckett was panting and moaning and goose bumps stippled his flesh from nape to flanks.

But with his dick sliding between Beckett's ass cheeks and Beckett moving against him, the driving need to *fuck* could not be ignored. Donovan kissed back down again, balancing on one hand as he slid his other hand to Beckett's rigid cock.

Beckett cried out, a noise that was half pleasure, half pain and *all* fucking turn-on.

"God...Donovan," he said, his voice strangled, "*don't.* I'm barely hanging in here as it is."

Donovan smiled against the small of his back, loving that he had Beckett so aroused he was in danger of losing his load at the slightest stimulus. Maybe he didn't need to worry about how long *he* could last after all?

Dropping his hand, he slowly lifted until he was upright again on his knees, his cock resting along the cleft of Beckett's ass. With his heart beating like crazy, he picked up the lube and dropped a dollop on the condom, smearing it a little. Then he squeezed another onto Beckett's hole, using the head of his lubed-up dick to smear it around, causing Beckett to gasp and his legs to tremble.

Looking at the size of his cock and the neat pucker of

that entrance, he had no fucking idea how it was going to fit, but people had anal all the time, so it must.

And if Beckett wasn't worried, then…

"Are you ready?" he asked, a shot of anticipation riddled with anxiety hitting his chest as his big hands anchored on Beckett's hips.

"Ready?" He gave a half laugh as he looked over his shoulder. "Donovan Bane, if you don't stick your cock in my ass soon, I'm going to die from all the wondering before you get the chance."

Donovan gave a small smile as their gazes meshed, but it died a quick death, a sudden bout of nerves making him hesitant. He'd come here wanting to…rut. To bump and grind and work off the heady mix of victory and horniness with this guy who'd had him all at sea from their very first glance. As quick and as dirty as he could. It had obliterated all else.

Now all he wanted was to not screw this up. To be all Beckett needed him to be.

"I…don't know how to make this good for you."

"God." Beckett shook his head. "You really are the sweetest freaking guy, you know that?"

Donovan gave a half laugh. There was a hell of a lot of his opponents out there that would beg to differ, and that was the way he liked it. "Well, let's keep that between you and me, okay?"

They smiled at each other for a beat before Beckett said, "How about we just feel our way through it?"

"Yeah. Okay."

Glancing down, his cock poised at Beckett's hole, Donovan dolloped on some more lube to be sure, then slowly, gently, his pulse skyrocketing, he pressed forward. The tightness around the head of his cock as he eased in was *indescribably* good, tearing a groan from deep in his chest as the crown slowly slid inside, and the way Beckett moaned, then panted and said, "*Jeeeesus*," filled up his chest and his head and his heart.

"Withdraw slowly," he said, his voice husky and strained, "then come back in again. Slowly."

Donovan did as he was asked, the pressure gripping his glans mind-blowingly hot, pulling at the muscles in his belly and his ass and his groin. Sending sparks to the nerves that circled the bottom of his spine.

"Oh yeah," Beckett panted. "That's good. *So* good. Now come in a little more."

Easing in a little more, Donovan grimaced as the tight ring squeezed his cock, increasing the sparks. "Fuck." He groaned and clutched and unclutched Beckett's hips.

"God, *yes*, more, slowly. Slowly."

Donovan eased in some more, looking down. It was glorious watching his cock being slowly swallowed by Beckett's ass, but looking up, his gaze locking with Beckett's, a dark flush of arousal staining his cheeks, his mouth fallen open, his dilated pupils, the grimace of pleasure written all over his face, was something else entirely, and he pressed in a little more.

"Ah..." Beckett shut his eyes for a moment, his face twisting. "*Oh God.*"

"What?" Donovan's heart banged to a halt. "Too much? Should I stop?"

"No, just...wait. *Fuck.*" His eyes flashed open. "God. *Fuck.* That's good."

Donovan blinked. "It doesn't look like it."

Beckett gave a half laugh. "Oh, it is." He shut his eyes briefly. "Trust me, it is." When he opened them again, he found Donovan's. "It's okay," he assured, "keep coming."

Torn between pulling out and the overwhelming urge to *thrust in to the hilt*, Donovan tamped down on his inner caveman and advanced again, going even slower, if that was possible, until finally he bottomed out, his balls nestling against Beckett's perineum.

The unholiest sound he'd ever heard filled the air around them as Beckett collapsed down to his elbows, his forehead against the mattress, thrusting his ass higher and changing the angle from *fuck-this-is-good* to *Holy-Hell-I'm-dead*.

"Oh. My. God," Beckett muttered and then groaned. "Just there. Right there."

Donovan couldn't agree more. It felt like being enveloped in warm velvet at one end and being gripped by a vice at the other. It was confusing and contradictory and totally fucking *worked* as he held still, the sparks flying everywhere now. His balls, his belly, his spine. Ringing the base of his cock. Lodging in his groin and his brain and lungs.

"Okay," Beckett said after several long beats, pushing up onto his splayed palms again. "Now withdraw." His voice was low and rough and needy as he looked over his shoulder, piercing Donovan with his gaze. "Slowly. About halfway. Then come back in again. And keep doing that over and over. Gotta warn you, though," he said on a grimace, "I'm about to explode, so this is going to be over real quick."

Donovan gave a half laugh. "Like I'm going to last much longer."

"Oh yeah?" Beckett teased. "Where's all that famous rugby stamina?"

"I think I'm going to need a little more training to be match fit for *this*."

"That's good news for me." He grinned then twitched his ass, which caused a hitch in Donovan's breath and a humming noise from the back of Beckett's throat before he muttered, "Now *fuck* me, damn it."

"Well." Donovan laughed. "Because you asked me so nicely…"

And Donovan did. Slowly as requested, easing in and

out, the tight squeeze massaging his shaft, the slight suck at the end of his cock on every withdrawal its own fucking magic, the gentle slap of his balls a particularly tortuous stimulus. But it was Beckett, who craned his neck to hold his gaze through every thrust with heat in his eyes and a groan on his lips and a flare of his nostrils, that set the testosterone bubbling through Donovan's blood, that loosened the muscles in his belly and his ass and his thighs.

That lit a flare to the sparks and set them aflame.

Beckett, who bit his lip and shut his eyes and arched his back as he cried out, "*Donovan,*" then opened them again and said, "I'm coming," that tipped him over the edge.

Sliding his hand up the smooth, pale expanse of Beckett's back to his shoulder, Donovan anchored his hand there just as his climax hit. Pushing in right to the hilt, he held Beckett locked tight and hard, shuddering through a climax that burned hot and bright and so intense he thought he was going to pass out.

He didn't know how long it lasted, their combined cries a cacophony inside his head obliterating time and space and place. They could have been on Mars for all he knew.

For all he cared.

It only mattered that he was with Beckett. Doing *this* with Beckett.

At some point they collapsed on the bed. Donovan, on top, was very aware of the man beneath him and their very intimate connection. Connected in a way he'd never before connected with a man.

Connected in the only way he ever wanted again.

"I don't think I'm a gay virgin anymore," he said eventually, as the roar of body systems started to settle, his lips nuzzling Beckett's neck.

Beckett laughed, but his voice sounded a little constricted, and Donovan realised he was probably squashing the guy. He was too damn heavy for this kind of intimacy. Easing away caused a delicious internal shudder and a low groan from Beckett. He rolled onto his back, his bones heavy but super aware of the condom, and he hauled his ass out of the bed to discard it. His legs were a little on the wobbly side as he made his way to the ensuite.

Catching a glimpse of himself in the mirror, he smiled. He looked…content. And he'd *never* seen that looking back at him from a mirror before. Not really. Not like *this*. Striding back into the bedroom, he discovered Beckett had pulled the covers down and moved so his head was on the pillow, the sheet pulled to his waist. He rose on his elbow and smiled tentatively. "You need to go?"

Fuck no. Not unless Beckett was kicking him out. "You want me to go?"

"No."

"Good. Me neither." He hadn't spent the night with Beckett before, he'd always left—no matter how increasingly hard it was becoming—but he didn't want to go home. Not after this. Hell…not ever again.

And there he went again, getting ahead of himself…

Beckett pulled the sheet back. "Come to bed."

Chapter Twelve

Beck woke with a big male arm, thick and tattooed, slung across his chest a couple of hours later, temporarily disorientated. Then he smiled as the memories flooded back, turning his head to find a sleeping Donovan lying on the other pillow, his mouth slack in slumber.

And then he freaking beamed.

Christ, that had been an experience. He'd been so close to coming when Donovan had been sucking him off, which had been really freaking *good*, but the escalating need to feel Donovan inside him as he lost his load had risen like a tide. It had started when Donovan had arrived sans hoodie. Knowing that the rugby pro's desire to be with him had been greater than his need for anonymity had really pushed Beck's buttons. And it only got worse at the hot, wet pull of his mouth, the rising urge for more clawing at his throat.

Still, he hadn't meant to say it out loud. Anal was a deeply personal choice and not something he'd been obsessing about with Donovan. Sure, Beck had been impatient to try it when he'd first become sexually active, but he knew plenty of gay men who didn't like it or preferred not to indulge, and Donovan had been freaked out enough by the *sex stuff* to go there at this point.

But he sure as hell wasn't sorry now that he'd given voice to his desires.

Beck had had a lot of good sex. He'd had a lot of terrible sexual experiences, too, particularly in those early years, but on the whole it had been positive. Tonight, with Donovan, had blown it all out of the water.

Tonight, *he'd* felt like a virgin again. Like it was his first time. The anticipation, the crazy kick in his pulse, the impatience, the need. Sure, it was usual to feel all that with a new partner, but this had been next level. He'd never felt this needy. This *greedy*. This desperate for someone.

And the way Donovan had been. The way he'd wanted to make it good for him when Beck wouldn't have blamed him for a second for thinking only of himself. The way he took direction, his eagerness to please…

He was such a big, powerful lug of a guy, who was so damn sure of himself on a rugby field, dominating and leading and taking whatever he wanted, and yet in bed, he'd been so willing to follow, to learn, to give.

To please.

Christ. That had made Beck's heart thump the hardest.

And then after, he'd expected Donovan to leave—like he had every other night. Not that Beck had ever asked him to stay. It was only practical for him to leave, after all. The man had to get up early for training, and it allowed Beck to hold the line on what was happening between them.

Boyfriends stayed the night—not whatever they were.

But Beck had worried about what Donovan was thinking and feeling when he'd taken himself off so quickly to the bathroom. What they'd done was a *lot* to take in. He knew how easy it was to get carried away in a sexually charged

moment and how hard it could be to face the consequences
when all the happy-sexy-times juices had stopped a'flowing.

So, he'd invited him back to bed. Invited him to stay.
Even though it was a breach of the line he'd put in place. And
they'd snuggled and slept.

And it had been so freaking good.

Beck grinned again, suppressing the desire to lean in
and wake Donovan with a kiss to that mouth. To his cheeks
and those eyelashes and that fascinating white scar bisecting
his right eyebrow. Because he could. But Donovan *had* to be
exhausted after such a physical night—both on and off the
field—so he'd let him sleep.

Easing out from under his arm, Beck slid quietly out of
bed. Donovan stirred but only briefly, and Beck tiptoed to
the bathroom for a leak then out of the bedroom in search of
a drink of water. Grabbing a bottle out of the fridge, he took
several long swigs, gazing out the glass doors to the moonlit
balcony and the darkened buildings opposite.

Too restless to go back to bed and *not* wake Donovan,
he made his way outside. Cold air nipped at his naked skin,
but he could bear it for a while, and it might help to cool his
ardour. Besides, he liked it at this time of night, with the
traffic below practically nonexistent and only the buildings
standing silent sentinel around him for company.

The full moon was bright as it beamed down, bathing
everything in cool, white light, and despite the wintery night,
there was something cosy about being out here while his lover
slumbered on in bed.

His clandestine lover.

Beck wasn't sure how long this situation would last. If
Donovan was *that* good at the sexy times this early in his
tutelage, Beck was going to be quickly superfluous. He hoped
not, because although he was dicing close to that line, their
secret tryst was…nice. Donovan was good to be around—

warm and funny and *eager*—and there was something just a little bit naughty about the risqué nature of what they were doing that put a skip in Beck's pulse.

It was nothing like his closeted relationship with Dieter, which had felt like some terrible addiction he hadn't been able to quit. Intense in all the bad ways. He'd never felt this good, this...positive during his time with Dieter. There had always been drama and fights and make-up sex that had felt more like exorcism than recreation, more hate than love.

Being with Donovan was so damn easy. And he'd miss it when it was over. Unless...it didn't have to be?

A flood of happy surged in his chest at the mere thought, which brought Beck up short. Oh no. *Absolutely not.* Christ, was it the moonlight or the sex fritzing his brain cells? He shook his head to clear it of the incredibly fanciful, incredibly *dumb* idea. No anal was worth contemplating something long term in this situation. A no-strings fling in the closet he could handle, but a relationship?

He couldn't do that again. Dieter had scarred him for life.

"It's freezing out here."

Beck, whose brain was too busy calling him names to hear the door slide open, started at the voice. Half turning, he found Donovan drawing close, also stark naked. Despite his inner turmoil, his body practically burst into flame.

Man...he wanted Donovan all over again.

"Sorry, I didn't mean to wake you."

"It's fine," he dismissed, coming up behind, pressing the hulking mass of roaring heat that was his front into Beck's back, aligning their hips as he slid his hands onto the railing on either side of Beck's and kissed his neck. The prickle of his whiskers spread a rash of goose bumps from neck to knee.

"What are you doing out here?" Donovan asked as he continued to nuzzle.

His sleepy voice did delicious things to Beck's insides.

And his outsides as blood flowed to his groin. Shutting his eyes, Beck forced himself to forget about his earlier panicked thoughts and relax. Live in the moment. "Cooling down. Trying to resist temptation."

Given that Donovan's lips were pressed into Beck's neck, he could feel them lift into a smile. "Am I the temptation?" he muttered, his voice a low, sexy rumble.

Beck chuckled. "What do you think?" Then Donovan's hot tongue snaked out and licked where he'd been kissing, and Beck groaned. "That's not helping."

On a surge of lust, he turned in the tight circle of the other man's arms, Donovan's hands on the railing either side of Beck's waist. Their erections crossed like swords—taut, hot skin sliding against taut, hot skin—as Donovan pressed in *real* close, caging Beck between the hard wall beneath the railing and the even harder wall of his chest and abs and hips.

It was madness to be out on the balcony on a freezing night when there was a warm bed inside, but Beck couldn't think of a place he'd rather be.

A rush of emotion flooded his chest as he inspected Donovan's face. The strong jaw covered in dark, heavy whiskers. The broad forehead and cheekbones, the full mouth. The white scar through his eyebrow silvery in the moonlight. This face...when had it become the first thing he pictured when he woke up and the last thing as he went to sleep?

When had it—had Donovan—become the predominant thought in his brain?

"I..."

Beckett wasn't too sure what he'd been about to say, but, as he didn't get a chance to finish, it was a moot point. Donovan's head lowered and his mouth touched down, his lips sliding gently, seductively against Beckett's. Eating him up, licking him up. Killing him slowly, killing him softly. All big and hot and badass but so freaking gentle Beckett wanted to crawl inside Donovan's skin.

Unfortunately, or fortunately as the case may be, the balcony light from next door flooded them in artificial light, and they broke apart. Beckett pressed his forehead into Donovan's shoulder, his pulse skipping madly. Bloody hell—what were they doing?

Making out on the balcony for all the freaking world to see when they were supposed to be keeping this behind closed doors?

"Let's continue this inside, shall we?" Donovan murmured, his lips close to Beck's ear before tugging on his hand and leading him inside.

• • •

Monday's training session was a breeze. Training was *never* a breeze, but Donovan doubted anything could wipe the smile off his face. The fact that Beckett was up there perving on him, hot on the heels of their entire day spent in bed yesterday, was giving him all kinds of feels.

Sexual *and* otherwise.

He couldn't remember the last time he was this happy. Deep down in his bones happy. And he knew who he had to thank for that. If Beckett hadn't come into his life, he'd still be living his half existence and pretending it was enough. But now, he was living his true life—rugby *and* a man—even if it was a secret.

No training session could fuck with that.

It didn't seem to matter how hard Griff worked them—and he worked them *hard*—Donovan took it all in stride and did it with a grin on his face. Something that had clearly not gone unnoticed.

"Fuck's sake, Dono," Linc grouched as he yanked his

jersey off in the locker room after training was done. "Must you look like you've spent the morning at a fucking spa instead of running your ring out on the field?"

Donovan grinned. "You young guys. No stamina." *He shouldn't have any stamina given how few hours' sleep he'd had last night, but he'd never felt so fucking energised.*

"Yeah, leave it to the old guys," John Trimble—already in his mid-thirties—agreed and high-fived Donovan as he passed by bare-ass naked.

Linc eyed him suspiciously for a beat or two. "Hang on a moment, I know that look. You're getting laid."

The accusation cut through the murmur of conversations as every eye in the locker room swivelled in his direction. *Fuck.*

Bodie swaggered over to stand next to Linc, joining in the inspection. "You're right."

Dex also joined the clutch. "Yeah." He nodded. "He does seem…happy."

Oh, for fuck's sake. Donovan shook his head. "I don't date, you know that."

Linc shrugged. "Who said anything about dating?"

"C'mon, dude, spill," Bodie pushed.

"Yeah," Dex demanded. "Who is she?"

Aaand there went all his happy. He'd never faced this kind of scrutiny before—damn his stupid happy face. And damn Linc who was worse than the paparazzi if he sensed some juicy gossip.

"It's okay, you can tell us you're in a relationship with a sheep." Linc grinned as everyone laughed. "We know how you Kiwis roll."

Donovan also laughed. Sheep jokes were their thing, their running Aussie-Kiwi shtick with the guy who came from a country where sheep outnumbered people five to one. Still, the immediate assumption that he was seeing either a woman or a *sheep* over a man was telling.

"Dono?" The interruption by Eve was so perfectly timed he could have kissed her. "Why are you the only one who hasn't signed the goddamn approval form for the website updates? I'm not your wife or your mother," she grouched. "Can you please get your ass in my office and do it now so HR will get off my back?"

Everyone protested as Donovan grinned and said, "Yes, ma'am." He turned back to them. "Sorry, guys, gotta rush. Can't keep the lady waiting."

Ordinarily, the tedium of paperwork was something Donovan avoided, but right now it was a fucking lifeline he was grabbing with both hands. He left to a cacophony of protests and chicken noises, to which he responded by exercising the middle fingers on both his hands and departing the locker room with a smile on his face and a spring in his step.

• • •

The spring in his step lasted all day. It lasted all the way to Beck's apartment and all through dinner and right into Beck's bed. The sex was…well, Donovan had no words for what the sex *was*. It just kept getting better. But more than that it felt *right*. Being with Beck. Being close. Getting closer. Lying face-to-face, holding the other man's gaze as he moved deep inside him, watching the ecstasy play out on his face. The way he sucked in a breath and bit down on his lip at the same time, and the way he moaned, "*Donovan*," like he was in a trance.

In fucking *thrall*.

Donovan had always shut his eyes when he'd had sex with Annie. Concentration mixing with guilt and shame driving his eyelids closed. But with Beck, they were wide open.

With Beck, he didn't feel shame or guilt. He didn't need to *concentrate.*

And he didn't want to miss a thing.

A flood of emotion welled in Donovan's chest as they lay panting in the dark in their post-coital buzz. The condom had been disposed of, and Beckett's head was on his shoulder, his top leg draped over Donovan's thigh. The flood became a geyser, gushing until his chest was so big and full it felt like his ribs were about to crack open.

It felt like he was drowning. In a good way.

It felt like *love.*

Like how he felt about Miri and Annie and his family and his Smoke teammates. And rugby. But it was different, too. It was attraction and obsession and *possession.* It was very, very male, but it wasn't sex—it was far, far deeper than that. And every atom of his body was consumed by it.

"I love you."

Donovan blinked as those three little words slipped out in what felt like slow motion even as his brain scrambled in fast forward to take them back. But then he stopped, and the hot slick of panic ebbed, because although Beckett had warned him that this thing was only supposed to be short term, that he wasn't after a boyfriend, he *did* love Beckett Stanton.

He may be new at this whole gay thing, but he knew what love felt like. Even if it did feel different to the other kinds of love he'd had in his life.

Especially because it felt different to the other kinds of love.

But the sudden stiffness of Beckett's frame didn't bode well. "You shouldn't say that," he said after a beat or two before rolling away. Scrambling off the mattress, he reached for his clothes, leaving Donovan alone on the bed.

"Why?" Donovan asked, watching Beckett's back as he

stepped into his jeans and yanked his shirt down over his head. "It's the truth. I love you."

"Don't." Beckett's voice was gruff. "Don't say that."

Donovan's heart beat like crazy as Beckett stood with his hands on his hips, his back to him. His chest, that had been overflowing only moments ago, now felt like it was caving in on itself. Pinpricks of pain, like a thousand tiny darts, found their targets, puncturing his lungs, making it hard to breathe.

"I'm sorry, I know I wasn't supposed to…develop feelings for you, but…it happened anyway. I'm in love with you."

"It's not love."

The other man's swift, toneless denial clobbered Donovan in the chest as he, too, swung out of bed, grabbing his pants. "I think I know how I feel, Beckett," he said, shoving his legs into his shorts. He had no idea where his shirt had landed.

The other man turned to face him, and yes it was dark, but there was enough ambient light to pick up every anguished line on Beckett's face. "What you're feeling is not love." Unlike his face, his voice was flat. Expressionless. "It's relief and gratitude and appreciation. And anxiety and apprehension. All rolled into one heady mix. It's a lot to deal with in a short space of time, and this is all new, and I'm your first, and the sex is off the charts, and you're…projecting."

Donovan took a moment to inspect each one of those characterisations to see if they fit. If this feeling coursing through his veins and bubbling in his chest was related to any of them, and he called bullshit. "I'm not projecting."

He *had* experienced all those things, but his love had not evolved from a place of thankfulness *or* the dark, swirling cauldron of his uncertainties. He knew without a shadow of doubt that it had come from a place of purity.

It had come from his heart.

"It's been a month. You barely know me," Beckett dismissed.

God, the desolation in his tone was hard to bear. "I know you."

"Donovan…" He gave an exasperated huff—his first show of emotion. Then he leaned over and scooped something off the floor, tossing it in Donovan's direction. He caught it on autopilot—his shirt—as Beckett continued. "You don't tell a guy you love them for the first time just after you've stuck your dick in his ass and come loud enough to bring the building down. That kind of *love* comes from the genitals, not from the heart. And definitely not from the head."

A hot, sinking feeling started at Donovan's throat and travelled all the way down to his belly button. Okay, yeah. Beckett was right. He'd fucked that up. But it didn't make it any less true.

"I'm sorry, you're right." He threw his shirt on over his head, because this was the type of conversation where he should be at least as clothed as the other guy. "That was stupid and impulsive. But…it's not like that."

Donovan took a step closer, halting abruptly as Beckett stiffened.

"I know it's quick, but it *isn't* coming from my dick. It's coming from here." He tapped his chest. "When you've never felt like *this* about someone before, it's pretty damn obvious when you do. And I really do love you. Not because you've opened this door for me, but because you're good and kind and funny and thoughtful. Because you could have outed me by openly flirting that day we first met and you didn't. Because you offered to show me the ropes even when it meant lying to your friends about where you were and who you were with. Because I hate it every time I have to leave you, and I count the hours until I can see you again. Because I can barely breathe when I think about you and you're the only other person, the only *thing* other than Miri, that can wipe rugby from my mind."

Donovan paused to draw breath to try and find the words to articulate this seething mass of emotion boiling in his gut and pressing in from all around. How could he do that when there were no words?

"Because I just…do. It's there, deep and glowing and burning in my chest, and it's nothing to do with sex or gratitude or you being my first. It's just…*there*. Like gravity. And oxygen. And the goddamn moon. It just *is*."

If Donovan had hoped to sway Beckett with his words, he was disappointed. His jaw practically turned to granite right in front of him as he shook his head. "And how does this play out in your head, Donovan?"

"I…" He wished he could answer that, but Donovan hadn't thought past the *L* word. And that had just slipped out. He'd *meant* it, but he had no plan for what happened next. "Don't know."

"Right." Beckett nodded like he already knew the answer.

"I want to…be with you." Of that Donovan was sure. So sure he took another tentative step forward. "I want to have a relationship with you."

"And how's that going to work in with your rugby career?"

"I…"

He nodded again. "Don't know."

"Christ, Beckett." Donovan shoved two hands through his hair. He wasn't used to feeling helpless, and he didn't like it. He didn't like how far away Beckett was or how damn *remote* he felt. "I haven't had any time to think about this."

"No shit," he said derisively.

"Can't we just…keep doing what we're doing? For now?"

Beckett's eyebrows raised. "After the L-word?" He shoved his hands in his pockets. "No."

Yeah, Donovan supposed not. It was out there now, and he couldn't take it back—not that he would if he could. He *wasn't* sorry he'd said it. Just exceedingly fucking sorry it appeared not to be reciprocated.

That he'd been falling in love while Beckett had been keeping one eye on the door.

Drawing in a deep, unsteady breath, he asked, "You want me to come out?" Maybe it would make a difference?

Beckett drew back as if the question had slapped him in the face. "*Christ*, Donovan. *No.* I do not want you to come out. Nobody should *ever* force you to do that. That's something you do when you're ready, for your own reasons. Hell, you *never* have to come out. This isn't me giving you some kind of ultimatum."

"Then what is it?"

"It's me...setting you free."

"*What*?" He didn't fucking want to be free.

"You don't need me, anymore, Donovan. You can do *gay* just fine without me."

What *the* fuck? "I don't want to do *gay* with anyone else."

He gave a sad kind of scoffing noise. "You will. Maybe not straight away...but you will."

"No." Donovan shook his head, the thought like a thorn in his chest. "I only want you."

"Yeah, well"—he shrugged—"we can't always have what we want."

Donovan blinked. "You think *I* don't know that?" He'd spent *years* telling himself he couldn't have what he wanted. Until Beckett. "Is this about the guy?" he demanded. "From your past?"

"No." But his denial was a little too swift and his jaw clenched and unclenched beneath the scruff of his whiskers. "This was never going to last long."

"Talk to me about him," Donovan pleaded, taking another step forward.

Beckett shut his eyes, shook his head. "Please just...go, Donovan. Leave." He eyes fluttered open. "I don't want to argue with you, but I can't do this anymore. Please don't make this harder than it needs to be."

The defeat in Beckett's voice blew like a desert wind through Donovan's bones. The rigidity of his body was like an axe to his heart. He wanted to stay, to plead his case, to get to the bottom of what this was really all about, but Beckett was so remote, so shut down right now, he doubted any words would reach him. His mind was made up.

And sometimes, Donovan knew—all *parents* knew—it was best to retreat. To give space. And time. Before circling back.

"Okay…fine." He huffed out a loud breath. "I'm sorry for ruining the evening." And he was. But he'd never be sorry for telling the guy he loved how he felt.

There was no response, just Beckett standing stiffly in the dark, his hands crammed in his pockets as Donovan headed for the door. It took all his willpower not to stop and *beg* as he neared. "I'll call you tomorrow," he said as he brushed past, taking care not to get too close.

Beckett's definitive, "Don't," followed him out the bedroom door, out of the apartment, and all the way home.

• • •

By the second week, Beck wished like crazy he hadn't said *don't*. It would have been easier to press cancel on multiple daily phone calls from Donovan or let them go through to voicemail and delete them without listening than to be greeted with zero missed calls at the end of the day.

Zero.

Yeah, he'd pushed the guy away, asked him to leave, told him it was over. But Beck hadn't expected Donovan to just give up. And yes, he knew how freaking perverse that sounded, but he couldn't help it, either.

Beck hadn't split with Donovan, hoping to be chased—he wasn't into playing bullshit games like Dieter had been—but he'd braced himself for it and when it hadn't come, well...

It was for the best, he knew. A clean break. But that didn't mean he hadn't spent every waking minute thinking about the man.

He swore his heart actually skipped several beats when Donovan's *I love you* had slipped into their dark, cosy bubble. He'd been lying there in that lazy space between dissipating pleasure and encroaching sleep, and it had jolted him out by the roots of his hair. And in those immediate few seconds, his heartbeat had soared. But then reality had sunk in and had kept sinking in as the conversation had progressed.

Beck understood that Donovan hadn't really thought about the impact of his words. That he, too, had been lying in that gloriously sexual pre-slumber. But he *did* say them. And he did *mean* them.

Hell, he'd doubled-down on them.

So Beck hadn't been able to ignore those three little words. Nor, apparently, *not* freak out about them. He'd been coasting along, living in the laughter and the sexy times of the moment, deliberately not thinking about the next week, the next two weeks, the next month. Or the hard tug of yearning he felt every time Donovan looked at him. And in the space of one heartbeat, that had all ended.

Donovan had forced him to confront things he hadn't wanted to confront.

Like the feelings he'd been ignoring from the start. He'd never had such a visceral reaction to a man in his life. Sure, he'd met guys where there'd been an instant attraction, but that had always been fun and flirty. Meeting Donovan for the first time had *not* been that.

It had been hard and sharp. A slap to his face, a jolt to the chest. A giant neon sign flashing above his head.

One he should have heeded.

Because he'd been kidding himself that he could have *just a physical thing* with a man where there was so much more than chemistry in the mix. And when that man had confessed his love and asked if they could just keep doing what they were doing—*for now*—he'd realised just how deep he'd gotten himself into the liaison with Donovan.

Emotionally.

And he'd hit the panic button.

The truth was, they *could* just keep doing what they'd been doing, because ultimately his attraction to Donovan was potent and he wanted to be with the man. But could he do that on the down low? Potentially for years? For as long as Donovan had left in his career? Plenty of gay men had in the past and plenty all over the world still were. Beck, though, had been lucky not to have to hide. Fortunate that he could be who he was, openly and freely.

How long before being Donovan Bane's secret lover caused the kind of divisions neither of them could come back from? Before the strictures of their situation affected their day-to-day lives? His job performance? *Donovan's* job performance?

Their friendships?

Pete had shaken his head and hugged Beck two weeks ago when he'd discovered him watching a replay of an old Smoke game. He hadn't said *I told you so*, but if Beck was to voluntarily put his head back in that lion's mouth again? Pete wouldn't hold back his opinion on Donovan's gross stupidity.

Beck's phone rang, and he almost laughed out loud. It'd be Pete. His bestie had the most freakish ESP and always seemed to call at the exact moment Beck was thinking about him. Striding out to the balcony, where he'd left the phone ten minutes ago, Beck picked it up.

It wasn't Pete. It was Donovan.

An image of him flashed onto the screen—the one Beck had taken of him cooking shirtless in the kitchen what seemed like a thousand years ago now—and the conviction that he'd done the right thing tangled into a great big knot in his chest.

Beck almost didn't answer, but his pulse was fluttering madly and there was a demon on his back and *god*, he missed Donovan's voice.

"Hey," he said after he pushed the answer button, concentrating hard on steadying his breath, wishing he could quell the tremor of his hand as easily.

"Hey."

The low rumble wrapped fingers around Beck's heart and places much lower. Oh, sweet baby Jesus...he sounded *good*.

"How are you?" Donovan asked in another rumble as silence grew between them.

Beck shut his eyes. It was so freaking nice to hear Donovan's voice, but it was also just too damn hard. He shouldn't have answered. "Why are you calling, Donovan?"

"To see how you are."

"I'm fine."

"And your job?"

"Fine." Beck supposed he should be enquiring about Donovan, too—that was how conversations worked. But hearing him again was harder than Beck had imagined.

There was a pause for a beat or two. "I...miss you."

Beck opened his eyes and gripped the phone tighter. "Donovan..." He drew in a ragged breath. "Let's not do this. I'm going now—"

"No, *wait*," Donovan interrupted. "Please, don't hang up."

Shutting his eyes again, Beck murmured, "Donovan."

"I wanted to ask you about him. About the guy...from your past."

Beck's eyes flashed open. "Why?"

"Because I'm not sleeping and I can't think straight and my game *sucks* and I pick up my phone to ring you ten times a day because I miss you and I'm just…trying to understand."

His impassioned diatribe wormed its way past Beck's defences. Something about knowing Donovan had almost rung so many times broke through his barriers. Maybe if Donovan understood what had happened, he'd get why Beck had called it a day? "Okay, fine."

Another pause. "He hurt you."

It wasn't a question. It was a statement. And it was curiously touching. "Yes."

"Want me to rough him up a bit? I could sit on him?"

Beck laughed at Donovan's attempt at humour. It was unexpected, and for a few seconds, his chest hurt a little less. "No. But thank you." He didn't wish Dieter ill will. His ex was firmly in the past.

"How long ago was this? What happened?"

"About five years ago."

There was a long pause before Donovan prompted. "And?"

Beck sighed. He was surprised to realise he still felt a little foolish over the whole affair. "He was from a fundamentalist Christian family and firmly in the closet."

"Okay."

"Yeah. Except, not really. When he was *out* he was *out*, if you know what I mean? Partying in clubs far away from the suburbs and hanging with my friends, he revelled in being gay, but he was *really* fucked up about his sexuality, which he took out on me."

"What does that mean? Was he…violent?"

"No. God *no*," Beck hastened to assure. "Just mind games. Really fucked-up mind games. But he was very good looking and charming, and I was *obsessed*. I thought he was misunderstood. That I'd be the one to bring him out for good. To make a difference. I just didn't understand that when you don't like yourself, it becomes everything in your life and there isn't any room for anything or anyone else."

It had taken a year of therapy for Beck to figure it out. To be able to articulate it and not blame himself.

"You loved him?"

"No." He shook his head, a sad smile lifting the corners of his mouth. "I thought I did, but what I actually loved was the *idea* of him. The guy in the club being hot and charming and basking in his identity. I loved his...potential."

"I'm sorry."

Beck shook his head. "It's not your fault."

"I know, but I...compounded what you went through."

Maybe. The closeted situation was similar, but everything else about the two of them was night and day. Dieter had been a mere infatuation compared to Donovan. Yeah...the sexual attraction was similar, but *every* part of Beck's body yearned for Donovan—every cell, every tissue, every organ.

Not just his dick.

Hell, he felt the presence of the rugby pro right down in his *spleen*. And it had been that way from the first moment he'd lain eyes on the guy.

Infatuation was light and dizzying, like champagne bubbles floating in the blood. This, what he felt with Donovan, was heavy and grounding, sinking into his bones like cement and setting up camp.

Oh, *fuck*. Jesus. No...

He didn't just have *feelings* for Donovan. He was in *love* with him.

The knowledge filled his heart, resonating like a bass note that had been composed just for him. And he *could* be with Donovan. He could be with him right now. All he had to do was say the word and climb back into Donovan's closet.

Because the other man had an elite sporting career that was grounded in heteronormativity and a daughter he wanted to protect from people who weren't tolerant of *other*.

Both of those things were admirable. And important. For Donovan.

But neither of them negated *his* life. His right to be himself. To have a happy and fulfilled life.

"I wish the world was different," Donovan said, his voice a chasm of regret in Beck's ear.

"Yeah." Beck's heart broke clean in two. Because he could see how good they could be together, but he'd paid the price of not being himself once, and he couldn't do it again. It had been too high, and he was too damn proud to beg. "So do I." A long silence grew between them, pregnant with what could have been. When Beck couldn't bear it any longer, he said, "Have a good game on the weekend."

"Will you be watching?" Donovan asked.

His voice was strained, husky, and picked at Beck's fraying resolve to stay strong. He shut his eyes. "Yes," he said, then hung up the phone.

Chapter Thirteen

Two weeks later, Donovan, who was usually even-tempered whether things were going his way or not, was in a foul mood after training, and everyone in the locker room was giving him a wide berth. The Smoke had lost three out of the last four games, which was, in large part, due to his sudden shitty form.

And this Monday morning training session had totally blown. He couldn't concentrate worth a damn, and everyone on the team was irritating the absolute crap out of him. He'd been snapping at people for weeks, and he actually almost barrelled Linc to the ground earlier just because he'd been running his mouth—as usual.

"*Dono!*"

Oh, and Griff was pissed at him.

The thunderous bellow echoed around the locker room as several sets of eyes swivelled in Donovan's direction. He sighed, his head falling back against the locker behind him. *Great.* This reaming had been coming for sure—he was surprised it had taken the coach so long—but it didn't mean he was looking forward to it.

Donovan didn't bother making eye contact with anyone as he strode out of the locker room. He couldn't bear to be pitied right now when he was so goddamn *pissed off.* At himself, at his form, at the team. At the traffic this morning. At the goddamn weather.

At being fucking *gay.*

Griff's door was open when he got to it, and he was sitting behind his desk. Donovan walked straight in, throwing himself in the chair and glaring at the man opposite. Lucky for him, Griff was impervious to petulant rugby players.

The coach leaned his elbows on the desk and said, "What the fuck is going on with you?"

A whole *month* of pissed-off raged and boiled in Donovan's chest, clawing at his lungs and his ribs and his throat. Absently, he cracked his knuckles. "I'm having an off couple of weeks."

Expressive red brows beetled together. "Dono, there are *dead* people having better weeks than you."

"I'm fine," he huffed testily.

Griff's frown deepened as he shot Donovan a look that would have had him pissing his pants as a rookie player. But then, to Donovan's surprise, the coach sighed and flopped back in his chair. "Look"—he shoved a hand through his mane of hair, pushing it back off his forehead—"I know I'm not one of those coaches you talk to about personal stuff."

Donovan gaped at the understatement. Griff *had* come a long way the past year.

"But," he continued, "there's clearly something fucking wrong, and you *can* talk to me." This was hardly touchy-feely territory, but for Griff, it was the equivalent of a session with a cuddle therapist.

"Okay..." Donovan said because he seriously didn't know what else to say to this man. He sure as shit *couldn't* talk to him.

"Is everything all right with Miri? And Annie? Your parents?"

Donovan flapped his hand dismissively. "They're fine."

"Some of the guys mentioned that you might have broken up with a woman you'd been seeing?"

A derisive snort slipped from his mouth before Donovan could stop it. Jesus—Griff must be hating this. Almost as much as he was. "There's not a woman," he said not bothering to hide the bitterness in his voice.

Close, but no cigar.

"Well, it's gotta be something. Because there are eight-year-olds out there playing better rugby than you. So, you need to sort your shit out or I'm going to have to bench you."

Annnd that was the end of cuddly Griff.

But it worked, because the only thing Donovan had right now was rugby, and if he didn't have that to concentrate on, then he'd be truly fucked. He sighed as he shook his head, the squall of rage inside changing tempo, losing its intensity and taking on mass. It was heavy now, heavy in his chest and his heart. So damn heavy he could hardly bear it.

"It's…" Nope. It was no good. He swallowed against the fullness of his vocal chords. He couldn't say the words.

"What? You got money problems? Booze problems? Drug problems?"

Donovan half laughed. It said a lot about the state of his emotions right now that any of them seemed preferable to the truth. Griff was staring at him across the table, and Donovan couldn't stand it any longer. He stood and prowled over to the massive whiteboard on the wall. He cracked his knuckles as he examined a play Griff had plotted out with a blue marker.

"Are you having an affair with one of the WAGs?"

Oh, dear God. Donovan shut his eyes. *Please make him stop.*

But there was only one way to make it stop. Make the adrenaline charging through his system stop. Make the swelling in his throat go down. He turned to face the man he respected most in the world after his father, and he must have looked pretty grim, because Griff sat forward and said, "Oh, Jesus."

He reached across and picked up the soft, squishy miniature rugby ball that Eve always made sure was on his desk so he could squeeze it when he was feeling stressed instead of yelling at her.

"Please tell me you're *not* having an affair with one of the WAGs."

The irony that something as heinous as that would be more palatable to a lot of people was not lost on Donovan. "Hardly," he said, dropping his hands to his side, giving his knuckles a rest. He cleared the tightness from his throat. "I'm gay."

Donovan held his breath as he watched his words sink in. The rhythmic squeezing of the ball paused as realisation dawned across Griff's face. Not that it was easy to tell, given the coach's generally inscrutable expression. About the only emotion Donovan could easily pick out was displeasure, and he definitely wasn't seeing that.

Shuffling over to the chair, Donovan sat back down, waiting for him to say something. *Anything.* His silence was fucking unnerving. When he did open his mouth, he just said, "Are you okay?"

That was it. Quiet and simple and…caring. And absurdly, Donovan wanted to cry, which didn't make sense, and he blinked back the sudden hot prickle of moisture behind his eyeballs. He was a six-foot-four, tough-guy, rugby badass.

There was no crying in rugby.

Donovan's instinct was to brush off the enquiry. Pretend he was okay. After all, he'd been doing it for years now. But he was fucking *tired*. And he wasn't okay. "Not really."

"There's someone?"

"There…was."

Griff started rapidly squeezing the ball again, his knuckles going white, and Donovan cringed a little inside. He'd probably already pushed the big ranga guy well out of his comfort zone today. "It's fine. I know this isn't a topic a lot of straight guys like to talk about so—"

"*Donovan!*" Griff cut him off with an exasperated voice and a fiery glare. "I don't give a good goddamn who you sleep with."

His gaze bored into Donovan's, and his sincerity was startling. He knew other coaches who wouldn't have been so generous, who'd have worried about Donovan's *influence* on the team, worried his mere *presence* would be disruptive.

"All I care about is how you perform on the field. And right now, you're not. So what are you going to do about it?"

Donovan had no fucking clue, but he didn't think that would be an acceptable answer for Griff, who had always been solution based. "I'll…double-down. I'll work harder. I'll train longer."

Griff made a disgusted sound just before he threw the stress ball at Donovan's forehead. It bounced off and landed on the desk again. "That's not going to solve the problem. That's just a distraction. I don't have to tell you that players play with their heads first. No one at an elite level can afford to bring their personal life onto the field, Dono."

"Yeah." It was the same thing Griff had said to all of them many times: *whatever's happening at home, leave it on the sidelines for eighty goddamn minutes.* If a player was on the field, he expected total commitment. The same thing he'd expected of himself when he'd been one of the top rugby players in the world.

"So, I repeat. What are you going to do about it?"

Donovan dropped his face in his palms. He didn't know. He knew time would eventually make a difference, but he didn't have that luxury.

"Don't you think it'd be better if you just…got it off your chest?"

Frowning, Donovan lifted his head. "What do you mean?"

"I mean come out."

"I…" Donovan blinked. That was not what he was expecting. Not from Griff. "I didn't think that was an option."

"Well, what *was* your plan?" he demanded.

"I was going to wait until after I retired."

"Okay. Sure." Griff nodded slowly. "That's standard practise. But that's a good four or five years, maybe more, barring injury. Except it won't be." He picked up the stress ball and squeezed. "You won't *have* a career past this season if you keep playing under this…burden you're carrying around."

The thought of his career evaporating was like a hot fist to Donovan's gut, and he ground his teeth. He couldn't accept that. "I've managed being gay and playing perfectly well for the last seventeen years."

"No, you haven't," Griff barked. "You haven't managed being gay at all. And…" His voice gentled. "There's never been this guy before, right?"

"He doesn't want me to come out for him."

"Nor should you. But maybe you should come out for *you*."

It was stated so earnestly Donovan was forced to examine what he *did* want. He hadn't been exaggerating before, about being tired. About not being okay. His time with Beck had given him a glimpse into how things could be, and life without him—without love—stretched bleakly ahead. Once upon a time, rugby was all he needed.

Now, he knew it wasn't enough.

"I know better than anybody how hard it is to bear something silently," Griff continued. "I did that for way too long, and I burned every relationship I had in the process. I hurt my daughter. I almost missed out on connecting with my grandchild. I could send you to a sport psychologist, but I can tell you what they'll say. Secrets eat you up, Dono. And they make you a shitty player."

Donovan snorted. "You were never a shitty player."

"Yeah, but I was dead inside. It was the only way I could play. Is that what you want?"

The bleakness in Griff's voice was chilling. And although their circumstances were very different, Donovan knew he didn't want to shut himself off like that. He wanted to *live*, damn it. *Fully*. Whether his life included Beck or not, he was tired of hiding. A little spark of hope lit in his chest, and his pulse beat a little faster. But...

"It'll be a whole *thing* if I come out now."

"Sure." Griff nodded. "There'll be a bit of a storm in a teacup. A bunch of stuff will be said about you."

If it wasn't so serious, Donovan would have laughed at Griff's robust ability to understate. There would be some A-grade homophobia going round. The *F* slur would be thrown at him in scrums and in tackles and from the stands. Some people would tear up their club memberships in disgust. There'd be so-called journalists going through his rubbish and peeping through his curtains. The social media trolls would be out in force.

"But the club will have your back. *I* will have your back. We'll handle it. We'll be right behind you. The only question is...can *you* handle it?"

A flood of relief rushed blissfully cool through Donovan's system. A weight he never knew he was carrying suddenly lifted from his shoulders. Coming out whilst still playing elite rugby had *never* been in his plans, but he knew now he *never* wanted to play another game living under this lie.

He wasn't just a rugby player. Some machine that could be flicked on at a game and then powered down after. He was a person, too. *A man.*

And he had Beck to thank for that particular revelation.

He wasn't stupid. He knew it would be tough and rocky for a while. But if Griff, his hard-as-nails coach, had his back, then he could handle anything.

"Yeah. I can."

"Good." Griff put the stress ball down. "Are you okay to announce it this week?"

Donovan shouldn't be surprised at Griff's eagerness. He didn't believe in pussyfooting around. And really…what was the point in delaying when his mind was made up? "Sure."

"Does your family know?"

"Only Annie."

"You need to talk to them."

He nodded. "I should be able to get a plane to Auckland this evening. If I can have tomorrow off?"

"Yep. As long as you'll be at training on Wednesday morning?"

Donovan almost smiled. God forbid he should miss *two* days of training. "Yeah. I'll be there."

"I'm going to work you twice as hard to make up for that lost day."

He laughed out loud this time. "I would expect no less."

Griff cracked a brief smile. "When you're back, we'll sit down with your agent and work out a plan. But I'd like to get this done before Saturday's game."

A slick of adrenaline spiked his pulse. Man, this was *really* happening.

But it was time. Past time. And he was ready.

• • •

The next morning Donovan sat in the kitchen of his old house with his ex-wife and her husband, drinking coffee and waiting for Miri to wake up. His family had been shocked when he'd confided in them last night, but taken it well. His mother had hugged him and told him she loved him. So had his father, who had cried because Donovan hadn't felt he'd been able to share that part of himself until now.

His sisters had reacted similarly but recovered more quickly, demanding that he spill about Beckett, then teasing him mercilessly when he reluctantly did so, before suggesting they all go and get rainbow tattoos to honour their baby brother.

"That explains it," Dale said, shaking his head incredulously as Annie filled him in on why Donovan had flown over from Sydney last night and was here at six in the morning.

"What?" Donovan frowned as the other man looked at him with a grin on his face.

"I've never been able to figure out why on earth you let this one go, especially when you clearly love her." He slipped his hand over top of Annie's. "I mean"—he laughed—"I'm grateful and all, but dude, she's one hot mamma. I thought you had a few sheep loose in the top paddock."

Annie beamed at Dale, and Donovan rolled his eyes. They were so cute they were sickening. "I know." He smiled at Annie. "She's one in a million and you're a lucky guy."

Dale grinned. "Amen to that."

"Dad?"

He turned to find Miri barrelling across the living room toward him, and he stood just in time to sweep her up in his arms and swing her around and around. She was getting bigger—longer and ganglier—but she would always be his little girl. Two more bodies, Miri's little brothers, crashed into his legs, and Donovan, who was like an uncle to them, picked them up and swung them around, too, and the next hour was all wonderful family chaos with breakfast and dishes and school lunches and two energetic boys and a chatty, excited Miri.

But when Dale took the boys outside for a kick of the footy at the park across the road, Miri turned to her father and said, "Is something wrong?"

Donovan glanced at Annie before returning his attention to his daughter. People said she looked like him, but all he could see was her mother and maybe a little of *his* mother. Soft brown eyes and curly brown hair that bounced around her head. Beautiful in that way of old souls. A calm demeanour and wise eyes. And utterly direct.

Fourteen going on forty.

She wanted to be a lawyer when she finished school and then a judge in the Maori Land Court. She was going to be a fierce adversary in the courtroom, and Donovan could not wait to watch her kick ass.

"Not wrong, exactly. But I need to tell you something. To do with me. It'll be on the news in a couple of days and I wanted you to hear it from me, first."

Miri glanced at her mother then back to Donovan as she took a seat opposite him. "Have you resigned?"

"No."

"Been dropped?"

"No."

"Sacked?"

"No." He gave a half laugh at her persistence. "It's nothing to do with rugby. Well, it'll affect it but…"

"Okay…now you're freaking me out. Are you sick?" She glared at her mother, obviously thinking the worst. "Is he sick?"

"Hey, hey, no." Donovan reached across the table to cover Miri's hand with his. "It's nothing bad like that."

"So just tell me," she said, bugging her eyes out, giving him her very best exasperated *judge* look as she turned her hand in his and linked their fingers.

Typical Miri. She'd always been that kid who'd preferred the Band-Aid being ripped off instead of slowly removed. "Okay." He flicked a look at Annie, who nodded. "I'm…gay."

A slight frown crinkled Miri's brow. "Oh God, Dad…is that *it*?"

Donovan blinked at the complete lack of give-a-fuck in her voice. "Yes."

He filled her in a little on how long he'd known, and Annie talked about when Donovan had come out to her and how it had been the cause of their breakup, but there'd never been animosity between them and that they still loved each other and she only wanted the best for Donovan.

"Okay." Miri nodded as they came to the end of the scripted explanations Donovan had worked on with Annie last might. "Thanks for telling me."

"You can ask me anything, you know," Donovan prompted. "Anything."

She shook her head then obviously changed her mind as her clever brain pieced things together. "Is there a reason why you flew over from Australia mid-season to tell me now?"

"Yes." Donovan glanced at Annie again before returning his attention to his daughter. "I've decided to come out. Publically. And it'll be a bit of a *thing*."

"Wow, Dad." She shook her head solemnly. "That's *big*."

The fact that even Miri could see announcing it to the world would be a bigger deal than announcing it to her said a lot about the state of the world. Miri ate, slept, and breathed rugby and was old enough to be aware of the potential implications. She clearly knew exactly how big of a thing it would be.

"It is," he agreed. It was *huge.*

She tipped her head on the side for a moment, scrutinising him. "Have you got a boyfriend? Is that why now?"

Donovan blinked. Trust his fourteen-year-old daughter—his very own, self-appointed matchmaker over the years—to burrow straight into the heart of the matter. "There…is a guy," he admitted hesitantly. "But he's not why I'm coming out."

Beck might have been the catalyst and Griff might have turned up the heat, but ultimately this had been Donovan's decision.

"I'm coming out for me. Because it's time. Because I'm sick and tired of pretending to be someone I'm not."

Miri nodded thoughtfully. "But you like him?"

Donovan gave a half laugh even as his heart almost collapsed in on itself. *Like* was such a paltry word compared to the gargantuan state of his feelings for Beckett. "Yeah…I do. It's just…kinda complicated right now." Which was easier than admitting he'd screwed up. "But I'm working on it."

"Well…" She gave his hand a squeeze. "I hope it works out. Mum's happy, why shouldn't you be?"

Donovan didn't know what he'd ever done to be so lucky with the amazing people that surrounded him, but he was more grateful for it today than ever.

If only everyone could be so accepting.

"Some people might not be so kind or generous, Miri. They might say terrible things about me that could hurt you. If you get any trolls on social media or if anyone hassles you, you know—"

"Yeah, yeah. I know what to do."

Most people at Miri's school knew who Donovan was and they were very protective of her, but some people were just assholes no matter their age. She knew how and who to report them to at school and to tell her mother and Dale immediately. She'd never needed to, but Donovan wouldn't be surprised if that was all about to change.

Miri stood and Donovan followed suit, opening his arms. She walked right into them, accepting his hug as she slid her arms around his waist and lay her head just under his sternum. Her soft curls tickled even through the cover of his whiskers as he bent his head and dropped a kiss.

"I've got to get ready for school. Will you take me?"

"I will. And I'll pick you up, too." He wasn't leaving until nine tonight, taking the day to spend some more time with family.

She unhooked her arms and departed, and Annie stood also, slipping her hand around Donovan's waist and they stood side by side, watching her go. "Well...that was easy," he murmured.

"Kids today are growing up in a totally different world. Gender and sexuality are more fluid and diverse than ever, and kids are more welcoming and accepting than ever."

"Maybe." He slid his arm to her shoulder. "But you and Dale have to take some credit there, too."

"Oh, I will," she said with a grin. But then she sobered, tipping her head back to look him straight in the eye. "I'm sorry about asking you to wait to come out. That was wrong of me."

"No." He shook his head. "This situation isn't your fault. We made that decision together, one I was happy to make because I was just fine hiding away."

"Until you weren't."

He smiled down at her. "Yeah."

"You going to be okay?

"Sure."

"It could get rough."

"Yeah." It was ridiculous to think in a world that had

pulled down many of its barriers to gay people that coming out should still be so fraught, but he wasn't naïve enough to think it was going to meet with jubilation by everyone in rugby circles.

"When will you be fronting the media?"

"Thursday after training."

She nodded. "I love you, big man." Then she slid her other hand around his waist and hugged him tight.

"Love you, too," he said, leaning into the hug, grateful for Annie and Miri's and his family's support.

He suspected he was going to need all of it for what was to come.

Donovan contemplated texting Beckett when he'd landed back in Sydney from Auckland late Tuesday night and letting him know what was happening. But he resisted. He didn't want Beckett to think he was coming out because of the feelings he had for him or put some kind of expectation on him because he was announcing to the entire country he was gay.

No matter what came next, this was about *him*. About Donovan Bane. And he was going to hold his head up high as an elite gay rugby player whether Beckett was in the picture or not.

Which didn't stop him from feeling ill as he sat down around the poker table on Wednesday night, contemplating the bombshell he was about to drop. He hoped the guys would take it as well as his family had.

Sure, he loved his fellow players like brothers, but they *weren't* brothers, and what was going to be shared at the press conference, which was being set up for tomorrow afternoon, was going to bring some major disruption into their lives.

To explain his absence, the team had been told he'd had a family situation back in NZ, and the five guys around the table were being very circumspect as they went through the motions of their poker game, but Donovan knew it was only a matter of time before Linc started to pick.

It was just what the bastard did.

He was playing shit poker—not that there was anything new about that. But despite his poor track record at the cards, he enjoyed these nights with the guys, drinking beer and smack-talking, strengthening their bonds outside of rugby. Not tonight, however. Tonight, he was waiting for that opening to announce he liked dudes to five of his closest dude friends who had not one single fucking clue he'd been keeping this big gay secret from them.

"You know what this poker game needs?"

Everyone groaned as Linc went into his usual refrain. Once upon a time, the answer had been *women* as poker night was guys only. But since everybody here except Donovan was hooked up already, he'd taken to making other outlandish suggestions.

"Light sabres."

"Yeah, that's just what we need," Tanner said derisively as he took a sip of his beer. "You. With a sword."

"Hey," he said, affronted as everyone sniggered. "I would totally rock a light sabre."

"I thought you already had one of those in your pants," Dex mused.

Linc never missed a chance to extol the virtues of his dick. Considering how free he was at flashing it around in the locker room, he needn't have bothered. Just as well, Em thought his *infantile obsession with his penis*—her words— was cute.

He grinned and grabbed his crotch. "I've had no complaints."

"If it's glowing in the dark, you might need to see a doctor about that," Bodie said, which was followed by more laughter.

"Or donate it to science," Ryder suggested as he pushed

back the brim of his Akubra and reached for a discarded pizza crust from the box near his elbow.

"I intend to," Linc said. "Upon my death, it's being bequeathed to the Icelandic Phallological Museum."

Dex, who was swinging on the back legs of his chair, said, "Iceland has a phallological museum?"

"That it does, my friend."

Donovan snorted. "Only *you* would know there's a dick museum somewhere in the world."

Tanner shook his head. "Man, your search history must be interesting."

"What makes you think they'll want it?" Ryder piped up.

"They have a sculpture of the cocks being packed by the Icelandic silver medal winning hand ball team. *Hand ball*. What kind of bullshit sport is that? Why wouldn't they want the real deal from a bona fide rugby god?"

The guys cracked up at Linc's ego. "Jesus." Bodie shook his head when the laughter had settled. "How does Em even fit in the bed with that big, fat head of yours?"

"Two." Linc grinned. "Two big, fat heads."

Bodie rolled his eyes as Dex made gagging noises and Tanner said, "Are we listening to this walking hard-on all night, or are we playing poker?" He glanced at Donovan. "Your call, man."

Donovan, who had been thankful for the distraction of Linc being Linc, stared blindly at his hand. His pulse throbbed in his chest and echoed dully in his ears as he contemplated not waiting for an opening, just blurting it out right now. *I'm gay.*

"Three, please," Donovan muttered, chickening out and absently discarded his two worst cards.

"You mean two?" Linc said.

"Huh?"

"You only threw out two," he prompted.

Donovan glanced at the two cards in question. "Oh."
Shit. "Sorry." He tossed out another. There was plenty of
choice in this dog of a hand.

Linc, apparently now over talking about how well-
endowed he was, banged his hand on the table. "Ha!" he
proclaimed. "You went to New Zealand for sex, didn't you?"
Linc glanced around the table triumphantly. "The babes on
Dick-a-Licious are going to be pissed."

Donovan's heart rate sped up as Linc presented him with
the moment, but suddenly, he felt naked in front of them as
five sets of eyes lifted from their hands and scrutinised him.
He took a chug of his beer.

"Is the reason you don't want to tell us because her name's
Dolly?" Bodie asked, trying to keep a straight face but failing
as he cracked up, followed by everyone else.

"Or *Baaa*rbara," Ryder added to much more hilarity.

"C'mon, now," Linc said with a half laugh. "Those
rumours are completely untrue. He was just helping that
sheep *over* the fence."

Usually, Donovan would laugh along and tell a dumb
Aussie joke in return, but tonight he was too tied up in knots
to find anything funny. With dread sitting like a nest of vipers
in his gut, he looked around the table at his teammates. The
guys who were like his second family.

"Actually," he said, his voice tremulous, his throat dry as
wool, "I'm...gay."

There was more laughter. "Whoa, dude," Linc said. "No
need to switch teams. I was just joking."

He swallowed again as an invisible hand squeezed his
throat. "I wasn't."

The finality in his voice penetrated the air of joviality.
Laughter cut off, smiles disappeared, everyone stared at him
owl-like. Dex's chair *thunk*ing back onto four legs was like
the thudding of a gong in the sudden silence.

Everyone looked to Tanner, the same as they always did in team situations. He led the charge, and they followed. But it was clear Donovan had confounded them all. Tanner glanced at Dex then back at Donovan. "Dono?"

"Surprise," he said with a hesitant half laugh, the weight of their stares like bricks against his chest.

Tanner put down his cards. "You want to start at the beginning?"

The light patter of cards sliding against the tabletop followed as Donovan looked around the circle. Every one of his friends was watching him. He could see surprise and astonishment and...concern, but not horror or disgust or rejection, and the tight squeeze around his windpipe eased.

Throwing his cards on the table, Donovan took to knuckle cracking as he started at the beginning. From when he first knew he was gay up to and including meeting Beckett. He left out the alley incident and didn't name Beckett, because it was none of their business, and if nothing else, he could protect the man he loved from whatever three-ring circus was sure to spring up when the news broke.

For once, there were no wise cracks from Linc. In fact, they all looked a little stunned, and the thickness in Donovan's throat returned as the silence built.

"But...you were married, right?" Linc asked. Donovan was not surprised his was the first question.

"So was Elton John," Dex said.

Ryder nodded. "And Freddie Mercury."

"And don't forget about Rock," Bodie added.

Linc's eyes practically bugged out of his head. "The *Rock* is gay?"

"No, dickhead." Bodie shook his head. "Rock Hudson." When Linc looked at him blankly, he sighed and said, "He was a famous actor back in the golden days of Hollywood."

Thankfully, Linc was laissez faire about his general

knowledge shortcomings and didn't take any affront at being schooled. "Well *anyway...*" He glanced at Donovan. "I always knew you were checking out my ass."

Linc's urge to brag in any situation was typical and broke the tension.

"It's impossible *not* to check out your ass," Dex bitched. "You practically shake it in everyone's faces."

"Yeah," Ryder agreed. "And if he was staring at anyone's ass, it was mine."

Donovan laughed at two of the straightest men he knew vying for an ogling from a gay man. And then everyone else laughed, too, and it didn't feel weird or fraught anymore. It felt just like any other Wednesday poker night.

"Firstly," Tanner said when there was some hush again, "I think I speak for all of us when I say we're sorry that you felt you couldn't share this with us sooner. And secondly, we're here for you."

"Here, here," Linc agreed. "Women, sheep, dudes... Whatever, man."

There were chuckles but also unqualified agreement, nodding and murmurs of *hell yeah* around the table, and the thickness in Donovan's throat was back with a vengeance.

"I guess I'm wondering," Tanner continued tentatively, "if there's a particular reason you're telling us now? Has something happened?"

He looked around the table at his teammates—in rugby *and* in life. "I'm coming out tomorrow at a press conference. Because it's time. And I want to. And I know it's going to cause a shit storm and will put the Smoke under all kinds of scrutiny and pressure, and our opponents will try and exploit it, and I'm *truly* sorry for that."

"No." Tanner shook his head as he reached out, sliding his hand onto Donovan's shoulder, squeezing it hard. "You gotta do what you gotta do, man, and fuck the rest of them.

Let them think we can be exploited. We'll show them that if you put *us* under pressure, we'll shit diamonds right back at them."

"Fucking A," Bodie said as he raised his beer bottle, and everyone followed suit. "To shitting diamonds."

Donovan laughed as they all drank. He wasn't sure the analogy really worked, but they were running with it as they laughed and toasted and grinned at each other, and he knew, just as Griff had his back, these guys did, too.

And he'd never loved them more.

"So what now?" Linc asked as beer bottles clinked back onto the table top. "You want to all hug it out?"

"Jesus." Donovan rolled his eyes. "Get a grip." Hugging it out was for the field. "How about we just play fucking poker?"

And with that, they all picked up their cards and got back to the game.

• • •

Donovan wished he wasn't nervous as he travelled down to the first floor in the stadium lift—but his unconscious knuckle-cracking said otherwise. Even flanked by Andy, his agent, on one side, Griff on the other, and the club CEO and three of the executives in front of him, the enormity of coming out publicly for the first time at a nationally televised press conference was shredding his nerves.

"You ready for this?" Andy asked as they walked toward the press room. Donovan could already hear the low hum of reporters lying in wait like buzzards, ready to pick over the bones of his private life for *entertainment*.

He knew they were expecting him to announce his retirement. There'd been chatter all day on TV and social media ever since the presser had been booked. The news had been given some credence due to his recent poor form. But the *real* reason was going to blow their fucking minds.

"Not really."

"You'll be fine," he said, giving Donovan's shoulder a squeeze. "And we'll be right behind you. The whole club is right behind you."

Donovan nodded. He'd told the entire team this morning, and as expected, they'd been amazing. He knew they'd all be glued to their TVs, rooting for him.

"Remember," Andy said as they neared the door, "I'll announce that you're making a statement and that there'll be no questions, then it's you. Okay?"

"Yeah." They'd been through this several times already, but it helped to have it reiterated. A bilious slick roiled through his stomach. "Got it."

And then it was action stations as they headed into the room. A few flares and some camera-clicking went off as soon as the assembled media spotted Donovan amongst the group walking to the podium.

In a suit.

Normally press conferences were done seated and players were usually in their jerseys, but Donovan had wanted this to be formal in every way.

Andy stepped up to the lectern. "Donovan has a written statement to read at this time. He won't be taking questions after."

Donovan stepped in front of a bunch of microphones. Adam had placed the statement on the podium just as they had discussed. Trying to zone out the crowd of reporters, he concentrated on the words in front of him. He opened his mouth to speak, but before he even got a single word out, there was a murmur that rippled and rose from the assembled press corps, and all the cameras suddenly swung away and pointed at the opening door as the entire Sydney Smoke team trooped in, one after the other.

Beneath the scrutiny of clicking cameras, they took up formation just behind him, in two semi-circular rows, their blue-and-silver jerseys worn with pride and meaning. Tanner, Dex, Linc, Ryder, and Bodie stood immediately behind, all of them sliding a hand onto his shoulders. He *felt* their love, their support, right down to his fucking marrow, their message loud and clear.

He's on our team and we're *on* his. *He's one of* us.

Swallowing hard against the lump in his throat, Donovan started to speak. "Since I was old enough to kick a ball, I've played rugby. It has been my everything for a very long time. It's all I've ever wanted to do. It's still the only thing I want to do. But it's not just *what* I do. It's who I am. It's my identity. And that made it very easy for me to ignore the part of me that wasn't compatible with rugby."

Donovan took a moment to still himself. His voice was shaky and his heart was racing. Apart from the click of cameras, there was absolute silence in the room.

"Marrying young and having a daughter at eighteen also made it very easy to ignore that part of me. The part of me that had always felt *other* that I could never quite put my finger on."

A restlessness spread through the assembled media. They were starting to realise this was *not* a resignation announcement.

"I was fifteen when I realised what that was, and even then I knew I had to make a choice. Being gay—"

A murmur broke out and the cameras went ballistic at the G-word. The guys behind squeezed his shoulders again, and Donovan cleared his throat and continued.

"Being gay, or following the trajectory I had been slogging away at since I first laced on my boots—an elite rugby player. Because even then I knew the two weren't compatible. There were no—there *are* no—elite football players of *any* code in this country that are openly gay. That's not to say that I am the only elite football player who *is* gay in this country, just that others like me understand that being gay is not compatible with professional football."

A glass of water had been left on the lectern, and he picked it up and took a slug to dissipate the claggy feeling in his mouth. The adrenaline was settling now, but his skin still felt too tight. So did his lungs.

"Despite the advances in gay rights in recent years, the perception that a gay team member will disrupt a team and the locker room persists, and with no other role models to show the world differently, I accepted that I could play rugby or I could be gay. But I could not do both. So I chose rugby and left being gay for later. For retirement. Until recently."

Donovan dragged in a breath, mentally girding himself for the next bit, wondering if Beckett was watching this somewhere, wishing he was here instead.

"I recently met a man and fell in love. Despite this, I still had no intention of coming out, fearing my doing so would cause a paparazzi-style sensation for the team they did not need while trying to win rugby games. This man understood what was at stake for me and sacrificed his own freedoms to keep my secret. But that is not an easy life, and I was wrong to ask it of him."

His voice husked over, and Donovan had to take another swallow of water to clear it.

"This is not how I planned to come out and, in fact, I probably would *not* have done so at all, continuing instead in a clandestine relationship until my retirement, as I have no doubt others in my position have done before me. But I've realised recently this man I love deserves more than being a dirty secret, and *I* deserve more in my life than *just* rugby. And most crucially of all, young gay men wanting to become elite rugby players deserve role models so they know they don't have to choose between *what* they love and *who* they love. I want them to know they can have both."

Donovan breathed out a shaky breath as he reached the end. He glanced up and was almost blinded by the flashes. "Thank you," he said, and a lot more calmly than he felt, he picked up his paper, slipped it inside his suit jacket, and left the podium followed by his teammates.

The room erupted into chaos as a couple of dozen reporters all pushed forward, snapping pictures and hurling questions. It was the longest walk in Donovan's life, and he was sweating by the time he was halfway to the door. When it opened suddenly, it felt like a lifeline, but he wasn't prepared for Beckett to burst through it, clearly out of breath, phone in one hand, pulling his earbuds out with the other.

Donovan stopped abruptly, his heart slamming to a halt, which, given his sudden dizziness, must have been for several beats. Beckett came to a halt, too, his gaze locking with Donovan's as he panted, and they just stood staring at each other, eating each other up amidst the chaos, several feet and a whole world of possibility between them.

It had been over a month since he'd seen the other man, and his heart, that had been slowly falling apart, seemed whole again. But...what was he doing? Donovan couldn't protect Beckett's identity if he crashed a press conference like Hugh fucking Grant.

As the silence grew between them, so too did the noise in the room. One by one every reporter fell silent until there was just the noise of clicking cameras as if everyone gathered knew that they were witnessing *a moment*.

"I was just outside at the café when the press conference started," he said, clearly dazed, holding up his phone.

Donovan nodded, because he didn't know if it was a good thing or a bad thing, and apparently his vocal cords were completely malfunctioning.

"I—" Beckett started. Then stopped. Then after a beat or two he steamed purposefully toward a dumfounded Donovan. And he didn't stop. He just kept coming until his body was hot and hard against Donovan's and his hands were sliding to either side of Donovan's face and his forehead was pressed firmly into Donovan's, his blue eyes glittering with purpose.

He was still slightly out of breath, but Donovan didn't miss the husky, "I love you." Those words wrapped around his heart and squeezed. Beckett *loved* him.

And then, in front of every person in the room—every person in the whole fucking country—Beckett, the man who had shown him he *could* have rugby *and* a life…kissed him.

The media scrum roared then, cameras loud as shotguns, questions battering them like rams, but Donovan only had time for the hard glory of Beckett's mouth as the other man kissed him with such possession *no one* gathered could be in any doubt they were lovers.

Thankfully, Beckett managed to keep some control. Breaking off, he whispered, "Let's get out of here."

Donovan nodded. Today had been a lot to take in—not least of all that Beckett *loved* him—and he sure as shit didn't want to process it all on live television.

Without answering a question or looking at any of the baying journalists, Donovan grabbed Beckett's hand and pulled him toward the door. The media surged forward and Donovan turned, prepared to use force to repel them, but the team were forming up, putting a barrier between them and the pack, and Donovan grabbed the door handle and yanked, just hearing the CEO saying, "The club would like to make a statement at this time," as they stepped outside.

• • •

Beckett's ears were ringing by the time the door shut behind them and muffled the cacophony of noise. They were standing in the foyer outside the press room all by themselves, and he was still shaking a little from what had just happened.

"You okay?" he asked, lifting Donovan's hand to his mouth and pressing a kiss to his knuckles like he'd done that very first time at Donovan's house.

"Yeah." Donovan nodded. "I am. I feel *good*." He smiled then. "I feel…lighter."

Beck returned the smile. He *looked* lighter. Also incredibly hot in a suit that strained *everywhere*—pulling around his shoulders and his thighs—his hair dragged back into his regulation man-bun. It had been a month, but it felt like forever, and Beck's gaze ate him up for long seconds before he glanced around, searching for a place to talk.

Spotting a room across the foyer with an open door, he said, "C'mon." Beck wasn't sure how long the team would be able to keep the media corralled after the CEO had finished his statement, and he wanted some privacy.

The room was small and windowless but empty, which made it perfect. When the door shut, they were standing in the middle, facing each other, just out of reaching distance.

"You didn't have to do that, you know?" Donovan said.

"What?" Beck waggled his eyebrows. "Kiss you?"

Donovan smiled. "I was trying to protect your identity."

Beck smiled back at the man who had become his everything in such a short space of time. He appreciated Donovan's chivalry, but he didn't need it. For better or worse, he was in this. "It's not like me being gay is a secret."

"I know, but…the media scrutiny will be pretty intense."

"Maybe." But the enormity of what he'd witnessed on his phone screen had sent Beck into a spin, and he'd reacted without much thought.

He'd just had to get to Donovan. It had felt wrong not

being there when the man he loved was announcing to everyone he'd been keeping a secret for two decades. When Donovan was exposing the innermost corners of his private life.

"But, on the other hand, my gay friends will probably throw me a parade for bagging a rugby hottie, so"—he shrugged—"swings and roundabouts."

The chuckle that slipped from Donovan's mouth glowed warm in Beck's chest. And when he reached out and interlaced their fingers, Beck nearly freaking swooned.

"So…" Donovan glanced from their joined hands to Beck's face. "You love me, huh?"

Beck grinned at the hope and anticipation he saw in Donovan's eyes. "Yeah." Of course, he loved the guy. He'd been struck silly from the moment their gazes had met across a crowded café. He just hadn't realised it at the time.

"Why? Because your friends are going to throw you a parade?"

He hooted out a laugh. But then he realised that beneath Donovan's attempt at levity, the question was serious. Why did he love Donovan Bane?

God…he couldn't even count the ways.

Beck took a step toward him, his eyes locking tight with Donovan's. "Because you picked me up in the rain when I know you just wanted to drive on by. And you got a little old lady's cat down from a tree in the middle of a storm. And because you tried to push me away in the beginning and tried to protect me just now."

That unique blend of aromas that was quintessentially Donovan invaded Beck's senses—shampoo, liniment, and 100-proof testosterone—and he knew he wanted to live all his life surrounded by that scent.

"And then there's the way you still love your ex and are so supportive of how she parents. And the way you talk to

Miri on the phone, never in a hurry, always just that little bit in awe of her."

Beck loved how wrapped around his daughter's little finger Donovan was and how he just didn't care.

"And because it's just...*there*," he said, repeating Donovan's words from that night back at him. "Like gravity. And oxygen. And the goddamn moon." Beck smiled. "I love you, Donovan, and I'm sorry I freaked out when you told me."

He shrugged as he stroked his thumbs over the backs of Beck's knuckles. "I'm sorry I freaked you out."

"It just felt too big and too...soon, and I...was trying to keep you in this neat little box so I could...justify you to myself, and I panicked. I was worried you were confusing sex and desire and gratitude for something more. Letting the sex and the newness of it all do the talking."

"I wasn't." He shook his head. "Sure, I *am* grateful to you. And yeah, I have the hots for you, and for fucking sure I want to do dirty, *dirty* things with you as often as we possibly can." Beckett laughed at the growly emphasis, and Donovan grinned. "But it's more than that," he continued in earnest. "It's deeper. Just because I've never been with a man doesn't mean I don't know what love feels like. And this *is* that. And yeah, you might be my first, but I want you to be my last."

Beck sucked in a breath. Donovan was looking at him with such zeal, vibrating a righteous kind of energy—except he was standing very, very still. It was incredible and humbling and sexy as fuck, and he wanted nothing more than to launch himself into Donovan's arms. But the rugby pro's celebrity meant they'd be starting this relationship under immense scrutiny, and he needed Donovan to be sure.

"And when the dust settles and life in the spotlight makes things *hard*?" Beckett held Donovan's gaze. "When it isn't new and easy and fun? When long lenses are taking pictures of us from the high-rise apartment across the road and people in the crowd boo you and it starts getting in your head and it affects your games? Will you still love me then?"

"I will love you harder. I promise."

Beck practically melted into a puddle. "And I will fucking hold you to that," he muttered.

They reached for each other then, and when Donovan's mouth came down on his hard and deep and good, Beck groaned and melted and clung, his hands sliding up the back under Donovan's jacket. *This*. He wanted *this*.

Donovan. Forever.

Handfuls of him, mouthfuls of him. Around and in and over him. Taking up his space and his air and his heart, and he wanted it to start right now. Today. Tearing his mouth away, he pressed his forehead to Donovan's as they both struggled to calm their breathing.

"What do you want to do now?" Donovan asked, his voice husky.

"I just want to go home with you and shut out the world and tell you I love you a thousand times until I know that you believe me."

"I *do* believe you."

"Okay, well, I'm sure we'll think of other things to do."

Donovan grinned. "Oh, I can think of *plenty*."

Beckett's pulse leaped crazily. "Good. Let's go."

And then, with the press conference still in full swing, they walked out of Henley together, hand-in-hand, into their future.

Epilogue

"C'mon, Beck, it's starting!" Miri called.

"Yeah, Beck, get your ass in here now," Pete hollered. "Henry Cavill awaits." He turned to Miri, offering her the warm popcorn he'd just dumped into a bowl. "What are they doing in there?"

"Probably kissing," she said, her hand disappearing into a mountain of fluffy kernels.

"Eww." Pete wrinkled his nose. "Gross," he said, then he laughed.

Miri laughed, too, and threw a piece of popcorn at his head. Pete retaliated, and by the time Donovan entered the living room a few minutes later, a full-scale popcorn fight had erupted between all the usual crew from the Monday night Netflix crowd.

"You two are going to be cleaning that up after the episode finishes," he interrupted, hands on hips as he shot his daughter and Pete as stern a look as he could muster, considering his head was still spinning from a bare-ass naked Beck kissing him senseless.

Miri smiled at him sweetly. "What makes you think it was us?"

"Yeah," Pete concurred just as sweetly. "What she said."

Donovan snorted. "I wonder." Pete and Miri were thick as thieves.

It was hard to be annoyed about the mess, though, when his heart swelled at how easily Beck's friends—*their* friends—had welcomed his daughter into their circle. Miri texted Pete all the time about teenage boy stuff, and Pete, who thought all teenage boys were horny little toads, had turned out to be an excellent sounding board for his daughter.

"Tell Beck his hair is pretty enough," Pete said. "*The Witcher* waits for no man."

Donovan grinned. "He'll be out in a minute."

"Good. In the meantime..." Pete waggled his almost-empty wineglass. "It's your round."

Donovan grinned. "Who needs another?" he asked.

Five hands went up, and he was in the kitchen, choosing a bottle of wine, when Beck made an appearance. His pulse did its usual triple jump. Even after a year of living together, he still couldn't get enough of this man, his love an ever-expanding thing.

"Need a hand?" Beck asked.

"As most of the popcorn is now on the floor, you could pop some more?"

Beck laughed. "On it."

Donovan strode over to the couches and topped up glasses before returning to the kitchen to grab a beer for him. He smiled as he watched Beck pottering around.

"What?" Beck asked as he glanced up, full popcorn bowl in hand.

"Nothing." He grinned. "Just thinking how good you

look in the kitchen."

Beck rolled his eyes as he returned the grin. "You happy?"

Donovan nodded. He'd never been happier. Sure, there had been challenges this past year. He'd faced his share of trolling and even lost a couple of sponsorships, but he'd also gained a couple. And the Sydney Smoke had led the charge for more inclusion across the entire rugby organisation. They'd even entered a float in the gay and lesbian Mardi Gras.

Linc, looking cute in blue-and-silver hot pants, had been a hit with the community.

"I didn't know it was possible to be this happy," he murmured.

"Me neither."

"Thank you," Donovan whispered.

Beck smiled. "Back at ya, big guy."

And for the forty-six-millionth time since they'd met, Donovan swooned...

Glossary

I've probably used some words in here that some readers may not know—both rugby ones and strange Aussie-isms alike. So I thought a handy dandy glossary might help. It is, of course, written entirely from my perspective so is heavily biased, female-centric, and quite possibly dodgy. It probably wouldn't stand up to any kind of official scrutiny...

Footy – We love this term in Australia. The confusing thing for most non-Aussies is they never know which game it refers to because we have three separate but distinct codes of football in Australia:

1. Rugby League (Jarryd Hayne played this code before he went and played Gridiron).

2. Rugby union – The code the Sydney Smoke play and the one this series is based upon (Jarryd Hayne tried his hand at this code for a bit after the whole Gridiron thing didn't work out but is now back playing League).

3. Aussie rules football – Different altogether. Tall, fit guys in *really* tight shorts.

There is also soccer but we don't really think of that as football in the traditional sense here in Australia.

The confusing thing is we refer to all of them as *the footy,* e.g. "Wanna go to the footy, Davo?" And somehow we all seem to know which code is being referred to at any given time. Even more confusing, the ball that is used in each code is often also called *the footy,* e.g. "Chuck me the footy, Gazza."

Pitch – Apparently the rugby field is called a pitch but colloquially here we just call it the footy (see, I told you we liked that term) field. A pitch is more a cricket term. No, don't worry, I won't ever try to explain a game that lasts five days to you…

Ruck – No, not a typo. That's ruck with an *R*, ladies! Happens after a tackle as each team tries to gain possession of the ball.

Line-out – That weird thing they use to restart play where each team lines up side by side, vertical to the sideline, and one of the guys throws the ball to his team and a few of the guys from that team bodily lift one dude up to snatch the ball out of the air. It's like rugby ballet. Minus the tutus. And usually with more blood.

Scrum – Another way to gain possession of the ball. I'm going to paraphrase several definitions I've read: A scrum is when two groups of opposing players pack loosely together, arms interlocked, heads down, jockeying for the ball that is fed into the scrum along the ground. It's like a tug of war with no rope and more body contact or, as I like to call it, a great big man hug with a lot of dudes lying on top of each other at the end of it all. Very homoerotic. Win/win.

Maul – The good kind. It's when at least three rugby players from either side—one with the ball—are in contact together to challenge possession. Yes, another man hug! Sounds positively delicious, doesn't it?

Try – A goal. Except in rugby union we don't say someone scored a goal, we say someone scored a try after they've dived for the line and a bunch of other guys have jumped on top to try and stop it from happening. Very homeerotic. Win/win. A try is worth five points.

WAGs – Wives and girlfriends. These are partners of the dudes that play rugby. Although we also use the term here in Oz to refer to partners of our cricket players. I think in the UK WAGs is also a term used for football (soccer) partners.

Akubra – An iconic Australian brand of hat worn by country guys and gals. Vaguely similar to the Stetson but I'll probably have my nationality revoked for saying so! It has a distinctive shape that's about as Aussie as vegemite.

Arvo – In that long tradition of shortening everything and sticking an o on the end, this is Aussie for afternoon, eg. "Hey Robbo, whatcha doin' this arvo?"

Wank – To wank is to masturbate. Pretty much always referring to a guy. Although we embrace all terms for this biological process. Jerking/jacking/tossing off are well known, as are spanking the monkey and choking the chicken (or chook as we say here). There's also the term wanker which is actually rarely used to describe one who wanks. We much prefer to use this as an insult for someone who is a bit of a jerk, eg. "That Johnno is a wanker."

Boardies – Shortened (of course) from board shorts, the knee-length shorts worn to the beach by blokes, although women wear them as well.

Togs – Some Aussies call swimming suits togs. No one knows why.

Starkers – Completely, utterly, 100 percent naked.

Bum bag – Known as fanny packs in the USA. But a fanny here in Australia is a "front bottom" on a woman and none of us can keep a straight face calling them that…

Hard yakka – Yakka is work. So, any job that's heavy or difficult or requires muscle is hard yakka. Also a rugged brand of clothing designed to survive said yakka.

Cattle station/property – A farm or a ranch where cattle (and sheep) are raised. Usually has to be a big ass property to be considered a station. When someone's taking a betting game too serious here, we'll often say, "Come on, Richo, we're not playing for sheep stations."

Woop woop – Out in the middle of bloody nowhere. Usually where you can find most cattle stations!

Out past the black stump – another way of saying woop woop. No, nobody knows where the black stump is exactly…

Jackaroo – a station hand on farm/station/property. In other words, an Aussie cowboy. Yeehaw!

Softdrink – this is what we call a soda. Soft refers to it being non-alcoholic/wussy.

Ute – Short (just for something different) for utility vehicle. Similar to the pickup.

Fair dinkum – Slang for something that is true or genuine. "Fair dinkum, mate, that bloody cattle station out woop woop got six inches of rain last night."

Cooee – An Aussie bush call used to attract attention. Or a way of describing how near or far something is. "I was within bloody cooee of Bazza." Or "I wasn't in bloody cooee of Bazza."

Yobbo – An uncouth individual. Or Aussie for dickhead.

Dill – an affectionate term for a fool/idiot. "Don't mind Robbo, he's a bit of a dill."

Trackie daks – trackie refers to a tracksuit and daks refers to trousers. So these are tracksuit bottoms. Generally not the most sophisticated choice of clothing, usually just something to slop around the house in. Loved by authors all over this big, brown land!

Dag/daggy – a dag actually refers to the matted wool around a sheep's ass but we also apply it to people, usually affectionately. A person can be "a dag" which means someone who's funny but not very hip or fashionable. And you can "look daggy" by wearing your oldest/ill fitting/ill-kept/out-of-fashion clothes (trackie daks is a classic example) and generally just not really care about how you look.

Ranga – this is an affectionate term for a person with red hair. It has its roots (snorkel!) in the word orangutan, those ranga apes of the jungle.

Bogan – this is Aussie for redneck.

Tinnies – these are the cans that beer comes in, usually down in huge quantities by Aussie bogans.

Torch – Aussie for flashlight

Slammer – the clink, the jail, the big house. If you're in the slammer, you'd better look good in an orange jumpsuit.

Swagman – an old fashioned term for an itinerate man who wandered around and camped out in the bush with his swag (bedroll) They weren't often jolly as described in the famous Waltzing Matilda song but probably a few of them did camp by billabongs. And possibly stole sheep…

Squicky – something that's icky and grosses you out (as we say here).

Biscuit (or bikkie for short) – this does not refer to the biscuit that US readers eat with gravy. This is Aussie for cookie. Nomnom.

Across the ditch – affectionate term for the body of water between Australia and New Zealand.

Acknowledgments

My thanks, as always, go to the team at Entangled Publishing for all the behind the scenes work that goes on to get these fabulous books into your hands. Special thanks to the sensitivity readers and to Lydia Sharp for their editorial oversight.

I've already dedicated the book to these two wonderful people but I wanted to add some extra thanks here to Daniel de Lorne and Courtney Clark Michaels. I want to thank them for not only being my first readers, but reading the book with a critical eye to the sensitivities involved from their unique perspectives. Writing my first ever MM story after 80 plus MF books was something I did not want to screw up and these two people kept me on track and gave me faith that I had done it right. I'm very lucky to call both Dan and Courtney friends. Not only are they top people but they're also fabulous authors in their own right. Dan writes his own deliciously sexy MM romance and Courtney is an award-winning debut author, so please do go check out their books!

And to my rugby gurus David Grice and Jon O'Brien. Thank you both for your technical help, it is always very much appreciated. Particular thanks to Jon – I know we had our differences over this one but you still took all my calls because you're that kinda guy.

About the Author

Amy Andrews is an award-winning, *USA Today* bestselling, double RITA®–nominated Aussie author who has written eighty-plus contemporary romances in both the traditional and digital markets. She's been translated into more than a dozen different languages as well as manga. Her books bring all the feels from sass, quirk, and laughter to emotional grit to panty-melting heat. She loves frequent travel, good books, and great booze—although she'll take mediocre booze if there's nothing else. For many, many years she was a registered nurse. Which means she knows things. Anatomical things. And she's not afraid to use them! She lives in a sleepy seaside town with her husband of thirty years. Visit her online at http://amyandrews.com.au/.

If you love sexy romance, one-click these steamy Brazen releases...

ONE NIGHT STAND AFTER ANOTHER
a novel by Amanda Usen

Clara Duke lives to crochet wearable art. But right this second, she's looking at the one guy who has the uncanny ability to unravel her in every possible way. *Zane Brampton.* A whole night with this delectable, gorgeous man would be nothing less than a total sexpocalypse. But then Zane wants his chance to prove he deserves more than one night...and he might just be the thread that snaps all of Clara's perfectly crocheted plans.

HIS HOLIDAY CRUSH
a novel by Cari Z

One meeting away from making partner, Max Robertson is guilted into coming back home for Christmas. The plan is to go for just one night, but a wild deer and a snow bank wreck everything. Former Army Sergeant Dominic Bell of the Edgewood police has his evening turned upside-down when he gets called out to a crash—and it's his one and only high school crush. Everyone deserves a present this holiday season, right?

SCORING THE PLAYER'S BABY
a WAGS novel by Naima Simone

After divorcing her cheating football player ex, Kim Matlock would rather cut out her own heart than work at a wedding expo. The last thing she expects is to be kissed breathless by a hot giant looking to fend off a stalker. She doesn't want relationships, but she agrees to one scorching night with the sexy stranger. To her shock, she finds out afterward that a) he's a pro football player, and b) she's pregnant.

Lightning Source UK Ltd.
Milton Keynes UK
UKHW020334070223
416560UK00009B/253